# *The Ransom*

## Chapter One

*The days leading up to the Company's attack on France according to Thomas, the Bishop of Cornwall.*

I was visiting with an old friend, the Bodmin abbess, and just starting to get to know her again, when a messenger galloped in from my nephew bringing word that some of our galleys were coming up the Fowey. It was an inopportune interruption but I made the most of it and hurriedly withdrew.

Sure enough. As the horse I was riding came out of the trees I could see the camp in front of me was an ant hill of activity. There were three galleys tied up next to the riverbank just below our two floating wharfs.

And I could see that the archers who did their rowing were already ashore. One galley company was marching to the sound of its rowing drum into the big meadow where the apprentice archers were learnt to push arrows out of a longbow and the experienced archers practice their archery.

Several large groups of men were already in the meadow practicing with their longbows, almost certainly the men from the other two galleys. The sound of their voices wafted over the grass to me. They had obviously arrived whilst I was going over certain matters of mutual interest with the abbess and trying not to let myself be distracted by her muffled prayers.

In addition to the three galleys which had already arrived and discharged their archers, I could make out a fourth galley coming around the bend further down the river. Even at this distance I could hear the slow and steady beat of the approaching galley's rowing drum, and see its oars making the strong, smooth strokes that only veteran rowers would make. I was not sure, but I thought I could hear the faint sound of another drum coming from further down the river.

There was activity all around me as I rode into camp wearing my archers' hooded tunic with the six stripes of a lieutenant commander on its front and back. As a result, I was constantly smiling and nodding my head this way and that to acknowledge the men who knuckled their foreheads as I rode past them. The open area in front of the river was filled with men walking and running every which way, and a horse-drawn wain with squeaky wheels was heading up the muddy cart path towards the castle carrying what looked to be coin chests.

The scene in front of me as my horse trotted into the meadow would have looked hectic and chaotic to anyone who did not have enough experience to know better. It was rather like a recently dug up ant hill or a dead sheep covered by many bugs which were all moving around in different directions at the same time.

In fact, so far as I could tell, and expected, it was highly organized with everyone doing whatever it was he was supposed to be doing. And, as was always the case whenever a new galley arrived, women and children and the company's idlers were streaming down from the company lines and the hovels in and around the castle's outer walls to see who had come in on the new arrivals. They were as keen to get the latest news and rumours from the east as I was. It was a scene I had seen many times before as our galleys came in from long voyages.

A familiar voice hailed me as I swung out of the saddle and looped my horse's reins to one of the hitching posts that were scattered about. It was my nephew, George, a sturdy young man who scribed with a fine hand in addition to being one of my brother's battle-hardened lieutenant commanders.

George was the first boy from my school to join the company if you do not count William himself whom I learnt to gobble and scribe Latin and do sums in the Holy Land whilst we were crusading with King Richard.

It was hard to believe since it seemed like only yesterday, but William's second and much younger son, Edmund, would be joining my school in a few months. We had gotten him as a spare out of Helen and he had been born right here in Cornwall. I do not know why I thought of Edmund when I saw George, but I did.

"Hoy Uncle Thomas. I see my messenger found you. Peter's galley has not come in yet. But one of the captains said he was fairly sure he saw him to the south of Land's End yesterday afternoon, so he should be coming in any time now."

At least this time George did not make any humorous remarks about my visiting the abbess, her being so well-known as a result of her enthusiastic calls for more prayers when she was getting to know someone—even if they were quite funny and always made me laugh, George's remarks I mean.

"A good hoy to you too, George. I did not see you there amongst all the commotion. And how are Mistress Becky and the little one? The lads and I have been praying for her." *What else could I say? The poor lass had been sweating and not well ever since her new baby arrived. Probably the birthing pox, God forbid.*

"She was better this morning, thank you, but very weak. The midwife says she thinks her chances are good since this is her third, just that it will take some time for her to stop being so hot and sweating. Our new little girl is fine as well. One of the sergeants' wives is nursing her in addition to her own little one.

"Oh, look there, Uncle; could that be Peter on the galley that is just now coming up around the bend in the river? Up on the castle roof. Yes, by God, I think it is. One of the captains told me there are seventeen galleys in Peter's fleet, and perhaps even more in father's, though he was not sure how many there were in my father's fleet or where they might be headed." *He is changing the subject and looks worried. It must be bad.*

My nephew continued before I had a chance to respond.

"The captain who told me about Peter, Joseph Fine from Banbury, said he and the rest of Peter's fleet sailed from Lisbon before my Father's fleet arrived.

"He had obviously been kept in the dark because he did not know how far behind Peter's fleet my father's galley might be, or even that father and his galleys would be calling in at Lisbon for supplies and then sailing for Cornwall. But he certainly had some good news—he said Peter's galleys took a lot of prizes, and sent most of them to Cyprus because of all the reports of the Moors being out along the Spanish coast."

"That is good news," I replied. "I can hardly wait to hear their tales *and count the coins.* Are you having all the captains stay at the castle as usual so we can listen to them talk whilst we eat?"

"Oh aye, and their lieutenants as well. My mums expect it so they can get the latest news about my father. They have already got the bread going and some cheeses and ale out of the dungeon and Beth is helping the cook to cut up one of the old milk cows that went dry and has been hanging in the cellar. Her mother is sitting with the children because of Becky being all poxed up and unable."


\*\*\*\*\*\*

The evening was a great success and the good food and ale were greatly appreciated by the men who had just spent so many weeks at sea. Seven galleys including Peter's had come in by the time the sun finished passing overhead. The galley captains and their lieutenants, many of whom were newly promoted as their predecessors had recently gone for prize captains, had walked up the path to the castle to sup with us.

Our guests brought their blankets and hooded sleeping skins with them, as was the custom, since afterwards they would stay to spend the night sleeping in the great hall. So did Peter and the young apprentice sergeants assigned to me and George.

It had been the first visit to Restormel Castle's great hall for a couple of the captains and most the lieutenants, even though almost all of them had started with the company as apprentices in our nearby training camp. At first they were a bit overwhelmed by the grand size and high ceilings of their surroundings and the presence of the lieutenant commanders, but bowls of ale, good food, and being with old friends soon loosened them up most fine.

It was a fine supping. Three candle lanterns hanging over the long table lit the great hall and cast flickering shadows as the men moved about and waved their hands as they talked and ate. Everyone was wearing a hooded archer's tunic with the stripes of his rank on its front and back.

Some of the stripes particularly drew the attention of the lieutenant commanders and captains, and caused those who wore them to be singled out for approval and conversation—because they had obviously been quickly cut out of old sails and sewn on in the last day or so by newly promoted lieutenants. The commanders and captains knew the merit that their promotions suggested, and went out of their way to recognize and congratulate the new lieutenants.

And it was right that the newly promoted men be recognized; unlike the king and his nobles, and even the Templars, the company only promoted on the basis of ability and accomplishments, not the social rank conveyed by someone's birth. As a result, every captain and commander knew from his own experiences what it took to earn such a promotion, and greatly respected the new lieutenants for getting it.

Even my nephew George had earned his stripes with years of fighting and taking Moorish prizes, and because he knew how to scribe and do sums and gobble Latin; not because he was his father's son. If anything, George had done more to earn his stripes than anyone in the hall except, perhaps, Raymond and me.

There was little wonder in George having so many experiences; he had been on the company's roll ever since he had been a boy in the Holy Land when the company's prospects were dark and its current captains and lieutenants, and even its lieutenant commanders such as Peter and Yoram, did not even know the company existed.

Yes, there was no question about it, George and the handful of survivors from the company's difficult crusading years, even me I would like to think, were greatly respected for having been there and then doing that which had ended up making the company and its men so successful in terms of earning their daily bread and being feared and respected.

In any event, Peter and the new arrivals spent most of the evening regaling us with their tales of their voyage from Cyprus, and talking excitedly about the prizes they had taken off the Moorish coasts and what had happened and who had done what and been killed.

There was no doubt about it, Peter and his men had experienced a great success and taken many fine prizes for the company to either sell or to buy in for its own use. They were proud of themselves, and rightly so. It was their first chance to tell each other what they had seen and done, and ask each other how much prize money they thought they would receive and when they thought they would receive it.

Peter and George listened carefully and encouraged the men to talk. So did I. And at my request, young Edmund was allowed to come down the stairs and sit with the men at the table for the first time. He, of course, said not a word; he just sat wide-eyed at the end of the table with the apprentice sergeants and listened to the manly talk and boasting going on all around him.

As you might also imagine, Peter was in a particularly fine fettle, as well he should be seeing as he was about to be named as the company's new commander. At that moment, so far as I knew, only William's lieutenant commanders and some of their apprentice sergeants were aware of William's decision to step down, or that Peter was to be promoted and replace him when he returned from France.

Not even William's wives knew of his decision to step away from active service with the company, and it certainly was not my place to tell them. William would probably tell them and announce it when he arrived from Lisbon. At least, that was what I expected.

When William finally did make his decision public, I was sure it would cause great surprise everywhere. And, and I do not deny it, his decision to step down had set me to thinking behind my eyes about my own future and who should replace me. *Of course it set me to thinking; William was four years younger than me.*

Only Peter and a couple of the company's other lieutenant commanders knew that William and his fleet of galleys had followed along close behind Peter in order to raid the Moorish ports a second time. Peter's captains and their men did not know because they did not need to know. As a result, they were somewhat amazed and taken aback when Peter stood up with a bowl of ale in his hand and somewhat drunkenly told them about William leading a second round of raids on the Moorish ports which had followed close upon their own.

Peter said he finally tell them about the follow-up raids by the galleys sailing with William had undoubtedly already been completed by now. *Peter never was much of a drinker, was he?*

What neither Peter nor anyone else also did not tell the assembled captains and lieutenants was that William and his fleet were on their way to Cornwall, or what they would all be doing after William and his fleet of galleys arrived.

The fact that they had neither been told about the follow-up raids by William's fleet, nor heard even rumours about them, greatly pleased the men sitting at the long wooden table. To a man, they pounded their hands on the table and shouted to express their pleasure at having been so successfully kept in the dark.

Why were they so pleased? Because they were all experienced veterans and knew all too well that if they had been told or heard about it, one of them, or one of their men, might have let the cat out of the sack to someone acting as a Moorish spy. If that had happened, the Moors would have been ready and waiting when William and his men arrived.

As experienced fighting men, they understood that the next time it might be them and their men who were protected by their fellow archers being kept in the dark until it was too late for an enemy to find out they were coming. In any event, and rightly so, they all approved their not being told until just now, even the lieutenant who had been outside pissing and hurried back in shouting "What happened? What happened?" when he heard all the commotion.

There was immediately much speculation as to whether William's fleet hitting the Moorish ports again so quickly "would do as well we did since we got there first and took the choice cuts."

And, of course, all evening the captains and lieutenants talked about what they would be doing next, and looked at their betters with questions in their eyes each time the subject came up. They knew it was something big or they would not have been ordered to give up their regular pursuit of coins and sail all the way to England. They just did not know what it was or how big it would be.

Those who expressed their best guesses, and most of them did, were roughly divided between those who thought they had been ordered to come to England because the company had been hired to fight for King John against his rebel barons, and those who thought they had come to England to help the barons and the French allies fight against King John. We did not tell them it would be neither.

They also did not know about William's plan to combine the men and galleys of the two fleets and take them to France for the same reason of secrecy, or that Peter would soon be the company's commander with George as his second. Only the company's lieutenant commanders knew those secrets, and we were not about to say a word to anyone, not even our best friends.

It was a fine evening filled with good will and fond remembrances. I myself lasted until the moon had moved until it was well up in the sky above us. It was a lively session and no doubt continued for some time, perhaps even the length of another three candles, after I staggered off to bed in my room in one of the wall towers where the boys were learnt.

That the new arrivals would talk until the sun arrived was to be expected; some of men had not had a chance to talk to each other for years and everyone had much to ask and to tell and share. In any event, we all drank too much ale and made many trips to the jar outside the door that served as the piss pot. *The only tanner in Lostwithiel, the castle village, would collect the piss pot in the morning and use its contents to help cure his leathers.*

As I also recall about the food we ate, the buttered fresh bread and the burnt meat strips were most satisfying, and the cooks were rewarded with good belches and many requests for more food and ale. It was a fine meal even though some of the cheese seemed slightly off.

Everyone stayed up later than usual because there was so much to talk about. Accordingly, it was quite late and very dark except for some moonlight by the time I walked back to my room and climbed into my bed. It was in the tower next to the long hovel against the inner side of the inner curtain wall where the lads in my school were sleeping.

And then I could not sleep—it had dawned on me as I listened to the talk of the bearded company veterans around me that they were all young boys compared to me.

What kept me awake was the realization that I was some years older than William, and he would soon be stepping down from active service with the company even though he would keep his stripes and pay for the rest of his life. Henry was stepping down too. Should I do the same? It was all I had thought about ever since I received William's parchment announcing his intention to step aside. I did not think I slept a wink all night.

# Chapter Two

*Questions and Rumours.*

The next morning I was as tired as I had ever been as I settled myself on my wooden stool, and then asked my question of my older boys. I did so whilst I was giving a good scratch to the patch of lice around my dingle. They had started acting up more frequently of late, the lice I mean.

"Both the king of England and the crown prince of France claim the English throne, and so do a couple of their nephews and someone claiming to be one of King Richard's bastards; so which of them should *we* support?"

The "we" in my question, as the eleven boys sitting attentively in front of me all knew perfectly well, was the Cornwall-based company of archers in which I was a lieutenant commander with six stripes on my tunic and they hoped to someday join as apprentice sergeants.

I had served in the company as an archer in addition to now also being both the head of my school and the Bishop of Cornwall, the position I bought from the Pope some years ago for eight hundred silver coins. It was a bit much for such a poor diocese but we had paid it cheerfully; it was worth every penny of it to be able to keep meddling priests out of

Cornwall. They always ended up thieving and trying to separate people like my dear mother from their coins.

All the boys also knew, of course, that my younger brother, William, was the company's commander and had been ever since the captain before him had been killed fighting the Saracens in the Bekka Valley. They also knew that William was an experienced archer and had been in many battles by the time he became the company's commander—and that I had been there by his side during most of them.

It was all true. William had been in the company from its beginning, longer than everyone else except for me and Raymond and a couple of the other greybeards from the original company—the men who made their marks and joined at the same time William and I did. It seemed like just yesterday, but it was actually many years ago when I left the monastery and took William with me to go crusading with King Richard.

It was me who taught William to do his sums and to scribe and gobble Latin. And it was me who used that to convince the men to vote him to be their captain when the company's previous captain, a man from Liverpool, was killed of being hit in the head by a Saracen rock that came over the castle wall. It made a horrible mess of the old captain's head and William became the new captain.

In any event, the question as to which of the men who wanted to be England's king the company should support was the question I put to the eleven bright-eyed young lads in front of me. They were staring at me intently from where they were sitting on the three rickety wooden benches. *And as I did, I almost misspoke and started to ask them who they thought should be the next bishop and lead the school and the diocese.*

The boys, of course, were watching and listening carefully, as well they should. It was an important question with an answer I wanted to have firmly lodged behind their eyes—because someday they might be the company's captains and commanders and have to make just such a decision. What I wanted the boys to understand was that there were many things that had to be considered before such a decision could be made, and some of those things were more important than the others.

All of the boys to whom I had addressed my question were the oldest students in my school, somewhere between fourteen and sixteen years old of age, although neither they nor anyone else knew for sure when they had been birthed. The one thing they had in common was that they were all quite bright, as was to be expected since I made a real effort to only recruit likely lads for my school.

What was surprising to me, since it is well known that being learnt too much can weaken a man, they were already bigger and stronger than most of the archers they would be leading in the years ahead. *Being weakened by being learnt too much without taking the proper precautions, of course, explains why priests are usually too weak to make good soldiers.*

I attributed my boys' surprisingly good health and the death of so few of them whilst they were in my care, to the advice I got from a relatively young Greek physician in Damascus when I was first thinking about starting my school. That was way back many years ago when I was still a crusader and Richard was king. Over a cup of good wine I had asked the Greek how much a boy could be learnt before it would weaken him so much that he would not be strong enough to push arrows out of a longbow.

To my surprise, the Greek assured me that filling the boys heads with summing and scribing would not be a problem at all—so long as the boys ate meat or fish at least once each day and always got as much bread and cheese as they wanted to eat at least two times every day. He particularly said that every day they must each be required eat two or three eggs from red hens.

As I recall, he rounded on me most fiercely and shook a warning finger under my nose when I asked if the eggs from white hens would do in a pinch and suggested that young boys might not need so much food because they were smaller.

My assistant, the man who put the learning on the boys whenever I was away, white-haired Master Robert, was sitting behind the boys and listening as well. Robert was a former priest in Durham's cathedral who had run afoul of his archbishop as the result of getting to know a certain well-known and noisy abbess of our mutual acquaintance. Indeed, it was through her that I first learnt of Robert and ended up bringing him from Durham to be my assistant, and to take charge of the school and my students whenever I was away.

Unfortunately, Robert had been caught getting to know the abbess whilst she was visiting a sister nunnery of her order in Durham where he had been a priest at the time. Her loud and enthusiastic prayers when sinning had drawn a prissy visiting monk's attention to Robert's somewhat un-priestly behaviour.

His appearance at the scene of her prayers had, in turn, caused a rousing argument with blows being exchanged that resulted in an injury to the monk's nose. Robert was dismissed from the Church, and the abbess became even better known, when the injured monk reported Robert's behaviour to the archbishop—who promptly sacked Robert and hurried off to "examine" the abbess to see for himself if she could be "saved" for the Church. She obviously was.

I had not even been aware of Robert until the abbess told me some months later how guilty she felt about replacing him in her bed with the Archbishop. In the end, since it was too late to warn Robert about her loud prayers when she was getting to know someone, and I knew he could scribe Latin and was not interested in the dingles of young boys as many priests seem to be, I decided to offer him a position in my school. *I myself usually stuffed a rag in her mouth to keep her quiet; better safe than sorry, eh?*

All of the boys listening to me were sitting on three wooden benches set out on the stone floor of my room in one of the towers of Restormel's inner-most curtain wall, the tower nearest to the wall's drawbridge gate. That was where I slept and where Master Robert and I usually met with the boys so they could be learnt "what they would need to know in order to be successful in the company of archers in the years ahead."

At that moment, the boys were either looking at me anxiously or trying not to catch my eye by looking away. They were the oldest boys now in my school. If they did well when they went on active service with the company, and were fortunate enough not to die for some reason or get injured along the way, they would someday become its captains and commanders.

My boys' success was my hope and intention. In the brief moment of silence whilst the boys tried to avoid my attention, we could faintly hear a company of apprentice archers chanting as they marched through the nearby gate in the castle wall to the beat of a marching drum.

"What they would need to know in order to be successful in the company," of course, meant that they could do sums and scribe and gobble Latin in addition to knowing how to push arrows out of a longbow, march together on the same foot to the beat of a marching drum, and properly set bladed pikes and sharp stakes.

The boys were also learnt to swim in the river even though many people thought sailors never should be learnt to swim so they could drown faster and with less agony if their galley or transport went down. I disagreed and made sure my boys were learnt to swim; my nephew George was alive because of it.

My question as to who they thought the company should support to be the king was an important question because the lads were almost finished with their long years of being learnt. Soon they would be joining the company as apprentice sergeants and begin their careers in the company doing summing and scribing for one of the company's captains or commanders. And someday, if they survived and managed to get themselves promoted, they themselves might have to decide whether or not the company should support one or another of the insipid nobles or princes who always seemed to be trying to become England's king.

The choice of who the company should support on the day the boys sat in front of me was between King John, King Phillip or Prince Louis of France, and a couple of nobles who were either their cousins or their fathers' bastards, or both. They were all members of the family some long-ago Pope said God had chosen to rule England.

Those would be the men we would talk about today even though they had almost certainly be long gone into purgatory by the time any of the boys had to make such a decision. In fact, we did not give one whit or patch of lice about who was king—so long as he left us alone and untaxed, and never entered Cornwall to bother us. And that, of course, was the correct answer to my question.

It was understood that sooner or later the lads listening to me would be joining the company. Already half a dozen of my school's earlier graduates had the four stripes of an archer captain on the fronts and back of their tunics, one had the five stripes of a captain major, and two had the six stripes of a lieutenant commander if I included my nephew George.

Most of the lads who had finished being learnt in my school, of course, still only had the three stripes of a sergeant and were still only apprentices to their betters. *And two who had been caught knowing too much about each other's dingles and had been quickly ordained and sent off to be priests in Yorkshire.*

Now there were only eight of us left out of the original one hundred and ninety-two archers who had gone for crusaders with King Richard to the Holy Land. But we had recruited new men to fill our ranks; adopted the most modern of weapons such as longbows and bladed pikes with long handles; and grown the company to be quite large and successful.

We were wealthy too, with many chests of coins filling one of the two rooms above Restormel's great hall. The other room, the one at the top of the stairs, was where William lived with his sister wives and their children during that part of the year when he was not in the east looking after the company's affairs out there.

We did not, however, behave like the Templars and nobles who flaunted their wealth and hung about in the king's court to make everyone jealous of their successes, and in so doing attracted robbers, thieves, and churchmen. To the contrary, William and I did not want to tempt others to come against the company or into Cornwall and to try to take it. Accordingly, we always denied our wealth and pretended to be poor, even to William's lieutenants.

The importance of keeping the company's successes, strength, and wealth a secret was something I constantly hammered into the boys in my school. On the other hand, and there was no denying it, the company had come a long way since the eighteen of us who had survived crusading with King Richard had taken William's young son George with us and gone over the wall of Lord Edmund's castle to escape from the head-chopping Saracens.

Our most pressing recruiting problem had continued for many years. And it explained why I had started gathering likely young lads to be students in my school even before I returned to England. It was related to the fact that of all the men in our original company, only William and I, had known how to do the summing and scribing necessary to send parchment messages back and forth and to enter contracts with the unscrupulous merchants who overfilled the markets in every port.

Many men believed that knowing how to sum and scribe would dangerously weaken and overbalance a man by filling up the space behind his eyes with too many words and ideas. That was unfortunate, for doing sums and reading and scribing must be done if the company was to continue to successfully sell the prizes its galleys took and carry passengers and cargos.

We could have done what the king and nobles do, and employed clerics or former clerics such as Master Robert to do our summing and scribing. And, indeed, that was what the company had been forced to do at many of the shipping posts we had established at some of the ports we served. But it was not a satisfactory state of affairs—the priests and former priests were mostly untrustworthy around coins and young boys, and prone to selling our secrets or revealing them in exchange for not having their evil deeds exposed.

There were exceptions to the problems caused by priests and other churchmen, of course. One of them was Yoram, our very first recruit. He was now married and one of the company's most important lieutenant commanders, and in charge of all our merchant and shipping operations east of Gibraltar. In any event, and there was no doubt about it, the company needed the boys who were being learnt in my school and we all knew it.

Originally there had been sixteen boys in this particular class, but two had died of one pox or another soon after they arrived years ago as young tykes, and three more were lost last year when a plague of the sweating and shitting pox swept over Cornwall.

The boys who had survived were important to us. Their ability to scribe and do sums, in addition to their being learnt to lead men both at sea and on land, was vital to the continued success of the company. That would be particularly true in the years ahead when William and I were gone.

And that day was coming quickly—I had known it ever since I received the parchment from William informing me that leading the archers against the French this summer to revenge my imprisonment and ransom would be his last campaign.

After I asked the boys my question about whom the company should support for king, and why and how, I pointed to young John sitting in the rear in such a way as to indicate I wanted him to be the first to answer.

I had, of course, gobbled my question at John in Latin. It was the only language the lads were allowed to speak and scribe when they were in my school. That was for several reasons. One was because Latin was the only language available to be used for scribing parchments. Another was because it was useful when dealing with merchants and others who could not speak English since there was usually a priest nearby who could translate for them.

The third reason my school lads were also being prepared to be ordained as priests was so they would be able to find employment if they turned out to be morally or physically unfit to join the company for some reason. *We could not have them hanging about and starving to death outside our walls if they turned out not to be fit to be archers, could we? It would be bad for morale.*

Besides, and this turned out to be very important, being able to claim you were a priest could be quite helpful when dealing with people who were gullible enough to believe whatever a priest or bishop told them.

It was also helpful when dealing with people who were not always sure they believed what the priests told them, but would pretend to agree with them and make donations because they feared what the Church would do if they did not pay. Being burnt forever in the fires of hell, or even temporarily whilst tied to a stake, was not something to be taken lightly.

My brother's recent experiences in Lisbon, and mine last year in France, were good examples of why I always took the time to sprinkle water on the boys and gobble the Latin prayers needed to make them priests. In William's case, the king ruling Lisbon immediately freed William, instead of holding him for ransom at the request of King John.

Lisbon's king did so when William astounded the king's chamberlain by gobbling Latin at him whilst shaking his finger in the chamberlain's face and proclaiming himself to be a priest acting on behalf of the Holy Father in addition to being the commander of the company of archers.

In essence, the Lisbon king's fear of the Pope, for whom William rightfully claimed to be providing coins for the Holy Father's personal needs, and on whose behalf William claimed the archers were acting, outweighed the Lisbon king's desire to get his hands on one of King John's young daughters.

William, of course, had somewhat lied to Lisbon's king about the company's relationship with the Holy Father. The truth was that each year one of William's lieutenants, usually me or George because we were the only ones amongst the company's veterans who could gobble Latin, took a coin pouch to Rome containing some, but only some, of the coins the company's galley and transport captains had collected from their passengers "for the Pope's prayers for your safe arrival."

As you might imagine, we handed the pouch directly to the Holy Father so that none of the coins would mysteriously disappear into the purses and pouches of the Holy Father's assistants. It was a precaution suggested by the Holy Father himself.

We took the prayer coins to Rome each year because collecting money for the Pope's prayers from our passengers was a good earner of coins for us, and because the relatively small amount of "prayer coins" we did take to Rome kept the Pope and his courtier priests sweet.

Importantly, the coins we took to the Pope let us tell lies about the company supporting the Holy Father and being supported by him in return. Besides, who was to say the Holy Father did not support and protect us? No one was going to ask him were they? At the most, they would discreetly inquire amongst the Holy Father's courtiers and learn that we did indeed personally deliver coins to the Pope each year.

In any event, all it took was a small amount of coins every year and the ability to keep a straight face when we claimed that we were the ones who provided the coins the Pope used to pay his personal expenses, or that we were doing something because the Holy Father had ordered it.

John gulped in dismay and blinked his eyes when I pointed at him to start the talking. The other lads were visibly relieved not to have been asked to answer the question. They turned as one to look at John and listen to his answer. They thought it was a question intended to help me weed out those amongst them who were not yet ready to put the three stripes of a sergeant on their tunics and become a captain's apprentice and scriber. They were wrong.

What the boys, and everyone else, did not know was that William and a goodly number of the company's archers were on their way to Cornwall to take on supplies and prepare for a major raid on France. The raid, of course, being the revenge required in the company's contract for the French taking me to France last year and holding me until the company paid a ransom for my release.

Although they did not know it yet, all eleven of the boys sitting in front of me, each and every one of them, would soon be sprinkled with water and prayed at in Latin to ordain them as priests. I was also going to let all eleven of the boys make their marks on the company's roll and become apprentice sergeants.

I had questions about several of them, but their ability to gobble and scribe Latin was too important for me to set them aside—because their presence would let William and his lieutenant commanders send scribed orders to their galley and post captains and enable their captains to send in scribed reports. It was something none of the captains would otherwise be able to do because not a one of them knew how to read and scribe. As a result, the boys would get their chance despite my misgivings.

In any event, and there was no doubt about it, participating in the company's revenge raid on France would be good experience for those of the boys who survived long enough, and performed well enough, to become the company's captains and commanders in the years ahead.

There were already rumours flying about as to what was going to happen now that Peter and his men had arrived. And other rumours were flying about as to how soon some or all of the boys in my school would be joining the company. But nobody knew what would actually happen, and when, except me and my fellow lieutenant commanders.


****** 

My efforts to get the older boys ready to be ordained and join the company as apprentice sergeants was not the only preparation being made for the raid William intended to lead against France. No announcement had been made, not even to our own captains, because we did not want the French to know we were coming.

Indeed, none of William's galleys had yet arrived from the east and there had been no announcement that they would even be coming. Even so, it was plain for everyone to see from all the activity along the river that something was up. The arrival of Peter's galleys alone was enough to make it obvious that something was in the wind. But what could it be?

There were more rumours flying about the castle and our nearby training camp along the river, and in the castle's village of Lostwithiel and my school, than there were fleas on one of the castle's rat-eating cats. Some of the men thought they would be sailing to London to fight with King John against the rebel barons and the French knights who had been sent from France by Prince Louis to help them.

Others thought they would be going to London to join the barons and their French supporters and fight against King John.

In retrospect what happened was inevitable. As we should have expected, betting stalls had been set up by the owners of the village's two alehouses within hours after Peter's arrival. They were immediately over-run with archers and sailors seeking to make their fortunes on the basis of the latest news and rumours. *In the end, it turned out to be fortunate for everyone except one of the alehouse owners that we did not prevent them taking the bets, for it helped us catch a spy.*

Of all things, what had caused everyone to realize something really big was afoot, in addition to the arrival of Peter and his fleet, were the large numbers of cattle, sheep and other food supplies being assembled in hastily erected pens along the river. There were already more sheep, cattle, and live geese and chickens on hand than the galleys already on the river could possibly carry—and even more meat animals were known to be coming.

Similarly, the galleys in the river had already taken on full loads of firewood for their cooks and more was being brought in to the camp. It almost certainly meant that a large number of additional galleys would soon be rowing up the Fowey to take on supplies.

Moreover, George had intensified the training of the apprentice archers and brought forward the usual final two weeks of their being learnt to be archers. That made it obvious that many of them would soon be allowed to sew the stripe of a regular archer on their tunics and join the company.

And earlier in the week Raymond had ridden in from Okehampton with a large force of his horse archers and outriders—just as they would if the fighting men in the camp would soon be sailing off to parts unknown and the camp and the company's women and children in and around the castle needed to be guarded.

Taking everything together could only mean one thing and everyone knew it—something big was in the wind.

The more experienced men amongst the archers understood that no one could possibly know the strength of the army of archers that was being put together until the rest of the expected galleys actually arrived and could be counted. Similarly, no one would know for sure how soon the archers would sail until the order was given to nobble the legs of the cattle and sheep and tie together the legs of the stringers of chickens and geese.

Preparing them to travel would be done at the last minute so they could be carried live on the galleys' decks to help feed the men when their supplies of previously dead and butchered meat were exhausted.

In any event, we dared not tell the men they would soon be sailing for France. If we did, it would almost certainly soon be known by the French and they would be waiting for us and ready to fight or, in the case of the French king, long gone from where we might capture him and hold him for ransom. *It is always better to fall upon someone who is not expecting you.*

As a result, the only thing the rank and file archers knew for sure was that their captains and commanders were experienced fighting men and would not want spies to get a warning if they were going to be sailing off to fight somewhere. That meant the archers would, as was the company's custom, not be told where they were going, and why and who they would be fighting, until after they sailed.

As one might expect with rumours were flying fast and furious, there were many arguments and speculations. As a result, there was heavy betting at the betting stalls that had been quickly set up in all three of the alehouses in the castle's village of Lostwithiel.

Most of the bets they booked were either that the archers would soon be sailing for London to fight for King John, or sailing for London to fight for the barons who were trying to replace King John. There were other rumours and bets, of course, but those that the archers would soon be sailing off to fight for or against King John were by far the most numerous.

There was, however, a problem that was not fully appreciated by the gamblers, at least not initially. The secrecy as to the company's destination and who the archers would be fighting when they got there, meant that the men who won their bets would not know they had won until after they had sailed away from Cornwall and the coins that were due them—and then those who had won their bets would have no way to collect their winnings.

Despite the reality that the winners would not be around to collect, Lostwithiel's three alehouses were quickly overwhelmed with archers and sailors placing bets. They were so busy they almost ran out of ale.

No one knew it at the time, of course, but the gambling of the archers and sailors had a profound effect on what subsequently did *not* happen in France.

# Chapter Three

*William returns to Cornwall.*

William's galleys began arriving twelve days after the last of Peter's galleys slowly rowed its way up the river. Within minutes of the first of William's galleys mooring at one of the camp's floating wharfs, the word from its crew had spread and everyone knew that an additional twenty galleys would be coming in to join those already moored all along the riverbank.

It would be, without a doubt, the men excitedly told each other, the biggest force of the company's archers and galleys ever assembled in one place. Word of their coming and their numbers spread faster than London's public women ran to the tower when the French army was paid.

Almost immediately the gambling stalls in the village's alehouses were once again mobbed by archers and castle workers attempting to change their bets or add to them. William himself did not arrive until the next day.

I first learned that William's galleys were beginning to arrive when I heard someone shouting as he ran through the gate in the castle wall that was next to the tower where I lived. As you might imagine, I rushed outside to see what was happening. Moments I was lifting my bishop's gown so it would not drag on the ground and hurrying down the cart path to the river to see for myself.

I was not alone. People were pouring out of the castle and village next to it, the collection of hovels some of the castle workers living in them were now calling Lostwithiel, and heading down the path to the river. They included my brother's wives carrying and leading their children, and just about everyone else. It was an excited and happy throng. Our men were coming home after many months of being away.

Some of the excitement, but not all of it, disappeared when we reached the river and discovered that it was a galley commanded by one of William's captains, Sam Carpenter, which had arrived, not William himself. George and Peter were at the floating wharf talking to Sam when I arrived.

Sam said he had no idea how soon William and the others would arrive as he had lost sight of them almost as soon as his galley had rowed out of Lisbon's harbour. He was, however, quite pleased with himself when he discovered his was the first of William's galleys to arrive. He did not know it, but he made a favourable impression on everyone when he attributed his galley's fast voyage from Lisbon to his fine lieutenant and his sailing sergeant and crew.

George told Sam to bring his lieutenant to the castle tonight for supper when the sun was finishing its daily voyage around the world. "And you should both bring your bedding with you as well; you will be staying in the hall with Peter Barrow and some of his captains and lieutenants who are already there. They will be anxious to hear what you have been doing and where you have been doing it."

"Cheer up," I said with a somewhat forced smile as I walked back to re-join William's dejected and disappointed family, and we began slowly walking back up the path together towards the castle. "He will be back soon. It will not be long now, will it?"

George and Peter remained behind to see to the care and feeding of Sam's men and the resupplying of his galley. As I walked away I heard Peter ordering some of the galleys moored near the two floating wharves to move further down the river to make room for those who would be arriving shortly. *Good. They seem to be working well together.*

I listened to the women chatter as we walked together back to Restormel, but my mind was far away. I could not help but think of my own future now that William was about to arrive. Perhaps Master Robert would be the best choice to replace me as the head of my school with George becoming the bishop. The only other possibility I could think of for either position would be Albert Ditchling, one of George's fellow students who had been our spy in King

John's court ever since we bought a position for him as one of the nuncio's priestly assistants.

The idea of using the nuncio's assistant was behind my eyes because a few days earlier a message had arrived from Albert about the strength of King John's army, or perhaps I should say its profound weakness despite being led by the man that many people thought was England's best soldier, Sir William Marshal.

Albert was my former student who became our man in the nuncio's household using the name Father Alberto. In reality, he was our spy in London and Windsor who kept us informed as what the Pope's self-serving nuncio was doing and saying in his ongoing efforts to enrich himself. *He probably wanted to buy a cardinal's appointment in Rome. At least, that was what Albert thought.*

So far, at least so far as we could tell, the nuncio's various coin-earning treacheries and betrayals had not involved either Cornwall or the company. But that could change at any time because the nuncio was the Pope's ambassador to England and was now, according to Albert, secretly supporting the French as a result of a substantial donation to the Church from Louis of France, most of which had somehow found its way into the nuncio's purse.

We knew about the secret switch of the nuncio's support from King John to Prince Louis because Albert had scribed the nuncio's report to Louis about the King John's army and its commander, Sir William Marshal. Sir William, the nuncio told the French, was devoted to the king and probably could not be turned—but he could be defeated because King John's army of supporters was so small and poorly trained. *But is it the nuncio who wants the French to attack King John or is it the Pope?*

What the nuncio did not know was that a similar, but significantly smaller, "donation," thought to have come from one of the nuncio's friends in Rome, unfortunately recently deceased so he could not confirm his benevolence, had likewise bought "Father Alberto" a position in the greedy nuncio's household. And once in the nuncio's household,

Albert's ability and his fine hand at scribing Latin parchments soon led to "Father Alberto" rapidly becoming the nuncio's favourite scriber. His rapid promotion came when the priestly scriber he replaced suffered an unfortunate and costly injury to his hand whilst walking in London in the dark after visiting one of his gentlemen friends. *It cost me five silver coins.*

\*\*\*\*\*\*

The rest of William's galleys began coming up the river one after another the next day. A huge and growing crowd began assembling to greet them about two hours after sunrise. The people did not come out at dawn to wait for them because they knew that it would take the galleys at least that long to row up the river from its mouth. They were not disappointed. William's was the seventh galley to arrive and nine more came in after his before the sun finished passing overhead.

Each of the newly arriving galleys was greeted with great cheering and merriment, and then curiosity as the crowd inevitably surged forward to see who was on it and greet old friends. Some of the galleys came all the way up to our two floating wooden wharves where the lieutenant commanders were waiting to greet them, and then moved back down the river to tie up at whatever open space they could find along the riverbank.

The captains of other arriving galleys saw the galleys already tied up along the riverbank and moved in to tie up along with them without even trying to go on up the river to the wharves. The result, at first, was a cheerful chaos with a surging tide of cheerful people moving up and down the path along to the river to reach and greet each new arrival.

Helen and Tori and all their children were waiting anxiously, and broke into tears, when William's galley came slowly around the bend in the river with its drum booming and the water from its oars flashing in the sun. They knew immediately that it was his because they could see a woman standing amongst the men on the roof of its forward castle. I just stood there between the two alternately crying and laughing women with my arms around their shoulders.

William's actual arrival at the first of the camp's two wharves was the joyous event you might expect. He was waiting at the deck railing as one of the galley's sailors threw its mooring lines to the willing hands waiting to help tie it up. And then promptly, and very gingerly I noticed, he threw his leg over the railing and stepped on to the floating wharf even though it was still bobbing up and down. *My God, his hair has gone as white as mine.*

A few quick and careful steps on the pitching and bobbing wharf and William was in the arms of Helen and Tori, who were both smiling and crying at the same time. The three of them, in turn, were surrounded by a gaggle of children, all of whom were either jumping up and down with excitement or standing shyly to the side waiting to be recognized. Sarah, his travelling companion, was nowhere to be seen.

Seeing William alive and with his family once again moved me almost to tears. It was at that very moment that I made my decision to step down as Cornwall's bishop and take George's name and a pouch of coins to the Pope to make sure he became my successor. He could hold the diocese until he took over the company from Peter. *He would be a good replacement seeing as he was a younger version of me, a six-stripe lieutenant commander who long ago had the required Latin prayers gobbled at him to make him a priest.*

\*\*\*\*\*\*

The cheerful chaos along the riverbank continued long after William walked up the path to the castle surrounded by his happy family. I remained behind with my brother's other lieutenants and watched as the river got more and crowed with galleys.

In no time at all, the riverbank and the meadow alongside of it filled up with the several thousand archers and sailors coming off of the new arrivals and their even more numerous well-wishers from the castle, the training camp, and the galleys who had arrived a few days earlier with Peter. Never before had there ever been so many of our galleys or archers in Cornwall at one time.

After a while, right after William began walking up the path to the castle, a similarly pleased and excited George and the company's other lieutenant commanders began imposing a degree of order on the ever-increasing chaos and excitement. They did so by riding horses up and down the path along the river and waving the latest of the new arrivals into mooring places along the riverbank.

Raymond helped them. He had come in from Okehampton three days earlier in order to meet with William when he arrived. And he brought with him the surprising news of a spy in Cornwall. The man his outriders had caught was actually a mere lad. But he was carrying a message that neither he nor anyone else could understand: "The new mares are ready. There are three browns and a grey."

It sounded innocent, but it fuddled us and was worrisome because his father had instructed him to tell that message to both a Sir Gerard at the king's court at Windsor, someone I had seen at court several years ago and knew to be a captain in King John's army, *and* to a French priest at the Tower of London—where Louis of France had recently re-joined the French knights who were holding it and promptly proclaimed himself to be the King of England.

What was also worrisome was the boy himself. His name was Giles and he was one of ours. Not an archer, but rather the son of the couple who operated one of the two ale houses in Lostwithiel, the village nearest to Restormel Castle and the archers' training camp.

Raymond had the boy safely under guard at Okehampton; he had wisely not brought him back to Restormel so that his capture would become known and his parents would have a chance to flee before they could be questioned. Raymond had also reduced the number of horse archers in his escort to a handful of his most trusted men in an effort to prevent the boy's capture from being revealed by loose lips whilst his men were visiting Restormel.

It sounded to me as though the boy's father, also named Giles, was a spy. But for whom? And why was his message sent to both of the two deadly enemies? And why did he entrust the message to his rather simple young son instead of trying to deliver it himself or use another courier? It just did not make sense.

# Chapter Four

*Plans are made.*

William's return to Cornwall was greatly celebrated by both his family and his men. There was little wonder in their happiness because for a number of months in the winter everyone had thought he was dead and gone. As a result, we had two celebratory meals in Restormel's great hall one right after another on the day of William's return.

The first was an early meal for the members of his joyful family to welcome him home. It was probably significant that Helen herself had walked down to Harold's galley to fetch Sarah so she too could attend.

After William's meal with his family was finished and his women and children, including Sarah, made their way up the stone stairs to their rooms above the great hall, food and drink was set out on the hall's long table for a second meal for all of the company's captains and their lieutenants.

****** *Thomas*

Before the two meals started, William spent much of the afternoon in a private meeting with me and his lieutenant commanders. We each needed to bring the others of us up to date.

George, Raymond, and I were intensely questioned as to what we was happening in Cornwall and England. And we would listened carefully as William, Peter, Henry, and Harold told us what they had seen and done in the east. Young Edmund and our apprentice sergeants were, at Thomas's request, allowed to sit with us so as to be learnt about the company's concerns and considerations; they listened attentively from the end of the long table and, of course, never said a word.

William and the rest of us spent a good part of our meeting speculating as to what the latest news from London meant for Cornwall and the company. We had a lot to talk about because something very significant had recently happened: Prince Louis of France and a large force of French knights and their men-at-arms had returned to London to reinforce the French troops helping the rebel barons hold the Tower and the city.

More importantly, to everyone's surprise, as soon as he reached London, Prince Louis had issued a proclamation, with the rebel barons standing beside him nodding their agreement, proclaiming that he, Louis of France, was now the true king of England. It undoubtedly meant something that would end up affecting the company and Cornwall in some way; we just did not know how or when.

One thing was certain: Louis might well win and become the king of England. Therefore we decided to do everything possible to avoid associating the company and Cornwall with either King John or Prince Louis and, in so doing, turn the other into a serious enemy. It was a decision with which we all agreed. And it would dominate our planning for our raid on France.

Prince Louis and the French reinforcements arriving in London were almost certainly the cause of the two parchment messages that had been carried by the same courier and arrived at Restormel several days earlier. Both were addressed to William.

The first parchment was from King John himself. It offered to employ the company's archers as mercenaries to help his army fight the supporters of the French prince who was "defying God" by trying to take his throne. In essence, the king offered his stannary rights and holdings in Cornwall, meaning his tin mines, refineries, and two coineries, as payment for the company's assistance in his fight against the French prince.

What made the king's offer particularly interesting such that we immediately began to consider it seriously, was the parchment that accompanied it. The second parchment was from Sir William Marshal, the commander of the king's army, and well known to be an honourable man.

Sir William's message was as important as the king's. It said that the king had authorized him to negotiate and sign a mercenary contract in the king's name. Accordingly, he asked to meet with William or his representative in a mutually agreeable place as soon as possible.

One of the several things that made the request of the commander of the king's army so interesting was that he suggested London's moneylenders might advance enough coins against Cornwall's stannaries such that we could pay our men "enough to temporarily turn their eyes away from the Holy Land to help their king."

It was quite encouraging, we all agreed, that King John had not bothered to try to order us to recall our men and put them at his service. If he had, we would have assured him of our great loyalty with many fine oaths, and regretfully reported that our men were all far away and unavailable.

But he did not even try to order us to help him. We hoped that was because he and Sir William, and everyone else in the king's court, believed our oft-repeated lies wherein we said that Cornwall and the company were too poor to be of any help to anyone. Our constant refrain to everyone was some version of the following:

"The poverty of Cornwall and the difficulty the Company of Archers has in obtaining enough coins to pay its men are well known. They are, of course, "God's Will" and explain why most of the company's archers and sailors are usually in the Holy Land earning their bread and coins—and why they would almost certainly refuse to come back to fight in England or France unless they were paid in advance whatever coins they were promised for risking their lives as mercenaries."

It was a very good story and quite believable. In reality, the coin chests at Restormel and on Cyprus were numerous and full to overflowing.

If the parchments were to be believed, King John and his fawning courtiers, including the commander of the king's army, did not know about the company's wealth. Or, at least, it seemed they did not know. And if they did not know, it was almost certainly because of our lies and because we made them believable by not flaunting our wealth the way the Templars do.

We did not do so, flaunt our wealth that is, because it would ruin our fine excuse of being too poor to help the king or pay taxes. Even worse, it would almost certainly attract nobles and priests to Cornwall who would attempt to get some of it.

Our desire to discourage others from coming to Cornwall so we would be left alone and untaxed explained why we always lied and claimed that Cornwall and the company were so poor that the archers had to go to the Holy Land to earn their bread, and the company often had to borrow the coins it needed to pay its men.

It appeared that the king and his fawning courtiers and captains believed our lies. *Of course the men who are in Cornwall and lead the archers are too poor to be of any assistance to the king; otherwise they would be dressed in the latest styles and attending the king's court to seek his favours.*

We would normally have respectfully declined the king's offer to employ us because we had better and more profitable things for our men to do than risk their lives helping the king keep his throne or regain his ancestral lands in France. But things were not normal both because of the king's offer of his stannary holdings, and, more important at the moment, because we would soon be launching an attack on France even if we made no contract to support the king.

"So why did the king himself not borrow against the mines from London's moneylenders and offer us coins in payment instead of offering us his tin mines and other stannaries?" Henry asked of no one in particular. It was a good question.

"He has probably already borrowed against them himself from the moneylenders in Scotland or Germany, and thought we and the London moneylenders would not find out until after we helped him defeat the barons and the French," George suggested with a cynical tone in his voice. *The lad has a good head on his shoulders.*

"Well, George, how then do you think we should answer the king and Sir William?" was my brother's question to his son as we all nodded our heads in agreement with Henry's question and George's comment. *Good. William and the others can see it too; George will make a good* commander for the company, even though he will not be taking command of it until after Peter.

After much discussion, it was decided that we would have a go at trying to gull the king into paying us to do what we had already decided to do—attack the French in such a way as to bring ransom coins, chests and chests of ransom coins, to the company.

Accordingly, I was told to scribe a parchment reply and send identical copies of it to both Sir William and the king. All it was to say was that the proposals of the king and Sir William were most interesting, and that I, as the Bishop of Cornwall, had been asked to represent the company due to the absence of its commander. *Well, he would be absent from the meeting, would he not?*

More specifically, I was to respond by offering to meet with Sir William to attempt to reach an agreement for company's men to participate in one major battle against the king's rebellious nobles or their French supporters in France. I was also to say that I was fully authorized to put my mark on such a contract on behalf of the company in the event an agreement could be reached. *Of course we only said we would "attempt" to reach an agreement; we did not want the king and Sir William to think we were too anxious, did we?*

I, as William and my fellow lieutenant commanders knew full well, was the best person to represent the company and meet with Sir William. That was because I knew him slightly from my previous visits to Windsor to attend the king's ill-fated "peace council" and also from when Sir William and I were both in the party of nobles and churchmen who accompanied the king to Runnymede to meet with his rebellious barons.

As everyone now knows, the meeting at Runnymede resulted in yet another totally meaningless agreement between the king and the barons to end their differences. Indeed, if anything, the king's willingness to pay dearly to employ the archers to fight for him was more evidence of the agreement being just another meaningless failure amongst the many efforts to bring peace to England. So far as I could see, the only good that ever came out of it was that I got to know Sir William.

As you might imagine, my brother listened carefully to all his lieutenant commanders, including me, and then gave me very specific instructions as what to put into my parchment when I scribed it. One was that the company's captains understood that time was of the essence due to the recent actions of the dastardly French and against our beloved and rightful king. What was *not* to be scribed, or even hinted, was that time was also of the essence because we intended to attack France in the near future—in eight days when the tides and our supplies would be at their best.

Also to be scribed was that I would agree to meet with Sir William with the understanding that he would bring to the meeting a parchment with the king's seal on a deed transferring the mines and refineries to the Company of

Archers. Thus, if we reached an agreement, it could go into effect immediately before the company sailed for France.

I was also to say that I had been ordered to make sure the king's seal was on a parchment authorizing Sir William to make his mark on the king's behalf on any agreement that he and I might reach for the use of the company's archers against the French. *Notice that I did mention using them against the barons.*

Moreover, and only because it would almost certainly be required by London's moneylenders "because Cornwall and the company were known to be so poor," Sir William himself would have to personally guarantee that the agreement to turn the king's tin mines and his other stannary-related interests in Cornwall over to the archers would be honoured in full if the archers launched a major attack on the French during the current campaigning season. Sir William's guarantee, we had decided as we talked about the king's offer, was important.

Requiring Sir William's guarantee was a reasonable precaution for us to take. Unlike the king, Sir William was known to be an honourable man in addition to being powerful. He might be able to force the king to honour the terms of the agreement if the king changed his mind and decided not to abide by it after the fighting ended; a situation that was not only possible, we decided, but also highly likely unless we received Sir William's additional guarantee.

I ended my parchment by suggesting that Sir William and I meet in Bath in four days' time if the company's conditions were acceptable to him. I would, I scribed to Sir William, start out for Bath immediately because I understood from the messages we had received that he and the king thought time was of the essence. And it surely was since our fleet would be sailing in eight days.

The parchments, with identical copies going to both Sir William and the king, were carried by pairs of hard-riding horse archers acting as couriers. We expected, if the couriers had no trouble on the roads, my replies would get to Windsor and Sir William in two and a half days. That would give Sir William more than enough time to get to Bath to meet me before the archers sailed for France.

I selected Bath for our meeting because it lay between Cornwall and London, and because I had heard the city's lord was staying neutral—he was pretending to be poxed and unavailable in order to avoid taking sides between the king and his rebels.

My instructions as to how and what I should negotiate were precise. When I met with Sir William, and during our negotiations, I was only to offer the company's services to directly attack the French somewhere as "mercenaries employed by one or more of France's other enemies" with at least three thousand men sometime within the next six months. And I was to strongly *imply,* but not promise, that we would attack the French in London.

If asked where we intended to hit them, I was to say "probably London and very soon; because that is where they are, are they not?"

Only if it was absolutely necessary to get an acceptable agreement signed was I to admit that some of our men had already returned such that we would be attacking the French much sooner than six months. And if I did make such an admission, I was to lie and say that they had begun returning because we had expected the king's offer—and imply to Sir William that we had already been negotiating with the king.

In other words, I was to only agree that in exchange for the mines and stannaries, the company, acting as mercenaries along and with others so our force would be large enough to be effective, would undertake a major action against the French sometime in the near future. In fact, the archers were going to sail for France in eight days no matter whether or not we had gulled a mercenary agreement out of Sir William and the king.

Eight days would be enough for an agreement to be reached and a hard-riding pair of couriers to get back to Restormel with the news. But it would be three or four days more before I would be able to get back to Restormel in a two-horse wain. During the eight days whilst they waited to sail for France, the archers would practice their archery and fighting on land. One galley would remain behind to carry me to France when I returned from Bath.

The seven of us also talked about the spy courier Raymond's outriders had captured. Raymond had him in chains in the Okehampton dungeon where the hinds brought in by Raymond's hunters were hung to age and soften.

Raymond had questioned the boy and, to Raymond's surprise, the boy did not think he had done anything wrong. To the contrary, he was quite agreeable and willing to talk without being tortured. The problem was that the boy did not have any idea what the message meant, only that he was told by his father to deliver it. Raymond believed him.

"He is just a lad is all he is." *Hmm. Raymond clearly does not want him hanged or chopped as a spy.*

At first, we decided to immediately send a sergeant and some archers to Lostwithiel and arrest the boy's father and mother, and to try to turn them into sending false information to whomever it was that had them spying on us. The responsibility for doing so was given to George. But then, for some reason, and I cannot remember what it was, we decided to wait.

****** *Bishop Thomas*

Our family's early supper was a joyous occasion despite the howls of hungry infants who periodically had to be taken up the stairs to their wet nurses. When it ended, George went to his home in one of the towers in the innermost castle wall to check on poor Becky and his new son, and William's women and children climbed up the stone stairs to their private places on the floor that served as the great hall's ceiling and, at the far end of it, held the many chests with our coins and treasures. Sarah went with them.

Without a word being spoken it had become understood that Sarah had joined our family and, like Helen and Tori, would have her own private space on the floor above the hall. If William agreed, I intended to gobble the Latin prayers needed to marry her to my brother as soon as we returned from France. It was obvious from how warmly Helen and Tori greeted Sarah that they greatly approved of her. *So did I. She had seen to my brother and kept him alive, did she not? That is what Harold told me and I believed him.*

# Chapter Five

*A gathering of eagles.*

Restormel's great hall was filled to overflowing later that evening with all of the company's available captains and lieutenants in attendance. It was a splendid affair with many more candles lit than ever before in the castle's history, at least a dozen so everyone could see everyone else.

Normally, three or four candles would have been sufficient. Not this time; the hall quickly became so packed with men that William's wife Helen had to send servants from the village running down to the galleys on the river for more lanterns to hold the additional candles she hurriedly pulled out of the castle's household chest. She later told me she had given a great sigh of hopeless resignation as she did so because they were so precious.

Indeed, there were so many men in attendance that it was soon became clear that there would not be enough benches for everyone to sit down at the same time. The problem of not having enough places to sit was quickly solved by all the benches being moved outside so there were none in the hall. As a result, those who were hungry took food from the stacks of bread, cheese, roots, and burnt meat on the long table and ate whilst standing about and talking with each other.

The smell of so many men crowded into such a small space was overpowering, almost as bad as that of a galley's lower rowing deck. But it was all so familiar to most of us that we hardly noticed it even though it caused young Edmund to turn run outside to vomit, and greatly bothered the women and children who were gathered in the family's sleeping room above the great hall.

William attended the entire time and was constantly moving about to greet his men and listen to their stories. All of the company's lieutenant commanders were there and did the same, except for Yoram who had remained on Cyprus to oversee the company's continuing operations east of Gibraltar.

Our family's women and their children were not present, except for Edmund who was allowed to attend. The family, almost all of us including Sarah and George, and one of George's wives and all of his children except his new and as yet unnamed infant son, had eaten together much earlier.

The only two members of my family who had not been at the family supper were George's poor Becky who was still sickly and sweating too much as she tried to recover from the birth of her recent son, and the new boy himself because it distressed her so greatly when she could not see and hold him.

\*\*\*\*\*\*

That evening saw what was almost certainly the biggest gathering for a meal ever held in Restormel's great hall, and, of course, the reason for so many candles. Even George's friend and one-time fellow student, Richard, rode in from Exeter Castle wearing the five stripes of a captain major on his tunic. I had summoned him as soon as Raymond told me he would like to step down from his command of the horse archers and move to Exeter Castle as its warden and the reeve of its lands, the position Richard had been holding.

William conferred with his lieutenant commanders, and then informed Richard of Raymond's decision and his transfer to take Raymond's place and his promotion to lieutenant commander.

It all occurred within hours of William's arrival at Restormel. Richard's promotion was announced during our meal, to loud cheers, along with a number of other promotions including half a dozen captains to captain major—one for each of the lieutenant commanders. They would be their lieutenant commanders' seconds and take over their responsibilities if they fell or were down with a pox. Those who were promoted were greatly pleased; those who were not, and thought they should have been, tried not to show their disappointment.

Richard's promotion came about because Raymond announced he was ready to join William and Henry in throwing off some of his burdens and slowing down. And besides, Raymond had privately told us rather sheepishly, Wanda, his wife from the land on the other side of the great desert, wanted to live in a city big enough to have its own market. *She collected coin purses and pouches, of all things, and there were never any to buy at Okehampton because its village was small and had no market of its own.*

As with William and Henry, and now me, Raymond wanted to step down and move to Exeter immediately after the company returned from it raid on France. Accordingly, William had decided, and we all agreed, that Richard would sew on a sixth stripe despite his youth and take over Raymond's post at Okehampton as the commander of both the company's horse archers charged with guarding the approaches to Cornwall, and the outriders who patrolled our roads and paths.

Richard would, in other words, change places with Raymond and assume the command all of our men who served as riders. He and his riders, unlike most of the archers who were based in the Holy Land, would continue to be permanently based in England.

Neither Richard nor Raymond nor their men would be going with the company to France. But they too were charged with moving their men to new positions and getting them ready to fight if the need arose. Raymond would be temporarily moving to Restormel to command the men, mostly his horse archers, who would hold Cornwall whilst Richard moved to Okehampton from Rougemont to command the horse archers who remained on the other side of the River Tamar, the men charged with holding the approaches.

Not that we expected trouble, mind you. But if the news got out about the departure of so many of our men to France, it might encourage the king or some of Cornwall's own outlaws or a trouble-making noble to have a go at us or some of our more distant villages and mines. Raymond and Richard would take up their new permanent posts when we returned from France.

Me? I would be going over to join the company in France as soon as I got back from meeting with Sir William Marshal at Bath. Bath was the location I had suggested to Sir William for our meeting because its lord was neutral and there were relatively good roads to Bath from both Cornwall and London.

The company's raid on France, I had decided, would be my last campaign even though I was still not certain as to whether I should give up all my positions, or just my positions as the Bishop of Cornwall and its sheriff. If I gave up both of them, I could concentrate on improving my school and my students—and that is what I decided to do if I survived the fighting in France. *I so much enjoy teaching my boys.*

What continued to vex me was the question of who would be best to replace me in my positions as Cornwall's bishop and also its sheriff. We certainly did not want someone arriving from Rome to be the bishop, or a sheriff appointed by the king. Such men would almost certainly attempt to interfere and have to quickly come to a very troublesome end as the result of a pox or a fatal accident.

Accordingly, I was leaning towards George replacing me to become the bishop and sheriff, with Master Robert to be the head master of my school if I fell in France. The problem was that George being bishop and sheriff meant he would have little time left to also serve as Peter's second in command. It was a problem.

Another possibility for bishop was Albert Ditchling, my former student and George's school friend that the Pope's nuncio to King John knew as Father Alberto from Rome. We had bribed him into the nuncio's household to be our spy, and then used a few more coins to make sure he would be the only one left to do the nuncio's scribing. But who would or could replace Albert as our spy with the king and nuncio if he were to come back to Cornwall and take my place as the bishop and the deliverer of the refugees' prayer coins to Rome?

As I thought about it more and more, I was not certain that Albert was ready to be Cornwall's bishop because of the sensitive negotiations that were sometimes required. So it would have to be George who took the position of bishop with Albert as the sheriff of our lands and the archdeacon who managed the diocese of Cornwall and did most of the traveling needed to keep Cornwall's monks and monasteries in line.

It had to be George who waved a crosier as our bishop because he was the only student I had ever learnt who I knew to be experienced enough and strong enough to be able to make both the annual trip to Rome to deliver the Pope's coins, and engage in the periodic travelling and negotiations required of a bishop.

I was well aware that I had neither spent enough time in our villages as Cornwall's sheriff to make sure there was peace and order, nor as its bishop making sure the village churches were functioning properly using the monks from Cornwall's monasteries instead of having their own parish priests. All that and going to Rome each year was just too much for one man.

*Actually, truth be told, I was well aware that I had totally failed at both positions. It was almost certain that there were now felons from London hiding in Cornwall's forests and villages, and that some of the Bodmin monks were starting to collect coins for themselves and molest the village women and boys—the very reasons I was keeping priests out of Cornwall by claiming it was too poor to support them unless they were housed in a monastery, and preferably a monastery devoted to poverty wherein every monk had to work so he had no time to make mischief.*

# Chapter Six

*Bath and the unexpected encounters.*

My meeting with Sir William Marshal in the old Roman city of Bath started earlier than I thought it would. My gallopers were leading spare horses as remounts and were not interfered with along the way. As a result, they were able to carry my parchment to Sir William at Windsor in near-record time. He, in turn, quickly found a cleric to read it to him and was easily able to ride to Bath in time to greet me, instead of the other way around as I had expected.

I donned my bishop's robe, placed my mitre and crosier by my side in the wain in case I needed to wave them at someone on the road to get them to move out of the way, and departed from Restormel soon after the gallopers. I was in a hurry to get to Bath. Even so, I travelled at a much slower pace in a two-horse wain with a guard of ten horse archers under the command of a very reliable sergeant.

Perhaps I could have gone to Bath with fewer men, but Raymond insisted I needed at least that many to protect me both from the outlaws whose depravities and felonies were well known to occur frequently in and around Bath because of its purgatory-heated waters, and from the dangers of the road in the lands beyond the approaches to Cornwall. In any event, as my brother also cheerfully pointed out, I would need to travel with enough men to be able to lift the wain off the ground and carry it to where it could be repaired if it got stuck in a pothole or one its wheels broke and had to be replaced with one of the spares we would carry with us.

My trip would have been much faster, of course, if I had ridden on my own horse and had a remount available from one of my guards if my horse broke down. But I did not because William ordered me to use a wain instead of riding a horse of my own.

Sitting in a saddle many hours every day and the nights when the moon and stars were out would have been too much for me. I knew that, of course, but I did not want to admit it. In any event, William had laughed and given me a warm brotherly hug when he explained his decision.

"You would arrive with at least a sore arse and a bad back if you try to ride all that way and back on a horse, even if it is one of our best amblers. Besides, you might break down before you reached Bath and not get there in time to meet Sir William; and then where will we be? Better for us to lose a wheel or two off a wain than lose you to a blistered arse, eh?"


\*\*\*\*\*\*

The weather was good and the night sky clear enough for the moon and the stars to light the way. It enabled my men and I to travel almost constantly day and night with periodic stops to piss and rest where streams crossed the road so we could quench or thirsts and water our arses after we shite. It was during these stops that we typically made changes from amongst the spare horses being led by almost all of my guards except the sergeant and the chosen man who was his number two.

We carried three spare wheels in the wain, and had to use them all by the time we reached Bath. And, of course, the pieces of the broken wheels were thrown into the bed of the wain with me so our wain wrights could repair them when we got back to Restormel.

As a result of the broken wheels, and my own longbow and the bread and some of escorts' additional weapons also being in the bed of the wain, there was barely room for me to sometimes stretch out and sleep. But I managed at times despite the wain's constant bump and jerks.

Our trip went well and I never once had to put on my mitre and shout at people to get out of the way. One look at my ferocious looking guards riding ahead of my wain and motioning for everyone on the road to move out of the way, and everyone quickly moved off to the side and let us pass, even a couple of noblemen and a bishop who glared at me when I waved my cross cheerfully and blessed them without stopping to talk.

As a result of rarely being delayed by other travellers on the road, and despite three times breaking a wheel, we were able to travel virtually nonstop and make good time both day and night. It also helped that the sky was clear and the moon almost full so that we could see the road and where we were going.

It also helped that every man was leading a spare horse. Even so, twice we had to drop wain horses for one reason or another and leave men to guard them. We also had to drop one the horse archers' mounts when it developed a sore hoof.

It was a pleasant trip in many ways. For one, we had more than enough cheese, dried apples, and cooked bread to eat and no one was foolish enough to attempt to delay us whilst they tried to extract a toll. As a result, we only stopped when the horses needed a rest or to change out a broken wheel, and I reached Bath relatively quickly with seven men remaining in my guard of whom five were riding.

The nonstop trip was a bit hard on my guards who were constantly in their saddles, but not on me because I could, and periodically did, lay myself down to sleep in the bed of the wain. They could handle it, I consoled myself with thinking, because they were younger. *Of course they were; everyone in the company was younger than me.*

To pass the endless hours of bouncing up and down when I was awake, I studied the countryside and its animals and people, waved my cross to bless the people who got out of the way so we could pass, and practiced bringing out my wrist knives quickly in order to kill people before they even knew they were dead. Mostly, however, I spent most of the trip talking to myself about the thoughts behind my eyes. They were mostly about the future of my family and my school.

There should have been six riders with me when I reached Bath. But there were only five because one of the riders' horses, a gelded ambler foaled by a mare in the horse herd we keep on the Moor northeast of Okehampton, broke down from its hoof picking up a stone and had to be led. It stopped being led when we changed out a pair of the wain horses and left them all behind at a village alehouse with a couple of archers to care for them.

Actually, it was just as well that the ambler had gone lame, for it meant its rider had to ride in the wain with me and could act as its driver when the regular driver needed to rest. *He had fallen asleep at the reins late on the second night and the wain had gone off the road. The result was a badly broken wheel before anyone realized what had happened.*

\*\*\*\*\*\*

We never stopped for long despite there being an alehouse at almost every village along the road. As a result, we made a fast passage and it was the middle of the afternoon when we reached Bath after four hard days and three long nights on the road. Somewhat to my surprise, Sir William Marshal, the commander of the king's army, had gotten there ahead of me. He was already in Bath when we clattered into the city without a single remaining spare wheel.

Sir William had men waiting for me at the gate in the wall that ran around the compound containing the building with the pool of hot water. I had heard about the hot water of Bath, but this was the first time I had ever seen it.

Some people thought the water was hot because the water came from so deep in the ground that it was warmed by the fires of hell. They claimed that if you listened very carefully in the quiet of a clear night you could hear the people in purgatory screaming as they burned down below, and that you needed to have a monk make special prayers for your safety before you dared to even touch the water with your hand, let alone bath in it to wash away your sins. *Fortunately, the prayers were not very costly and a surprisingly plump Benedictine monk was there to collect the required coins.*

Sir William's men immediately hailed us and led me to him. He was waiting inside the old stone building that surrounded the courtyard pond where the hot water bubbled up, and greeted me with a bowl of ale and a table with a plank of bread, cheese, and burnt chicken on it.

I was famished and told him how much I appreciated his kindness. And I appreciated him even more when he said he had made arrangements for my sergeant and our men and horses to be fed and watered as well.

We began our serious talking even as I wolfed down my food and ale. Sir William had already eaten because he had had no idea as to when I might be arriving, but he courteously drank a bowl of ale with me and nibbled on some cheese.

Whilst we were getting reacquainted we both noticed what appeared to be the faces and figures of people on the floor under the table that were made of little pieces of stones of different colours. They looked quite old were, I realized when I leaned down to pick at them with nail of my pointing finger, somehow stuck most solid into the floor. We agreed that they looked so old that they were almost certainly from the days of the Romans. *It was the first time I really realized that the old Romans looked just like normal people.*

It was immediately apparent that the commander of the king's army was as anxious as I was to reach an agreement for the archers' services and get a contract signed and sealed. The arrival of the French reinforcements in London, Sir William freely admitted, had given new life to the barons' efforts to remove the king and put Prince Louis on the throne in his place. I nodded sagely and agreed when he announced "the frog eaters must be stopped."

*Frogs? I thought it was toads and snails they ate. Yuck. It probably explains why the French are so foul and smelly, which makes it quite surprising that there are so many of them.*

What overbalanced me, and caused me great concern behind my eyes when our meeting started, was who had also come to Bath with Sir William to meet with me—the Pope's very own treacherous nuncio and a party of priests in addition to a strong force of Sir William's guards to protect him.

*Does Sir William know the nuncio has switched to helping the French? Does the Pope? Should I warn either of them?*

The nuncio was all smiles as he and the rest of Sir William's priestly clerks walked into the room to join us. My surprise at seeing the nuncio and his priests so overbalanced me that I promptly swallowed some of my ale the wrong way and began choking and coughing with a slight burning feeling in my chest.

Sir William noticed my surprise at seeing the nuncio and his band of priestly assistants. The nuncio was there, Sir William immediately began explaining to me, with the kind of toothy smile that so endeared him to the king and everyone at court, as an expert on canon law who could help us draft the documents such that the Church would recognize and accept our contract if we reached an agreement.

The documents Sir William was referring to, of course, were the parchment deeds and royal orders that would be needed to transfer the crown's tin mines and smelters in Cornwall to the company or earldom of Cornwall in exchange for the archers' services against the French.

"The nuncio and the clerics he has brought with him to help with the scribing have already been most helpful," Sir William explained to me, as the nuncio blushed and attempted to look at the floor most modestly, "both with the drafting of my own guarantee to help assure the moneylenders, and in providing rough drafts of possible agreements, orders, and deeds for our discussions." *Of course, I should have known; Sir William is a knight and was never learnt how to read or scribe for fear it might weaken him.*

Initial drafts of both parchments had been scribed for my consideration, the nuncio assured me in heavily accented English, as he gestured and nodded towards one of the priests in his party, by the especially fine hand of one of his assistants, Father Alberto.

Albert, in turn, responded by pressing his palms together and bowing most respectfully and prayerfully towards me as I turned to look at him. I was probably mistaken, but I thought I detected a twinkle in his eyes.

Albert's and the nuncio's unexpected appearances had initially caused a great confusion inside my head—and then the confusion behind my eyes faded away and was replaced with an idea.

******

Our meetings and the surprisingly amiable and brief negotiations that followed occurred in the same bare stone room with the Roman floor people where Sir William and I ate and drank. The carved wooden plank holding what was left of the burnt chicken, bread, and cheese was removed by one of Sir William's men in response to a nod of his head and a gesture to do so. Albert then carefully swept the crumbs and a few stray chicken bones off the table with his bare hand and laid three piles of parchments on it.

*From the hungry look on the face of the man who carried the plank away, I thought it doubtful that the leftover food would get very far before it was eaten. Well that was to be expected. The king was famous for not feeding his men, only his favourites. His brother was the same way; it must run in the family.*

"These are proposed copies of the deed and royal order to transfer the mines and tin refineries to the Earl of Cornwall; these are proposed copies of the agreement between the archers and the king for the archers' service as mercenaries in the army of one of the king's supporters during the current campaigning season; and these are copies of Sir William's guarantee for London's moneylenders," Albert said with a confident and satisfied voice as he looked at me and laid them on the table.

I picked up one of the copies of the deed transferring the king's stannary holdings in Cornwall and began to read it as the nuncio explained why they had already been prepared.

"The king has already placed his seal on one of each of the drafts so you would know the contents are generally acceptable to him," the nuncio said. "He understands that changes may need to be made." *Who am I negotiating with? Who represents the king here?*

"Sir William has the king's seal with him so he can put it on the final copies if an agreement is reached. Sir William and you, Bishop Thomas, will, of course, only put your marks and seals on whatever are the final copies. I will then add my mark and seal to the final copies as a witness and evidence of the Church's approval."

*It all sounded so reasonable. I must be missing something.*

"I have blank parchments and my scribing inks and quills with me, so I can either make the necessary corrections and changes on one of these copies or I can scribe new and final copies of each of them when everyone is satisfied and an agreement is reached," Albert volunteered rather cheerfully.

\*\*\*\*\*\*

Albert and the others hovered nearby and stared at me whilst I started to read the documents. I intended to read each of them at least twice, and probably more since the nuncio and the Church were involved in their preparation.

It took quite some time for me to do so because I leaned close to the parchment and squinted my eyes as I pointed to each word with my finger and read it out loud to myself. I soon put my plan into effect and began pointing to words, complaining about my eyesight, and asking Father Albert "what is that word?"

At first, the nuncio and his assistants gathered close around me in an effort to help me. I immediately became a very crotchety old man and waved them away.

"Stand back, damnit. I want to read this and you are bothering me and standing in the light. Not you Father Alfredo or whatever your name is." ... "Thank you." ... "Now, young man, what is that word?"

We proceeded in this manner for a few more minutes. Then I turned angrily towards Sir William and the gaggle of priests hovering anxiously nearby and told them what I thought of their efforts to help me.

"Look here. You lot are distracting me by standing close and staring at me whilst I read. You have all read these parchments, probably several times, and I have not read them even once. So why not go out and have a bowl of ale or take a piss or something whilst I have a chance to read over these parchments with Father Alfredo, eh?" *I deliberately got his name wrong once again.*

I was quite huffy about it and glared at them as I motioned towards the door to order them out.

Sir William had a definite look of understanding and concern on his face as he spread his arms and shooed everyone towards the door. I waited until they were all out of the room before I turned back to Albert and the parchment and spoke softly with my face turned away from the door.

"Hoy Albert. It is good to see you again. How are you, lad? I have been thinking about you and your future." I muttered my greeting and questions under my breath as I leaned forward as if to see better and tapped on a word on the parchment I was reading.

"And a good hoy to you too, bishop. I am pleased to see you too." He said it softly as he too turned away from the door and leaned forward as if to study the word I had tapped.

Albert immediately understood what I was doing and began playing along. We talked in low voices with our heads close together as I periodically touched a meaningless word.

"Is there anything in here that I should be concerned about?" I asked in a soft whisper. "If there is, please point it out when I come to it."

"Aye Bishop, there is one thing that should concern you for sure. It is in the agreement parchment between the king and the company. It would let the king void the transfer of the stannaries to the Earldom of Cornwall and commit the company to permanently supplying soldiers for the king to use as he sees fit. It is easily changed. Just draw a line through it. Putting it in was the nuncio's idea."

\*\*\*\*\*\*

Albert and I worked through the documents very carefully line by line. It took some time. And, of course, I made some edits and corrections including drawing a line through the three sentences that would have allowed the king to reclaim the stannaries for the crown at any time by proclaiming the inadequacy of the archers' contribution to the defence of the realm.

I also changed the wording in several places to make it clear that our obligation to fight against the French ended after the company participated in one big attack as mercenaries in someone else's army.

Sir William and the others periodically peered in to see how we were doing. For the most part, however, they waited anxiously outside whilst Albert and I worked and talked in low voices, and not always about what we were reading.

"What are your plans, lad? Would you like to return to Cornwall in the summer be the sheriff of Cornwall and our lands in Devon, and the archdeacon of the diocese under George who would be the bishop? It would mean a promotion to captain major and the wearing of five stripes."

There was a hesitation before Albert replied. Finally he asked, "Would I have to wear a priest's robe and act like a priest so I could not marry?" *So that is what the problem is; there is a lass somewhere.*

"Of course not, lad, of course not. You would be just like George. He is married as you know. It is quite simple actually. You just resign as a priest, get married all proper-like in a church, and then a bishop of that church's diocese, that would be me, ordains you as a priest again and appoints you as his archdeacon. It is only a matter of finding the right bishop, eh?"

*We had given the Holy Father a pouch full of coins and a lot of blather about it being in the best interest of the Church to issue the indulgence that let the archer priests and bishops marry and the archbishop of Cornwall appoint all of Cornwall's priests and deacons.*

*It also allowed the Earl of Cornwall and his three next-in-line heirs to have multiple wives so there would always be an earl in the company of archers committed to the collection of the prayer coins and to delivering them directly into the hands of the Pope. My old friend of blessed memory, Antonio, said the Pope looked jealous when he signed the decree.*

\*\*\*\*\*\*

It took some time but I finally finished reading the documents twice. And then I read them again to make sure all the copies were identical and had my changes in them.

"Father Alfredo and I were able to make the corrections and improvements necessary for Cornwall's agreement on the drafts without having to use new parchments," I finally announced several hours later as I walked to the door and motioned for the others to return. "We can make them on to any other copies you might need if they are acceptable to you, Sir William. Or we can have Father Alfredo scribe new copies."

Most of my changes were quite minor and probably could have been ignored. The two big changes, the removal of the king's ability to void the agreement and keep the company beholden to him forever, and the ending of the company's obligation to fight after one attack on the French, however, were quite significant.

I noticed the nuncio scowl when he read the agreement edited with my changes and saw they were gone. I immediately wondered if the nuncio was scowling on behalf of King John, or on behalf of Prince Louis, or merely for himself because he was proud of what he had scribed and did not want it being changed or corrected.

*Well, I doubt I will have a chance ask nuncio; not unless I can get him off somewhere by himself and use my wrist knives to send him off to purgatory. On the other hand, perhaps that is not a good idea; we know this nuncio can be bought and the next one might be even worse.*

In any event, the minor changes were grudgingly accepted by Sir William and the nuncio with a few minor changes of their own which I found acceptable. The various edits and changes were immediately scribed by "Father Alberto" on the various other copies, and we all made our marks and applied our seals.

When everything was signed and sealed most proper, I rolled up my original copies and put them in a leather courier case, one that can be slung over a couriers shoulder like a quiver. When I was finished, I sighed deeply and somewhat sorrowfully told Sir William, with the eavesdropping nuncio and his priests listening carefully and pretending not to, a great lie as to what I really thought of the agreements we had struck.

"I must tell you, Sir William, that I would not have made my mark on these parchments were not Cornwall and its company of archers so poor, and so desperately in need of coins to pay its men the substantial arrears that are already due them. The company will fully honour the agreement, of course, and attack the French as soon as possible, although I fear the archers will suffer dearly in doing so. You have driven a hard bargain on behalf of the king and that is the truth."

Sir William preened at my compliment like a cock pigeon flashing his feathers at a hen, and nodded modestly with a somewhat apologetic look on his face in response to my congratulatory lies. The nuncio seemed equally pleased. I, of course, was suitably downcast and unhappy. *Hot damn and thank all the saints in heaven; it worked.*

# Chapter Seven

*We plan for France.*

My lieutenant commanders and I started planning the details of our revenge and ransom raid on France right after we watched and waved as my brother and his escorts rode off to Bath. We had seen him off to Bath in the hope he would be able to meet with Sir William Marshal and get the king's agreement to pay us for doing what we intended to do anyway.

After we went waved farewell as Thomas clattered off in his wain with his escorts riding behind him, we returned to Restormel's great hall and got back to work. It was time to make a go or no go decision about the plan we had come up with for the company's raid on France.

Should we proceed with our plan or should we drop the whole idea and seek the revenge required by the company's contract with its men in some other way? That was the question.

My personal position was quite clear and carried the day.

"Even if it is the last thing I ever do, the revenge required in the company's contract means those sorry

French sons of bitches are going to pay for taking one of our archers out of London and holding him for ransom in France.

"Besides, it is a great excuse for taking French prizes is it not? And, perhaps, with a little luck we will even catch the French king in his castle and be able to collect an even bigger ransom than we paid to get Thomas back. We can never have enough coins in our chests or pay too much prize money to our men, can we?"

Every one of my lieutenant commanders and captain majors was keen to proceed. The raid was a go. Our men would be pleased.

\*\*\*\*\*\*

During our first two days of planning, it was just my lieutenant commanders and three captain majors sitting with me at the long table in Restormel's great hall. We had two maps spread out in front of us. One was a large parchment map of the waters along the French coast. An even larger, but certainly less fine, parchment with the details of the city of Paris was spread out on the table next to it.

Richard acted as our scribe in the absence of Thomas who had gone off to attempt to gull Sir William and the king. It was the scribe's task to maintain a list of our decisions each time I said "make it so," and to draw a line through them when someone came up with a better alternative or thought of a serious problem.

This was not the first time I had looked at the two maps and talked about what would be the best way to conduct a profitable raid, although it certainly was a first for some of the men at the meeting. To the contrary, before Thomas left for Bath, he and I had poured over them together, and particularly the map of Paris. As a result of our maps and my brother's experiences whilst being held for ransom in the French king's castle, I already had a reasonably good idea of what could be done and how we might do it.

I explained my basic idea to the men at the table and, to my surprise, I found myself quite anxious that they would be agreeable to it. If it could be avoided, I did not want to order them to carry out the plan whether they liked it or not—which I was prepared to do unless someone came up with something even better.

"It is rather simple when you think about it," I told my lieutenants without telling them I was merely repeating what Thomas had told me a day earlier.

"King Phillip of France lives on an island in the middle of the Seine, the river which flows through the middle of Paris and divides the city into two parts—one part of the city is on the west bank of the river, and the other part is on the other side of the city on the east bank. Both parts of the city are surrounded by strong defensive walls and are connected to each other by bridges to an island in the middle of the river where the king resides in a strong castle.

"To get from one part of Paris to the other, you must walk out of a gate in the defensive wall surrounding that part of the city, cross the nearby wooden bridge over a branch of the river to the king's island, walk across the island, and then walk across another wooden bridge to get across the other branch of the river and enter the gate in the defensive wall that protects the other section of the city.

"King Phillip lives on the island in a great castle where Thomas was held as a prisoner for some weeks. Phillip and his courtiers and captains think of the river as a great moat that will protect them even if an invading army breaks through the city walls and takes one or both parts of Paris.

"We, on the other hand, are going to think and act as if the river that divides into two branches to flow around the island is a great wall that prevents Phillip and his noble courtiers from escaping until they pay us very large ransoms—a king's ransom in the case of Phillip."

It had been clear to Thomas and me, and now to me and my other lieutenants, that our most important task would be to put a siege on the castle on the island where the French king resides and maintain it to prevent him from escaping. Preventing the king from escaping to safety was the key to our being paid a reasonable ransom, meaning one that was quite large.

Preventing the king from getting away, in turn, meant we had to take the little island in the middle of the Paris where the French king's great castle was located, and quickly destroy any boats and bridges he and his courtiers might use to get off the island. If all went well, King Phillip would then be trapped in his castle and we would not let him leave until we were paid a king's ransom.

Among other things, I told my lieutenants as I pointed to the map of Paris, isolating the king and preventing him from escaping meant we had to hold both of the two wooden bridges that connected the right and left banks of the Seine to the castle island of the king until they could be destroyed. If we did not, he might just walk over one or the other of the bridges and get away.

"We will almost certainly need the galleys which do not immediately unload their archers to bring in reinforcements if the French quickly counterattack, or if it takes too long to tear the bridges down. And then we will need them later to bring in supplies if the siege drags on. It also means we have to use our galleys to quickly destroy all the boats and barges which the king and his nobles might otherwise use to escape from the island."

We would, of course, take French transports and galleys as prizes anytime and anywhere we came across them, but our main goal was to hold the island and destroy the boats and bridges so the king and his courtiers could not escape. Putting the king's Louvre Castle home under siege before he had a chance to escape, we all agreed, was the key to getting a big ransom.

"Indeed," I said as my lieutenants smiled and nodded their agreement at the thought, "we might get more than one large ransom if Phillip has same kind of high ranking nobles and nobles' sons flitting about his court as John does when he is at Windsor."

What I did not have to tell them is that we would get a very small ransom, if any, if we arrived and took the island when the king and his rich courtiers were not there. *Unfortunately, we did not have a spy in the Phillip's court; all we knew for sure is that the king was usually in his Paris residence at this time of year.*

"If we are successful, the prize money from the ransom and the French prizes we take along the way will content our men and keep them paid and well-supplied with food and weapons for many years to come. And it will so much the better, in terms of satisfying our men, if we can also destroy Louvre Castle where my brother, their fellow archer, was held."

It sounded simple enough. All we would have to do is hold the island's two bridges long enough to destroy them whilst at the same time using our galleys to prevent boats and dinghies from carrying the king to safety or reaching the island with food and reinforcements.

If we did that, the royal castle would be cut off from the supplies and reinforcements its defenders needed no matter how big an army the French assembled on one or both sides of the river.

Sooner or later, the castle would run out of food and everyone in it would have to surrender, including King Phillip if we were fortunate enough to strike whilst he was in residence. We were, as everyone around the table could see, and we told each other, aiming high and hoping our arrows would carry. *And I could kick myself in the arse for not thinking ahead and putting a spy in Paris so we would know when the king was in his castle.*

My lieutenants and I talked all that day and throughout the next. Everyone agreed about the importance of either holding or destroying the two bridges, and destroying all the boats and barges on the river. We also talked at length about whether or not we should land a force on the island itself so that no food could be brought to the king's castle from the existing supplies of the merchants who operated a small market on the island. After much discussion, we decided we had to do both.

"We have enough men and galleys, so we are going to do both. Scribe it so," I finally said to Richard who was still acting as our scribe.

There were many questions, however, that we talked about at length but could not answer. For one, we did not have a clue as to who or what French forces would be in the castle, or how long our siege would have to last before the French king and his men ran out of food and were forced to surrender. We also did not know how long it would take for the French to gather up enough coins to be able to pay us a ransom sufficient to cause us to leave.

As with any siege, how long it would have to last would be determined by how much food was in the island fortress when we arrived, and how many people were in it who had to be fed—unless, of course, our siege could be broken by a sortie from whatever French soldiers were in the castle or by the arrival of a relief force strong enough to cross over the river to the island and defeat us in a pitched battle.

We agreed that neither a sortie from the castle nor a river crossing was likely to be successful against the size and fighting ability of the army we would be bringing up the river. We also agreed that the French would almost certainly make an effort to drive us away before they would agree to pay a ransom. The French effort to relieve the king's castle, we all believed, was doomed to fail so long as we kept enough galleys in the river and enough archers and weapons on the island.

Our basic plan to hold the island after we took it was simple as all good plans must be—we would use our galleys to bring food and reinforcements to our men on the island, and we would confront the French with a battle force of archers whenever and wherever they attempted to set foot on the island or sallied out of the castle in an effort to retake it.

In the end, we agreed that a French relief force would not be able to do more than stand along the riverbank and shake their fists at us so long as we controlled the island and the river. And that, in turn, meant that we would have to be prepared to stay on the island for as long as it took for the French to agree to pay a sufficiently large ransom, and then raise enough silver and gold coins to pay it. In other words, we were likely to be there for some time and would need to bring in more supplies.

What the size of such a ransom would be would depend on whether or not King Phillip was in his island fortress and, if he was, whether we could prevent him from slipping away to safety on some dark and rainy night. If Phillip was in the castle, which we had been told he usually was at this time of year, the ransom would be significantly more than what England paid to ransom Richard back from the Holy Roman Emperor; on that my lieutenants and I were agreed. *And it was unfortunate England paid it for the damn fool promptly went off and got himself killed by a boy with a crossbow.*

A second set of unanswered questions was how the French would initially react to our arrival? Would they know we were coming and be able gather enough men together to fight us off and prevent us from taking the bridges or the island outside of the castle's walls? And would they be able to come at us in force whilst we were still trying to destroy the bridges and small boats and prevent us from doing so?

A third unanswered set of questions was, in many ways, the most important—what would happen afterwards when our siege was in place? The French would almost certainly try to break the siege before they surrendered or paid a ransom. But how would they try to break it? We assumed Louis would return from England to lead the French effort to rescue his father and the island castle that would be his future home when he became king.

But what would Louis do when he returned to France and how many of his men from England would he bring with him? And how many galleys could the French muster to throw against us and how good would they be? And would the French fleet be strong enough to fight its way up the Seine to break our siege and send our survivors scurrying for home with our tails between our legs? Or perhaps a French army would suddenly appear on the riverbank carrying dinghies and swarm across the river to try to liberate the island.

The possibilities were endless; anything was possible and we knew we would have to be ready for all of them.

We talked about what the French *might* do, and how we should then respond, until we all had aches and pains behind our eyes.

And most of all, of course, we did not know who we would catch if we laid a successful siege on the castle, and thus how much of a ransom they might reasonably fetch. It certainly would not be the French crown prince as Louis was in London claiming to be the king of England.

Hopefully, King Phillip and the rest of the royal family would be in the castle since it was the king's principal residence—and not be able to hurriedly escape across the river as we arrived or secretly escape across the river in the dark after we arrived. And, of course, we hoped the king's courtiers would be in his residence with him and many of them would be rich toffs interested in saving their skins instead of fighting us or helping us row one of our galleys back to Cyprus.

On the other hand, we had several fine advantages going for us in addition to our two splendid maps. One of them was that Thomas had been held as a prisoner in the castle for some months last year until he was able to give his parole and go to live with the priests in the nearby cathedral rectory.

Whilst he was being held on the island Thomas had learnt enough about the castle to know we would never be able to take it with a direct attack. On the other hand, Thomas had also seen the food supplies coming over the bridge each day and thought the castle was not at all prepared for a siege. As a result, it was Thomas's opinion that the castle would surrender fairly quickly if the bridges were cut and the island occupied so that no new food could get in. We had learnt all this from Thomas before he left for Bath and, hopefully, a successful meeting with Sir William Marshal.

It was also somewhat helpful that I and all of the company's lieutenant commanders who would be leading the raid, and many of our galley captains, had sailed against the French a few years earlier. That was when the company's galleys attacked the transports that were loading the French army at Harfleur for an invasion of England. It was particularly memorable for Thomas and me because George was almost killed. This time, however, our raid would be different. We would be going after French prizes both in the estuary where the Seine enters the English Channel, and all the way up the river to Paris and, perhaps, even beyond.

If we were fortunate and Jesus and the gods of war were with us, we would not take too many casualties and be able to stay on the island until either the castle surrendered or we were paid enough ransom to leave with our prizes.

Whether or not this would occur in response to the prayers we muttered was not certain. All each of us could do was mutter many prayers under his breath, knock three times on wood, spit over our shoulders, and do all the many other things that could conceivably curry favour with God; or, of course, the many gods if it turned out that there were more than one.

There were a number of good ideas including an absolutely excellent one from Richard as to how we might solve what appeared to be our biggest problem— supporting, and possibly evacuating, the galley companies under George's and Peter's command which would have to hold and destroy the two bridges connecting the island to the rest of the city of Paris.

According to the map and Thomas, the city-side entrances to the two bridges were both so close to the city walls that our men would be within crossbow range unless they worked in the middle or the island side of the bridges. There was no doubt about it, our men on the bridges would be in real trouble, and probably trapped and unable to escape, if the French held the island and could shoot arrows at them or attack them from that side of the bridge as well.

It was Richard surprised us with a suggestion as to how we might use our galleys to get our men off the bridges if the French retained or regained control of the island. It was quite simple and we were surprised that it came from Richard. He had, after all, spent all his time in the company as a horse archer and never served on a galley.

Harold got so excited when he heard it, that he shouted "yes" as he loudly slapped his hand down on the table and rushed off to get things organized. *And Richard, though he did not know it, had just taken a big step towards sooner or later having another stripe on his tunic in the years ahead if Peter and George went down.*

\*\*\*\*\*\*

Three days later our planning was completed and we called in the galley captains to tell them about our plan and help us put together the final details. We waited to bring in the captains until two days before we intended to sail. When they arrived at the great hall, we immediately swore them to secrecy with many great oaths and dire warnings as to what would happen to anyone who revealed even a hint of our plans to anyone outside the room. Then I climbed up on to the great hall's long wooden table so they could all see me and explained what we were going to do and how we were going to do it.

As you might imagine, before I told the captains anything about our plan I warned them what would happen to anyone who talked about what we intended to do and how we were going to do it. There was, after all, a very real risk with so many people knowing about our intentions and plans, that someone would talk and, so to speak, let the cat out of the sack to run away.

If our plans became known, the French would be waiting for us. It was a risk my lieutenants and I were not willing to take. That was why we waited until the very last minute to share our plans with the captains, and they would wait until after they sailed to reveal them to their men.

Our galley captains were greatly surprised when they heard me say that the company's archers would be going to France for prizes and ransoms, instead of to London to fight for or against King John. They were also greatly surprised when they learnt what they were to do when they got to France. We knew it would surprise them because going for a ransom was something the company had never done before, and it certainly did. Hopefully it would also surprise the French.

And, of course, Thomas's absence was noted. We did not explain it. We merely said that he had been called away; we did not tell the captains about him being off to Bath or why he was there. They did not need to know.

In any event, the captains absolutely loved the plan we had come up with, or so they claimed. It was, everyone agreed, and the captains told each other with great enthusiasm as juniors are wont to do in front of their betters, certainly different from anything the company had ever done before. To a man, they said they liked it and thought it had great prospects.

As you might also imagine, the captains nodded their agreement and understood when they were told that any man among them who was at any time found to have directly or indirectly talked about, or placed a bet on, what the company would be doing or where we were going, would instantly have his stripes ripped off his tunic, his belly cut open, and be hung.

I think the captains believed our threats, both because Peter made them most fearsome, and they knew we meant them. Of course they did; they were all veteran fighting men and understood the need for secrecy.

*I sincerely hoped the captains believed our dire threats for we surely meant them. Besides, it always bothers me when I have to hang someone or chop off his head. It makes such a bloody mess.  And then, to top it off, you have to haul them away and bury them or else they will start to smell. That is why it is always best to do it at sea so you can throw them overboard.*

# Chapter Eight

*We catch a spy.*

My lieutenants and I probably should have left it to others to go to the Lostwithiel alehouse and arrest the alewife's husband, the alehouse owner who was almost certainly a spy. But we did not. We wanted to make sure it was done properly and we were getting tired of sitting around talking to each other and looking at maps. So we decided to take a break from our labours and do it ourselves. It did not go well.

It came as a complete surprise to the alewife, and to her husband and their drinkers, when Peter and I and some of our archers bent our heads to get through its low door and entered what was arguably Lostwithiel's largest and finest alehouse. It was the one whose ceiling was so low that most men could not stand up straight. The ale, however, was uncommonly good being as it was all thick and black and frothy.

We entered the alehouse with the intention of taking the alewife's husband by surprise, before he had a chance to run, and then quietly leading him away to be questioned. We wanted to know all about the puzzling message his young son had been sent to deliver to a knight at the king's court at Windsor and to a French priest in the great London fortress held by a French army on behalf of England's rebel barons and France's Prince Louis.

Our plan did not work. Our quarry was a heavily bearded and rather portly man of some size as the owners of taverns and alehouses always seem to be as a result of having too much food and drink. He was in the room drinking with his customers when we came through the door. We saw him immediately and, at the same, he saw us as we came through the door.

What followed was chaos. After a brief moment of hesitation when our eyes met, the alehouse owner lowered his head and bolted for the side door on the other side of the room. Perhaps it was the look of determination on some of our faces, or perhaps the fact that the man who led us in was beginning to pull his sword as he started towards him.

Whatever it was that had informed him of our intentions did not matter. He knew we were coming for him and ran for his life. Or, perhaps, it would be more accurate to say, he tried to run.

We should have let him go peacefully out of the side door because we had men waiting there also. But we did not. The sword-carrying burly archer who had been chosen to enter first, because he supposedly frequented the place and knew what Giles looked like, started running after him whilst shouting for him to stop and surrender—and promptly banged his head into the big and even lower cross-timber that was holding up the ceiling of the alehouse.

The burly archer went tumbling down to the dirt floor to sleep for a few moments; and when he did, he knocked over a rickety bench and took its drinkers down with him. He also took down a couple of our men who had been following too close behind and tripped over him.

The result was many cries of surprise from the drinkers who had been sitting on the other benches in the room and around the wall, and a great deal of confusion and chaos. Some of the other benches and one of the tables were toppled as our men and the drinkers fell over one another. At the same time, the rest of the drinkers jumped to their feet and some began running to the front door to get away from whatever was happening.

There was little wonder in the efforts of the alehouse drinkers to flee. About half of them were wearing archers' tunics and were obviously supposed to be working or practicing somewhere. They had seen the stripes on our tunics, and knew that if they were caught it would go hard on them. And they were right; we would be taking their names and talking to their captains about them.

The alewife herself, also of a substantial size and almost as big as her husband, watched us enter from where she was standing in the corner of the room. She was holding a couple of bowls of ale that she had obviously just dipped out of her ale barrel, and she was standing with her mouth open in surprise as she watched her husband try to escape amidst the chaos and confusion that engulfed the room.

She promptly added to the chaos by screaming curses and running at us in an effort to slow us down so he could get away. The bowls of ale she was holding dropped to the floor with a great splash that reached a couple of her open-mouthed drinkers, and made a great muddy puddle on the floor that soon disappeared as the ale soaked down into the dirt.

A couple of heartbeats later, Giles was out the side door and everyone who had been sitting in the room had jumped to his feet, with many of them spilling their bowls of ale and some of them falling to the floor in the process. At least half of them began trying to push past us to get to the narrow entrance door. The others were just standing wide-eyed and apprehensively watching. The once-quiet alehouse quickly turned into a large group of pushing and shouting men crammed into a small space.

Our quarry got out the side door behind his wife's open tub of ale, but he did not get much further. The men we had waiting outside the side door with their swords drawn took him without having to use their weapons. He stopped running rather than impale himself on their outstretched swords. But it had been anything but a quiet capture. There was no doubt about it; our plan to quietly question him and turn him to our advantage was already in trouble.

\*\*\*\*\*\*

"Why did you do it?" an overly excited Peter shouted at the alewife's husband as he pulled the spy's arm up behind his back and frog-marched him towards the waiting horse cart. Behind us, at the side door to the alehouse through which her husband had just run, several of our men were attempting to restrain the shouting and swearing alewife.

"Not here, Peter, not here," I hissed at him as I motioned towards the rapidly gathering crowd of onlookers.

"He did not pay his taxes and rent," I shouted in desperation towards the rapidly growing crowd in an effort to salvage the situation.

*I did not know if my deception would work, but I had to try. The last thing we needed was for word to get out that he was being arrested because he was a spy. We could not successfully turn him around to begin sending false information to his patrons, whoever they might be, if they knew he had been captured for a spy, could we?*

\*\*\*\*\*\*

An hour later the alewife's husband was talking to us in the cellars of Restormel, and we had an explanation and a much better understanding of the situation.

Giles was the owner of the alehouse. He had sent his innocent young son, also named Giles, to deliver the messages because he was afraid someone might steal the large amount of gambling coins he was holding for whoever ended up winning them. And he did not want to run off with the gamblers' coins and leave the alehouse and his wife behind because the alehouse was so profitable. And he could not risk asking anyone else to carry his messages because they might have betrayed him to the company.

His only alternative, Giles told us with a great deal of resignation and bitterness in his voice, had been to send his son and hope the boy would remember who he was supposed to meet and the words he had been told to say.

The good news was that Giles had sent no recent messages to either the king or the French reporting the arrival of large numbers of archers and galleys in Cornwall, or so he claimed. If he was telling the truth, something that was not at all certain, neither King John nor the French knew we had gathered together an army of archers and a fleet of galleys that could be used to carry them to France.

Also good news, because it meant we would not have to waste time torturing him so he would do what we wanted, was that Giles was greatly concerned "for my innocent son and my wife;" he would tell us everything, he said, and send any messages we wanted to anybody we named if it would save his family.

And to whom did Giles send his earlier reports, and what did he tell them, and how did it all get started? The alehouse man's answers were very much along the lines of what we expected to hear. According to him, it was a friend named James from his village near Derby, one of the lower ranking men in the king's army at Windsor, who had recruited him to spy on us.

James, he told us, wanted to curry favour with the king and advance himself by getting information about the archers and our intentions. In particular, James wanted Giles to send an advance warning he could take to the king if the archers made a mercenary contract with the barons or the French.

Giles told us he had been given a pouch of coins three or four years ago and told to buy the Lostwithiel alehouse because that was where many of the archers drank and talked and gambled. But James must have had loose lips because, according to Giles, someone came to his friend soon afterwards and threatened to expose them both unless a certain French priest secretly received the same information. Giles was not sure, but he had gotten the impression that the threat had come from a priest. He had asked who it was, he said, but James refused to tell him.

If his "friend" James was really from Giles' village, it must be the village's lord or one of the lord's sons. Who else would have the coins needed to buy an alehouse and be trying to help the king in order to advance himself? And the priest? Almost certainly the nuncio or someone in his household; but perhaps not since our own spy in the nuncio's household had not known about it.

We were not sure what we should do about our alehouse spy, and we needed to get back to planning our attack on the French. Accordingly I told Raymond and Richard to explain everything to Thomas when he returned from Bath, and to tell him I said to handle it however he thought would be best.

"Tell my brother I said he is to have the alehouse spy send whatever messages my brother thinks should be sent to confuse and mislead the king and the French. In the meantime, both the boy and the spy are to be kept alive until Thomas returns and decides what to do with them. I will also send Thomas a parchment telling him what we know about the situation, but he will be on the road and may not get it."

Within hours a badly shaken Giles was back at his alehouse busily explaining to his suspicious wife and sympathetic customers that it had all been an unfortunate misunderstanding—the alehouse's prices had been set so low, he told them, that he had not been able to collect enough coins to pay his rent and taxes; but the castle had been understanding and he had worked out such a reasonable payment plan that he would not have to raise his prices very much or stop giving credit.


\*\*\*\*\*\*

What to do with Giles the alehouse spy turned out to be a decision Thomas would not have to make. His wife cut his throat that very night whilst he was sleeping. She did it after Giles told her that her son was being held at Okehampton, and why.

And, of course, we could hardly continue to hold the boy after he had just lost his father and was well on his way to becoming an orphan; so Thomas let him go home to help his mother run the alehouse.

*It was a case of the greater good prevailing, Thomas explained when he got to France and joined us; having an adequate supply of ale in the village, he said, was much more important than hanging boys who were ill-used by their fathers.*

# Chapter Nine

*From Cornwall to France.*

We sailed from Cornwall on tenth of July in the year of our lord 1216. It was the warm morning of a clear and sunny day. Even so, the path all along the river was quite muddy and churned up as a result of several days of rain and the large number of cattle and sheep being brought in to provide food for the new arrivals to take with them for their campaign in France.

Our intention had been to sail for France four days earlier, but we did not because the weather in the Channel had been particularly foul. As a result of the bad weather, and at the urgent suggestions of our sailing sergeants, our galleys stayed tied up along the Fowey until the skies cleared over the Channel and the waves settled.

The follow-on impacts of the delay were severe. For one, both of the Lostwithiel ale houses ran out of ale such that emergency supplies were brought in from the surrounding villages and sold at very high prices. Even so, spirits were high because the men knew something was brewing. As a result, there was much moors dancing and merriment, even in the rain, particularly after the additional ale supplies arrived to great cheers, well-shaken but drinkable, in the beds of a couple of wains pulled by pairs of trotting horses.

Our departure occurred about two hours after the sun arrived to begin another day. A galley stationed in the river estuary for the purpose had rowed out to be in the Channel at sunup, and then hurried up the Fowey to report that the skies over the Channel were clear and the wind moderate. I immediately ordered the waiting livestock to be slaughtered.

Two hours later I ordered the warning horns to be blown and the men ran to their galleys. Many, of course, were already there. They had been expecting the signal and were ready in near-record time. Morale was high.

\*\*\*\*\*\*

My command galley, actually Harold's since I always sailed with him, was the first to cast off its lines and push off from the riverbank. The other galleys pushed off as we passed them and followed close behind us. We would lead them down the river as was the custom. At that moment only the galley captains knew our destination, and what the specific role of their galley and its archers would be when we got there. They would call their men on deck and inform them after their galleys cleared the harbour and entered the Channel.

The riverbank and the training field behind it were crowded with well-wishers of all kinds who had come to see us off. They ranged from cheering and waving castle workers from Lostwithiel to weeping young girls holding infants. The men on the galleys were excited and pleased to be recognized. Those who were not at the oars waved back from their positions on the decks and masts. Mostly they were sailors because the archers were all on the rowing benches manning their oars.

It was a festive occasion, with the sad exception of George who was sailing with us despite one of his sister wives being terribly poxed. I had started to order him to stay behind to care for her and to see her properly buried if she died. But he protested so much when I began, that I stopped and reversed course. He was sailing as the captain in command of the fourth galley behind Harold's.

*George was right; there was nothing he could do and it would make him look bad if he was favoured by being left behind because he had family problems, particularly since there were other similarly situated men with family problems who were sailing with us.*

The decks of each our galleys were carrying the bodies of the recently slaughtered cattle, pigs, and sheep. They would be cut up by each galley's cook and the pieces burnt his cooking fire to feed its crew in the days ahead.

Also on the decks of each galley were live sheep and cattle thrashing about and loudly complaining because earlier in the day they had been led aboard and their legs had been nobbled so they could not wander about but still could be kept alive until they were needed for eating. There were also great stringers of complaining Cornish chickens, ducks, and geese fluttering about on every galley with all their legs of every ten tied together into great flapping and squawking bundles.

We were carrying enough food for a long sea voyage even though we were only going to France. It was the prudent thing to do because we might have to stay in France for some time, and we were not at all sure if we would be able to buy food locally or send galleys back to Cornwall for more supplies. Our departure was, all in all, quite noisy and very much like the start of every long voyage. The only difference was that many more galleys than usual were pushing off from the riverbank and sailing all at the same time.

I stood on the roof of the forward castle of Harold's galley and watched my family standing at the water's edge. They were waving until we went around the bend in the river and they passed out of sight. Everyone was there to see me off. All except George, of course, who was on his own galley somewhere behind me and Thomas who was on the road returning from his meeting in Bath.

And I now had three wives again. Yesterday we had all gone together to the village church and one of Thomas's recently graduated students, newly ordained as a priest and proudly wearing his new archer's tunic with the three stripes of a sergeant on its front and back, had gobbled the Latin prayers and sprinkled the church water necessary to add Sarah to my family in the eyes of God.

My marriage to Sarah was done all right and proper, and a parchment recording it and its terms was placed in the old wooden chest that holds the Lostwithiel church's records. *There were no terms except she was to have her own bedding, bowls, and spoons; I did not require a dowry and would not have gotten one if I did.*

I would, of course, have preferred Thomas to put the necessary Church words on us, but he was still away on his trip to Bath to negotiate with Sir William Marshal. It had gone well according to the brief parchment that came in from Thomas yesterday via a pair of hard riding couriers; he reported that an acceptable agreement had been signed and sealed.

He also said he had other interesting, but less urgent, news that he would share with me when he joined us in France. And would I please remember to leave a galley behind to carry him there. *I did.*

****** *Thomas returns to Cornwall.*

Thomas left Bath and was on the road to Cornwall as soon as the agreements between the company and the king were signed with each man's mark and sealed. He and his archers spent the first three nights on the road in the rain and darkness huddling under the wain, and their days moving slowly along the muddy and flooded old Roman road.

They made up for it by spending the fourth and fifth nights resting and recovering in the comfort of Okehampton Castle along with Richard who had arrived two days earlier to take up his new command. Whilst they rested, Thomas's sergeant had two of the wain's broken wheels repaired and used one of them to replace the spare he had been able to buy in Bath. It had been smaller than the wain's other wheels and had made the cart ride lopsided.

Richard had not even had time to sew on his sixth stripe as the new lieutenant commander of the horse archers and outriders by the time Thomas reached Okehampton. According to Thomas, Richard did not need to wear his new stripes to get his orders instantly and cheerfully obeyed; word of his promotion and new assignment had quickly spread through the company and, for the most part, been well received. Thomas reported that Richard was clearly elated and enthusiastic about his new position.

Equally enthusiastic about Richard's arrival at Restormel and his new responsibilities were those of the horse archers and outriders who had served under Richard when the Earl of Devon and some of his friends attempted to invade Cornwall in response to the horse archers taking Exeter— and were mostly destroyed by the horse archers under

George and Richard before they even reached the Tamar and William's waiting army of foot archers.

Those of the horse archers who had been with George and Richard during the fighting affected to know Richard personally, which some of them actually did, and were much envied by the other men as they told their exciting stories, some of which were true.

Wanda, Raymond's wife, was in an equally good mood. She had received a messenger carrying a message from her husband telling her that they would be moving to Exeter and briefly describing his new and greatly reduced responsibilities. So she too had gotten what she wanted and was similarly elated.

As a result, Wanda was cheerful and absolutely bubbling with joy when she joined Thomas and Richard for a fine meal in Okehampton's great hall—fresh bread with bowl-whipped butter, a fine bottom fish with white flesh grown soft from eating shite and garbage in the castle's moat for each of them, and slices of a piglet which had been constantly turned as it was burnt in the hall's great fireplace.

Thomas and Richard had much news to share with each other. Accordingly, as they ate, Thomas told Richard all about the stannaries and the agreement he had reached with Sir William. Raymond's wife, Wanda, listened attentively without saying a word such that they soon forgot she was there.

Richard, in turn, told Thomas that the archers are almost certainly already on their way to France. Unfortunately Richard had left Restormel before it was learned about the fate of the spy at the hands of his wife, so they spent quite some time talking about how they could use him to mislead the king and the French. And, of course, they talked about what should be done with the alehouse boy in the room under the castle where the meat was hung to cure. They also discussed which of the boys in Thomas's school might be assigned to be Richard's apprentice after the archers returned from France.

Their meal was served Wanda who also sat with them and listened. She did not say a word until Richard confirmed that Raymond would be moving to Exeter and he would be moving to Okehampton. At that point she could not contain herself any longer and began talking excitedly about Raymond's new position and her move to Exeter. She did so even though she was a woman and was not supposed to talk about family matters when her husband was not present.

Neither of the two men seemed to notice her mistake. To the contrary, her pleasure and excitement pleased them greatly and they both became very encouraging, telling her "you will like Exeter and Rougemont Castle, you really will," and that sort of thing.

After they finished eating, Richard and Thomas took their leave and went to sleep and talk in the room in one of Okehampton's wall towers where Richard was temporarily living until Raymond returned and he and his wife moved out of the commander's room above the great hall.

"It will probably take an entire wain to move everything of Wanda's to Exeter," Richard said with an agreeable laugh as he climbed into the bed they shared.

"In addition to her string bed and two stools, and all her coin pouches, Wanda has two flat sacks she sewed; one full of horse hair that she and Raymond sleep on and another full of goose feathers that they sleep under. The two sacks apparently keep them warm all night long, even when the cold is most fierce."

After a brief pause, and another appreciative laugh, Richard added another thought.

"If my wife sees Wanda's sleeping sacks she will be sewing some for us and we will all be eating horse meat and goose for weeks."

*And right then and there, without saying a word to Richard, Thomas decided to have the Restormel servants and some of the galleys' sail makers sew some sacks for him to try out. If they worked, he would have some made for the boys.*

\*\*\*\*\*\*

It was a good and friendly meeting between two men who not only understood and respected one another, but were also in the best of spirits. Richard said his wife was no doubt very pleased when she heard out he was getting another stripe and they would be moving to Okehampton. He had already sent for her, he said, and expected her soon.

Richard also cheerfully told Thomas what little he knew about the boy in the meat hanging dungeon under the castle, and they talked at some length as to how Thomas might use the alehouse spy in Lostwithiel to mislead the king and the French. Richard threw out several good ideas that Thomas made much of and said he would use.

Thomas, in turn, told Richard about his recent meeting with Sir William, but he did not mention Albert, or his plans for Albert, despite Richard and Albert being good friends from their school days. And he did not even mention that he had just seen Albert in Bath. Albert was a secret, after all.

Thomas did surprise Richard, however, by confirming that he would soon be withdrawing from all of his responsibilities except the school. That particular change in his life, he told Richard, would occur as soon as the campaign in France was finished and Peter took over from William as the company's commander with George as his second.

The only position he intended to retain, Thomas told Richard in confidence, was that of the school's master. He also confirmed that George would almost certainly replace him as the new bishop in addition to becoming Peter's number one lieutenant commander, the man who would take over command of the company if Peter fell.

"Those are the responsibilities that have been mine; now they will be George's just as Raymond's will be yours." Thomas told the man who had once been one of his students.

Then Thomas added, "keeping the Pope happy and the priests and the king's men out of Cornwall will by George's most important task until he takes over the company, just as it has been mine."

Richard merely nodded his agreement because he understood fully, or thought he did. The importance of the company maintaining its special relationship with Rome, and its distance from the king and his taxes and wars, was something that Thomas had constantly discussed with his boys when Richard was a student.

The various changes, both men knew, almost certainly meant that George would be sailing off to Rome each year to deliver the company's prayer coins to the Pope. It also meant, Thomas explained, that someone else would have to wear a fifth stripe and be both the archdeacon of the diocese and its sheriff with a small force of outriders to assist him. He was searching for such a man and considering several possibilities, Thomas said, but he did not mention any names and Richard instinctively knew enough not to ask.

Actually Thomas was not searching; he knew it would be Albert but he did not plan to tell Richard or anyone else who it would be in order to protect Albert from a vindictive king or nuncio. No one would know, including Richard, until Albert was safely back in Cornwall.

Thomas's decision about Albert was, after all, something that neither Richard nor anyone else needed to know. Accordingly, Thomas limited himself to merely commenting to Richard that "you will have to get along with whoever becomes the sheriff and archdeacon since you will have to supply him with some of your outriders to help him keep order and hang felons." *Richard told Thomas he agreed, and he actually did. Besides, what else could he say?*

The two men, one getting old and the other still young, talked until late in the night. They both were quite content with the state of their lives when they went to sleep that night. That and everything else would change as a result of what would subsequently happen in France and London, although they did not know it at the time.

****** 

Things changed a bit in the morning. Thomas got a good night's sleep in a dry bed, broke his fast with breakfast ale and some bread and cheese. Then he took a good shite in the trench next to the outer curtain wall whose contents would soon be spread on the onion fields to make the onions and corn grow faster. Afterwards, he went down to the Okehampton meat larder to visit the lad who had been carrying the message to the king and the French.

One look and a short conversation with the guileless, and obviously not very bright, young lad who had been caught carrying the secret message to the king and the French, and Thomas had known that he could not act like a sheriff and treat the boy as a spy. Instead, he decided to take the boy to Restormel with him. He was named Giles, the boy cheerfully told Thomas, as was his father.

"Well Giles son of Giles, you will be coming with me to Restormel. We will sort things out when we get there. And did they feed you this morning, lad?"

Thomas climbed into his wain about three hours after sunup to continue his return to Restormel. There was no hurry; William and his army had already sailed long ago. He had ordered the spy's young son to be unchained and fed, and taken the boy with him. They would talk on the way.

Raymond's wife was already packing for her move to Exeter. A new day was dawning for both the company and his family so far as Thomas was concerned. All they had to do was get past William's adventure in France.

*Bishop Thomas did not know that the departure of the archers for France had been delayed for four days because of bad weather in the Channel. If he had not tarried at Okehampton to rest and recover, he could have sailed with them.*

# Chapter Ten

*Our fleet reaches France.*

When Thomas finally reached Restormel, to his dismay, he learned from Raymond that bad weather in the Channel had caused the archers' fleet to delay sailing for France until that very morning. He was more than a little angry with himself because he had not made any particular effort to hurry back to Restormel; he had thought William and his army would have been long gone by the time he arrived.

Thomas had also heard about the death of Giles' father from some travellers they met on the road; and being the coward that he was when it came to such things as giving bad news to people, he gave the boy a pat on the back when they reached Restormel and sent him home to find out for himself from his mother.

After he had spoken with Raymond and told him he was freeing the alehouse lad, he said hello and accepted great hugs from William's wives who had come out into the courtyard to greet him, peed in the tanner's big jar in the inner bailey, and walked to his room in a tower of the innermost wall to see how the boys of his school was doing under Master Robert.

Following his brief visit to his school to reassure himself that all was well and none of his lads were poxed, he sent one of the stable boys to fetch the captain of the galley he could see moored in the river below the castle. He assumed it was there to carry him to France and wanted to know how soon it could sail.

As he waited, he realized it was a great joy to be able to see his likely lads being learnt and stretch his legs in the sunshine after spending so many days of constantly bouncing up and down in a wain and sleeping under it at night.

****** *George.*

I sailed for France on a fine Algiers-built war galley with forty-four oars on each side. It was captained by John Cartwright. John, as I soon learned because he was a non-stop talker, was one of the four sons of a cart wright for the Templars and had grown up in the village of Bermondsey near London.

John's story was quite common for an archer, and I heard all about it because we shared the bed in the forward castle and John liked to talk so much that it seemed as if he never stopped, even when I was trying to sleep. *And it was a good thing he did for it distracted me from thinking about poor Becky, my poxed wife, and my new son. Thank God, Becky's sister and mother, and my father's wives as well, were there to help care for her.*

John and I stood together on the roof of the forward castle with the fleet all around us. We were there so John could keep an eye on the galleys rowing nearby as we dutifully followed the "follow me" flags flying at the top of both of Harold's masts. Whilst we stood there, John told me all about himself in between periodically shouting out orders to his sailing sergeant and rudder men to make sure we did not collide with another galley or have some of our oars sheared off.

When John was not giving his sailing orders, he periodically roared with laughter, and made me smile, as he described his family and how it was he had decided to go for an archer. It was a familiar tale and the ease with which he told it suggested that he had already told it many times and come to terms with the sadness and heartache it implied.

"Your strong arms are surely those of an archer," John said the company's recruiting sergeant told him when he was little more than a village lad who ran errands for his father and his arms were anything but strong.

"And then he told me that my strong arms meant I would make a fine archer and I would soon be the captain of my own galley and earn enough coins to be rich when I came back to the village to find a lass after a harvest or two had been brought in. It was heady stuff for a poor lad with no prospects and not yet old enough to wed."

John had believed the recruiting sergeant's lies, he said. As a result, after an argument with his father some months later, he had walked into London and found the stables that had served as the company's first London shipping post. Right then and there he had applied to become an apprentice archer and, to his surprise, he had been accepted.

From London he had blistered his hands helping to row one of our galleys to Cornwall where he had been learnt to push arrows out of a longbow. That was many years ago back in the days when our training camp was new.

After he finally got his first stripe, and made his mark on the company's roll as John the cartwright's son, he had been sent out to the Holy Land to pull an oar and fight. He had served for many years, he was not sure exactly how many, until he had finally gotten his fourth stripe and his own galley. It was the one on which we were sailing, and he was more than a little proud of it and himself.

"She is Algerian built and a good one. Her hull is so uncommonly tight that I usually only have to have one man bailing water except, of course, when we are in heavy seas."

John and his galley had been based on Cyprus. For the past several years he and his men had mostly transported cargos, passengers, and money orders in a great triangular run from Cyprus to Athens to Istanbul. He and his men had been pulled off of their regular run to sail to Cornwall with my father's fleet.

According to John, he expected some prize coins for himself and his men when he finally got back to Cyprus, "but nothing like those that will go to the lucky devils who sailed with Peter in the other fleet, eh?"

My talkative new friend had never gone back to his village or seen his family again, and he still had not found a wife. But he had finally gotten the command of his own galley, he told me, because he had been named to be its prize captain after the galley on which he was the lieutenant, Old Jack Black's, took it with a wounded bird.

It had happened two or three years back, John said, when her Moorish captain took her out of the Algiers harbour to chase us after we looked in there on a whim. He and his prize crew had fought their way aboard the Algerian and managed to get it back to Cyprus where Yoram, "God bless him," had bought it in for the company to use instead of ordering it to be destroyed.

*John was referring, of course, to the fact that we had long ago started destroying the prize galleys we did not buy in for our own use. It started when we took the same galley for a third time—and discovered, when we looked into it, that selling our Moorish prizes to the merchants with whom we traded often meant they ended up being sold right back into the hands of the Moorish pirates such that we ended up having to take them again.*

****** *George*

The weather was clear and our fleet of galleys easily stayed together until we reached the coast of France. We saw it in the distance late in the afternoon of the day we sailed from Cornwall.

At first France was only a grey blob, and our pilot was not exactly sure where we were. But that soon changed. Someone on Harold's galley must have known the French coast, however, for it promptly turned to the left, dropped its sails because the wind was wrong, and began rowing west and north along the French coast.

Everyone in the fleet, of course, promptly copied Harold and turned to follow him. As we had gotten closer and closer to France, more and more sea birds of all kinds began to appear. They followed us with much swooping and calling overhead as Harold's command galley, with my father on board, led our fleet along the French coast.

We continued sailing close together until the lookouts on our mast could see the beginnings of the estuary at the mouth of the Seine. At that point, Harold's galley stopped moving forward, and all but one of the galleys in our fleet, including mine, stopped with it.

Stopping where we did was part of the plan. We would spend the night waiting outside the estuary even though the sun had not yet gone down. As a result, we would be able to enter the Seine after the sun arrived in the morning—and, as a result, have the light of the entire day so we could see what we were doing as we rowed through the estuary and up the river to launch our initial attacks.

The one galley that continued moving forward had been ordered to do so. It was our scout. Its captain, one of our new captain majors, continued rowing forward towards the mouth of the Seine to see if any French fighting ships were waiting for us.

Just after the sun finished passing overhead, our scout came back to re-join the fleet and report what it had seen at the mouth of the river—absolutely nothing except for some three-masted ships receiving and discharging cargos into barges and lighters because the river was not deep enough for such big ships to get all the way up to Paris.

\*\*\*\*\*\*

The wind was calm and the weather fair as John's galley and the rest of the fleet waited out the night together a few miles offshore. It was a clear and peaceful night even though many of the men, including me, were still somewhat poxed by the up and down motion of the waves. We were feeling weakly because we had not yet gotten our sea legs.

We spent the night bobbing up and down in a vast raft of lashed-together galleys. Candle lights were burning on every mast and their docking sacks were hanging down on the sides of every galley's hull to prevent it from grinding against the galleys lashed to it. Henry, Peter, and I tied our galleys to Harold's so we would be able to go aboard and get any last minute orders my father might give us. And going aboard his galley is exactly what we did.

We reviewed the plan for our French raid as we ate and drank whilst Harold's galley bobbed up and down in the waves. It did not take long to review it because absolutely nothing had changed; we would proceed as we had planned:

Father was in overall command of the attack and would remain on Harold's galley so he could move our reserves around to either side of the river island on which the French king's castle was located; Henry would lead the archers of eight galley companies on to the island itself to occupy it; Peter would lead six galleys up the river channel on the right to take the wooden bridge connecting that side of the island to the mainland; and I would lead six galleys up the channel on the left to take the wooden bridge connecting the other side of the island to the mainland on other riverbank.

All the rest of our galleys, those without special assignments, would form up immediately downstream of the island so my father could use their archers as a reserve to be thrown in wherever they might be needed most.

Once the island and bridges were taken, all the available galleys would commence destroying any small boats and barges which might be used to carry the king and his courtiers to safety.

Our plan was to row through the estuary such that we entered the mouth of the Seine several hours after sunrise. That would give the transports waiting for the tide at the river's mouth time to get into the Seine and begin moving up the river—so we could close off the river behind them, and take them at our leisure.

Three galleys with a large number of prize crews on board would remain behind to close off the river at its mouth. They would take as prizes any transports they found in the estuary or at the mouth of the river; and then wait in the estuary off the river's mouth to take any unsuspecting new arrivals coming to Paris or to Harfleur, Honfleur, and the other smaller ports that were in the immediate vicinity.

If any of the new arrivals could not be taken immediately for some reason, or the three river-closing galleys ran out of prize crews, the new arrivals would be allowed to enter the river to join those which had already been trapped in the river.

Somewhat similarly, two galleys each would go to Harfleur and Honfleur, also with extra prize crews on board. They would quickly take whatever prizes they could find and send them off to Cornwall, and then row along the shoreline and up the river destroying all the small boats they found and anything else that someone might use to escape from the king's island.

More importantly, whilst they were waiting to provide any reinforcements that might be needed, all the galleys without specific assignments would be in the river under my father's direct command.  And, of course, they and everyone else to the extent they could do so whilst carrying out their primary assignments, would destroy all the dinghies, barges, and small boats they could find—so whoever might be in king's castle would be trapped in it and not be able to get off the island.

Hopefully, of course, those whom we trapped on the island would include King Phillip and all of his family and his rich courtiers, people we might ransom in addition to the king and his castle.

Our basic plan, in other words, was quite simple.  We would take the king's island and cut it off from the rest of Paris by destroying all the boats and barges on the river and the bridges connecting to the mainland—and stay on the island until we were paid a sufficiently large ransom to leave it.

According to Thomas, the island and its castle had not been taken by an "invading army" ever since Louvre Castle was built.  It had not been taken, Thomas explained, because the river flowing on either side of the island acted as a great moat. Our concern, of course, was whether the French had thought of some way to fight off an "invading fleet" that we did not know about.

How the French would react to our arrival was something we had talked and worried about for some time. One possibility was that the French might bring warships into the river to fight with ours. Alternately, and much more likely and worrisome, the French would have soldiers on the island who would hurry to wherever we were trying to land and try to prevent us from landing.

We were concerned about the French using their soldiers to oppose our landings at the water's edge because that was exactly what we intended to do after we took the island—in addition to our main force on the island waiting to confront a sortie from the castle, we were going to divide up some of our galley companies into quarter-companies under the command of our steadiest sergeants and scatter them around the island.

The task of the quarter-companies was to rush to the shoreline to intercept any French efforts to retake the island by landing soldiers from small boats, or rush to reinforce our main army in the event of a sortie from the castle.

As you might imagine, we hoped that if the French responded to our raid and occupation of the island, it would be with war galleys or troop transports so we could take them as prizes. That was something we were confident we could do. It was the possibility of a strong force of French soldiers waiting for us on the river bank of the island that concerned us most of all. We knew from our own experiences fighting along the River Tamar that a small number of well-armed soldiers could hold a river bank against a much larger number of soldiers trying to cross the river.

Most of the talk after the final review of our plan was finished was, of all things, about the large three-room villas my father and Henry were building for themselves near each other on Cyprus. After a bit of talking about them, however, Henry stood up, said "enough, I am an old man and need some sleep if I am to be ready for tomorrow." That, in turn, motivated everyone else to stand up and leave, including me. My father, however, caught my eye and motioned for me to stay. He wanted me to sit back down and have a personal word with him. So, of course, I did.

My father eyed me thoughtfully for a few moments, as if he was weighing my worth, and then began talking. He talked about our family and, at first, he seemed quite pensive. It was as though he thought something bad was about to happen or, God forbid, had happened. *Had he heard something about Becky was my first thought? I felt a great relief when it quickly became obvious he wanted to talk about something else.*

My father and I talked to as the candle lantern lighting the little room swung over us as Harold's galley bobbed up and down from the waves. He was, my father said, both encouraged and worried about our family's future. He did not, he said very intently, want his daughters or his sons, or their heirs, to be married off so as to form any kind of entangling alliance with a noble family or anyone else outside of Cornwall, or to ever be at the king's court, not even for a brief visit.

Similarly, he did not want the family or the company or Cornwall to ever take sides in the constant conflict between the King and the Church that he expected would occur in the years ahead, and probably forever; and he particularly did not want the company to ever allow a single Templar or priest to set foot in Cornwall without either being immediately buried, left on the ground to be eaten by the birds, or thrown in a river.

He looked at me so intently as he spoke that I soon realized he was telling me what would be expected of me if he fell in the fighting in the days to come or if he was suddenly taken off by a pox. I nodded my head in agreement and said that I understood what he wanted and would never let those things happen. "I swear it, father."

Then he truly surprised me by bringing up something new, very new.

"When I step down as the company's commander, which I am sworn to do as soon this revenge and ransom raid is finished, I am going to spend time, both on Cyprus and in Cornwall, scribing a parchment with the admonishments and orders for you and your younger brothers and your heirs to follow in the years ahead.

"You would be well-advised to follow them if you are to keep the family and the company somewhat rich and powerful. You would also be well-advised to pass my admonishments on to your heirs and most strongly suggest they do the same for theirs. Indeed, they are so important that I am ordering you and your heirs to obey what I just told you and whatever else I scribe. Do you understand?"

"Yes Father." *What else could I say, eh? Besides, thinking ahead about the future made good sense and I agreed to do it; it was very similar to what Uncle Thomas had said to me over and over again whilst I was growing up and in his school.*

\* \* \* \* \* \*

The twinkling lights I saw as I climbed over the deck railings of the two galleys and returned to the deck of John Cartwright's galley moved me behind my eyes. It was an altogether strange and wondrous sight as the waves raised and lowered the lights from the candle lanterns that hung on the masts all about me. It was if I myself had somehow been raised into the sky and the stars were twinkling all around me.

It was late in the darkness of night when I finally returned to John's galley. John was waiting there on the deck to greet me. As I climbed aboard I noticed something much less wondrous than the twinkling candle lights—that the deck railings on John's galley and the galleys around us were crowded with men standing about and talking, particularly where the railings were not up against those of another galley so that the food and drink vomited by the men on one galley would not foul the other.

Standing near the deck railing gave the men something to lean on while they talked, and to lean over if the sea pox took them. It was a reasonable precaution; a number of men still had not gotten their sea legs and were still periodically losing their food and drink as a result of being weakened by the motion of the waves.

Until recently I had been one of them; but, as John greeted me with a friendly "hoy" and starting talking, I realized that my legs no longer felt weak, and that I had not felt the need to rush for the deck railing ever since I set foot on Harold's galley for the meeting. I was, however, quite tired and in no mood to talk. To the contrary, I was looking forward to going to the forward castle and climbing into the bed I was sharing with John. I had much to think about and proceeded to our bed forthwith. Henry was right; tomorrow was going to be a long and arduous day.

As I walked towards the forward castle and the bed we shared, I could see that others of the archers were already sleeping, or pretending to be sleeping, on their rowing benches. There were not many sergeants to be seen; they were probably asleep in the much bigger deck castle atop the galley's stern or still poxed by the sea and hanging over the deck railing in the stern by the shite nest.

Everyone who was awake, on the other hand, even those at the deck railings, appeared to be either subdued because they knew we would begin our attack in the morning, or talking much too loudly about what they and their mates would do to the French when we met them.

There were also a number of visitors from other galleys, archers and sailors who had taken advantage of our galleys being lashed together to visit friends and family members.

In other words, everything was normal to the extent that anything could be normal for men who knew they were on the eve of a battle and did not know what it would involve or what would happen to them.

****** *An unknown archer*

Our sergeants came around and shook us to wake us up early the next morning, long before the first light of the day arrived. Preparations for our attack began almost immediately at the same time the bread and breakfast ale were being handed out. We carried bales of arrows up from the hold, and the pikes and boarding ladders were laid out on the deck, including the new and much longer ladders for use on the French bridges. We could see that fighting was expected because the sergeants were all kinder and more friendly, and the cook and his helper had prepared more food than usual and let us take all we wanted.

We had not even finished eating and getting ready when there was a great deal of shouting and pointing all around me, both on our galley and the ones around us—the "follow me" flags were being waved from both of the masts of the commander's galley.

Our warning horn was immediately blown by old Charley Joiner, and my mates and I rushed to our oars, with many of us, including me, still carrying what was left of our morning bread and cheese. Almost at the same time, one after another, the warning horns of all of the galleys began being tooted, and the sound of rowing drums soon began booming out over the water from all around us.

The galleys in the fleet's great raft were quickly untied from each other by our sailors, and then pushed apart so their oars could get into the water without hitting those of the galleys around them.

As soon as our galley was far enough away from the others, our rowing drum began booming and we began rowing for the mouth of the river. According to Sergeant Dixon, we were going to row up the river to the city called Paris where a king had many chests of gold coins even though his people were so poor they ate toads and snails.

At the very beginning, when we were first getting underway, there were a few minor galley bumps, and much swearing by the captain when another galley came too close and we had to hurriedly bring in our oars to keep them from being snapped off or hurting those of us on the benches when they were pushed back.

Once we got underway, however, a light quartering wind helped push us along so those of us who were rowing did not have to row too hard. The sails of our galley and the others remained up, even though the wind was barely usable, until we got close to the mouth of the river.

My mate Fred from the rowing bench in front of mine said that when he had been back to the nest for a shite he'd heard someone say the sailing sergeant told a sailor that the river we were about to enter was called the Paris, or something like that. He said we would be rowing up it to a big city where the people talked funny and the tavern girls smelled bad because they ate slimy things like snails and such, but were easy to get into because they were rigged differently and the foul things they ate made them all slimy down between their legs.

The talk on the benches was that we would each get three silver coins just for being here. And then someone on one of the benches behind me said his older brother had come up the river and visited the city many times when he was a sailor, and had told him there were a lot of taverns and alehouses where we could drink, and that they all had slimy girls we could get to know if we had enough coins. I was looking forward to it and so was everyone else; we anxiously questioned him to learn more.

# Chapter Eleven

*We surprise the French.*

The rowing drum on John's galley was pounding out a steady beat as my apprentice sergeant, Freddie Short, and I stood with John and his sailing sergeant on the roof of the forward castle. Freddie was known to the men, and somehow got on the company's roll, as Freddie Short because he was short and broad, and very strong even if he was not very tall.

In the distance we could see the masts of the cogs and ships at the quays of Harfleur and Honfleur. A short time later we could also see the masts of the transports still at the mouth of the Seine and those that were just starting to be rowed or towed up the river towards Paris.

I found myself getting quite excited; it would not be long now, probably sometime this afternoon, before I would be going ashore on the riverbank with most of my men to destroy one of the two wooden bridges that connected King Phillips's island to the city of Paris which stretched out in all directions on either side of the river.

After a few minutes of looking around and listening to John, I decided to go up on the nearby forward mast to see what else I could see. Freddie, of course, dutifully climbed up with me despite his trembling lower lip and white face.

What we saw below us was the deck of John's galley and a great fleet of our galleys following close behind my father's command galley. He was leading them towards what was obviously the mouth of the Seine, the river that flowed right through the middle of the city of Paris. Ahead of us, we could see a number of transports and barges loading and unloading cargos at the mouth of the river.

As we watched, four of our galleys peeled off from the fleet, adjusted their sails, and began rowing rapidly towards the ports of Harfleur and Honfleur on either side of the estuary. Those were the ports where transports moored when they were too large to use the river. Each of the four galleys had additional prize crews on board and high hopes. *They did take prizes and sent them on their way to Cornwall. Afterwards, they came up the river and re-joined the fleet.*

A few minutes later John's sailing sergeant shouted the orders that brought our sails down and we rowed through a great mass of transports, barges, and towboats gathered at the mouth of the Seine, and entered the river itself. The good news was that there were no French war galleys gathered at the river's mouth to stop us from entering the river.

In addition, at least so far as I could see, there were also none in the distance which might fall on the three galleys we would be temporarily leaving behind to take prizes from among the transports they encountered in the estuary and at the river's mouth. Perhaps there were Frenchmen about and they were away in pursuit of the galleys we sent to Harfleur and Honfleur, but somehow I doubted it; everything was just too peaceful.

Our passage through the estuary and into the river without being challenged was important; it was a great relief and boded well for our attack on Paris's castle island that something had *not* happened—the French did not have warships waiting for us at the mouth of the Seine and they did not try to prevent us from entering the river in some other way. The alehouse spy had apparently failed to alert them, unless, of course, the French were waiting for us further up the river.

We were not moving particularly fast as we passed through the estuary and entered the mouth of the Seine. There was little wonder in that even though the river was quite placid and slow-—because we only had about one-third of our galley's oars in the water. Slow but steady was the right thing to do at this early stage of our raid; we had hours of rowing ahead of us before we reached Paris. We wanted our men who would be going ashore to do so with fresh arms, arms that would be strong enough to push out their arrows and hold their pikes and shields steady.

My father, through Harold, had given the order that unless there was an emergency or a great opportunity, only one man in three of each galley's archers, as chosen by each galley's captain, and aided by all of its sailors not immediately needed elsewhere, were to do all the rowing from the lower tier of rowing benches. They would then move to the upper tier and stay with the galley whilst the galley's captain, its lieutenant, and all the archers with fresh arms, went ashore with their weapons and supplies. As you might imagine, the men doing the rowing tended to be our less experienced men and their sergeants.


******

There were common folk everywhere as we rowed up the Seine. Almost without exception, everyone we passed on the river, or saw on the roads and in the fields that ran along the river, stared at us with some degree of surprise and a look of uncertainty on their faces. The men and women on the transports and barges we passed paid us particular attention. It was if they had never seen so many war galleys in one place at the same time. And, of course, they probably had not. We ignored them as we rowed for Paris; we would take them later.

What the men and women looking at us did not know was who we were or what we were doing or why. They were not hostile, mind you, just curious. A few of them even called out to question us as we rowed past them. We just smiled and waved back at them all friendly-like. *When I was in his school, Uncle Thomas called what we were doing an "audacity," and said it was one of the marks of a good captain; I am still not sure exactly what it means. "Be brave and succeed by doing something unexpected," I think.*

The ocean-going transports and some of the river barges we passed were being towed by small boats with from four to twelve rowers depending on the size of the tow they were pulling and which direction they were going. Many of the towing boats seemed to be the dinghies from the transports they were pulling. There were also teams of horses pulling on towlines with bargees using long poles to continually push their barges away from the riverbank and the sandbars in the river.

All in all, the river was quite busy in both directions. It was very much as Uncle Thomas had described seeing it from the window of his cell when he was a prisoner in the king's island castle, and then later when he was paroled to live with the monks and priests at the other end of the little island.

It took us a good part of the day to get up the river to Paris even though we did not stop to take any of transports or barges we came across; they would be taken by the galleys we had sent to Harfleur and Honfleur or by the three galleys waiting at the mouth of the river.

Harold's galley, the command galley with my father on board, did not lead the way as our armada rowed up the Seine. It almost immediately fell back and let other galleys take the lead.

It was a good thing Harold let others go first. Twice on the twisting and turning river we passed a stranded galley with its crew working feverishly to get it unstuck from a sandbar as the rest of our galleys slowly and carefully rowed past it. The twisting and turning river was full of sandbars and shallows, and we had no river pilots or experienced captains to guide us.

We were picking our way slowly and cautiously up the river because we had no one in our fleet who knew the Seine. That was because Paris was rarely a destination for our transports. And I could not help but smile as we went past one of our stranded galleys and I remembered my father's explanation as to why the company did not have a shipping post in France and our transports rarely visited here.

"The French king favours the Templars because they are foolish enough to lend him money for his wars," my father had explained during one of our meetings at Restormel.

And then, with a fond gesture and an affectionate smile towards my uncle, the bishop, he added: "Between the Templars and the Church they have the money transfers, pilgrims, and shipping in the French ports sewed up tighter than a bishop's purse; there is no room for the likes of honest men like us."

*Now there is a thought; maybe we could make a shipping post for the company part of the ransom? Umm, no; that might sooner or later bring us into conflict with the Templars. They may be foul smelling because they do not wipe their arses since they are trying to live like Jesus and he did not have to wipe his since he was a god, but they are good fighters and they have become rich and powerful of late, ever since they got their hands on part of the cross on which the Romans hung Jesus and began making people pay to see it and pray nearby.*

\*\*\*\*\*\*

We began to see the outlying villages and the buildings and city walls of Paris in the distance after we had rowed up the river for some hours and the sun was almost directly overhead. It was a warm day and the sky was clear. Our rowers were hot and covered with sweat despite not rowing intensely and only wearing their light summer tunics. Everyone else was either resting wherever they could find some shade or working on their weapons.

Finally, as we got closer to the city and came around a bend in the river, we reached the beginning of the great city walls on both sides of the river. And for the first time we could see the French king's great fortress on the near end of the island in the middle of the river. And there they were in the distance on the far end of the island, the wooden bridges connecting the king's island to the gates in the city walls on both the left and right banks of the river.

It was the bridge on the left that held my interest, the one that connected the king's island to the Right Bank if you were coming down the river instead of going up it. My men, the archers of the six galleys of my mini-fleet, were assigned to cut off the island from the Right Bank by holding that bridge until we could destroy it. According to my father's plan, three of my galleys were to land their archers at each end of the bridge where it touched the riverbank.

\*\*\*\*\*\*

We were as ready as we could be as we approached the bridge. Each of my galleys had its battle axes and galley shields laid out on its deck along with all of its bladed pikes and arrow bales. We also had several of long-handled axes that had been hastily acquired in Cornwall from the woodsmen who provided firewood for the castle and our training camp.

In addition, on every galley assigned to the island's two bridges, the galley's carpenter and his archer-helpers had spent the last few days carving new and longer handles for the sharpest of the galley's short-handled battle axes. They had also painstakingly chopped and shaved some oak timbers to make pry bars. *We did not know how long it took the French to build those bridges, but we intended to take them down quickly. It did not happen, as everyone now knows, but that was what we thought at the time.*

In the distance, at the far end of the island beyond the French king's fortress home, I could see the outline of the great cathedral that my uncle told us had been under construction for many years. Everything was where our map had shown it to be and my uncle had said it would be; and we had reached the city without meeting any resistance. We had gotten up the river to Paris exactly as we had planned.

In other words, so far, so good. Everything was going smoothly and we had spent several days planning and preparing so as to be ready for anything the French might throw at us. I could not think of anything that could possibly go wrong.

\*\*\*\*\*\*

The waters of the Seine divided when they reached the king's island, with some of the river's water flowing on one side of the island, and some of it flowing on the other side. We rowed into the waters of the river that were flowing downstream towards us from the river channel on our left. This took us into the northern branch of the river that passed between the island with the king's fortress and that part of the walled city of Paris that was on the Right Bank of the Seine.

As we approached the bridge, I could see that a section of it functioned as a drawbridge did over a castle moat. At that moment, the drawbridge was partially raised because a long and narrow river barge was coming downstream and passing through the open section of the bridge. The barge's nose was being pulled in the direction the barge's captain wanted it to go by a line attached to a small dinghy rowing in front of it.

People, common folk from the look of them, and horse-drawn wains were on the bridge waiting for the barge to pass and the drawbridge to be lowered so they could continue on their way; others were fishing from the riverbank or walking on the paths that meandered along the riverbank on both sides of the river. It was a peaceful scene.

From where I was standing atop the roof of our galley's forward castle, I could also see the streets and lanes on the island after we passed the castle and began slowly rowing past the middle of the island where the island's common folk lived. The island's streets and lanes, to my surprise, were paved with stones with people going about their lives as if we did not exist. I also saw, immediately after we passed the French king's castle, a small market in the middle of the island filled with merchant stalls, and a number of very tall hovels where the common people apparently lived. Everywhere the island's common folk were walking about in what appeared to be a normal everyday manner.

Some of the hovels we passed were quite tall with ladders and wooden steps such that people could live in rooms that were piled on top of one another. They were quite similar to the tall hovels I had seen in London and in other big cities such as Lisbon and Rome.

The market and the hovels where the common people lived were in the middle of the island between the king's Louvre Castle at the downstream end of the island nearest us and cathedral that was under construction at the other end of the island where the bridge came ashore. There were a number of dinghies and small boats tied up all along both sides of the river; and some of them had fishermen standing or sitting on them.

And there was something of great and encouraging importance tied up to the riverbank close to what appeared to be the entrance to the castle where the French king resided—an elaborate and highly decorated barge with a dozen or so blue-liveried servants sitting in it and standing around on the island's riverbank near it. It was almost certainly the royal barge and its presence suggested that King Phillip might be in his castle.

I briefly considered going for it, and then watched as, a minute or so later, Harold's galley and the other galleys of his mini-fleet trailing behind mine and Henry's galleys picked up speed and headed straight for it.

After a brief moment of hesitation, I ignored the barge and left it to the galleys behind us because my orders were to take and destroy the rapidly approaching bridge. And then I totally stopped thinking about the barge when John began loudly shouting orders to his sailing sergeant and rudder men, orders that headed us straight for the place on riverbank where the bridge came ashore a few feet away from a gate in the city wall. The gate was open and a steady stream of people and carts appeared to be passing through it.

At the same time that John's galley and two others were heading for where the bridge came ashore next to the city gate, my other three galleys were heading to the other end of the bridge where it came ashore on the island. We were part of a bigger plan: Peter and his six galleys would take the similar bridge that ran from the other side of the island to the left bank of the river.

Simultaneously, the galleys in the middle of the long line of galleys coming up the river behind me, those under Henry's command, would land most of their archers on the island itself. Then the galleys, under the command of their sailing sergeants, would go after and destroy all the dinghies and small boats they could find so that no one could get off the island unless they knew how to swim.

From where I was, it appeared that the big gate in the city wall near the bridge was open with people and carts passing back and forth through it. What I could not yet see was whether or not the ramparts and archer slits on the city wall near the bridge gate were manned. Those on the king's castle, and on the city wall we were passing, had not been manned.

That the French did not appear to be expecting us was good news, very good news. What was worrisome, however, in terms of taking the bridge and holding it whilst it was being destroyed, was that sooner or later the city wall and some of its ramparts and arrow slits would be manned—and it looked as though some of them would be within easy crossbow or longbow range of where we would be going ashore and the first half of the bridge.

Not that I expected longbows, mind you; the French never used them because their arms were not strong enough because of the foul things they ate. But the French had crossbows for sure.

# Chapter Twelve

*I have a Problem.*

Three of my six galleys, including John's, the one I was on, were closing in on the bridge. In a minute or two we would attempt to land John's archers on the riverbank near where the bridge joined the mainland. Across the river my other three galleys would soon be doing the same thing where the bridge joined the island.

I looked back for a brief moment and saw Henry's galleys coming up the river behind mine. And behind Henry's mini-fleet I saw the galleys under my father's direct command coming up very fast and heading straight for the fancy barge with all the little flags and a liveried crew.

When I next looked back, the first of Henry's galleys, almost certainly Henry's, was just reaching the riverbank in the middle of the island and beginning to unload its archers on to the island. I could not see who it was, but I was fairly positive it was Henry himself who was the first man to set foot on the island. I did not, of course, wait to find out; it was almost time for me to jump down on to John's deck and get in position to lead the archers from my three galleys on to the riverbank next to the bridge, and then on to the bridge itself.

The good news was that, so far as I could see, there were neither Frenchmen with weapons waiting for us on the riverbank to oppose our landing, nor manning the wall near the gate. The bad news was very bad—the city wall and the gate near the bridge were much too close for comfort to the riverbank where we would come ashore and to entrance of the bridge.

There was no doubt about it, my men and I would be in easy range of a crossbow bolt shot from the ramparts of the nearby city wall and vulnerable to a sally out of the city gate.

On the other hand, it was easy to understand why my father and Peter considered the two bridges so important to our success, and so many galleys and men had been allocated to destroying them: They were perfect choke points because people going from the walled city on one side of the river to the walled city on the other side of the river had to use the bridge to get to the island, walk across the island, and then use the other bridge to get over to the other part of the city.

As I jumped down from the roof of the galley's forward castle, I could see that the men who would be going ashore with me had already picked up their weapons along with the additional quivers of arrows they each would be carrying. And right behind them on the deck were the men carrying the axes and other tools we would be using to destroy the bridge in addition to their weapons. The deck was crowded.

Every man including me would be going ashore heavily burdened, carrying everything he could carry in case the galley had to push off from the riverbank to avoid a French sortie from the gate or crossbow bolts coming from the nearby city wall. The only thing we were not carrying was water skins. We did not think we would need them because we would be so close to the river. It turned out to be a great mistake, especially for me, because the entrance to the bridge was within crossbow range of the ramparts on the city wall.

The hot sun and the heat of the day were initially forgotten as John's galley approached the riverbank. Some of the men were actually jostling each other for the right to be amongst the first to go ashore.

They would not be the first. I would be the first man to set foot on the riverbank with John and his lieutenant and my apprentice sergeant right behind me; it was expected of us. Being first was my right and duty as the commander of the landing party that would try to take both ends of the bridge, even though we probably only needed to hold one end or the middle to succeed.

I picked up all the quivers of arrows I could carry with my right hand and carried an upright bladed pike with my left. My longbow was strung and over my shoulder as I bumped and pushed my overloaded way through the crowd of excited men to get to the railing at the very front of the galley.

It was obvious to everyone that I intended to lead them ashore as they rightfully expected. The men smiled and nodded their approvals, and several shouted "commander's coming through," as I made my way through the tightly pack mass to the deck railing.

John and his lieutenant were similarly overloaded and right behind me just as they should be, with Freddie, my apprentice sergeant, right behind them. Under my tunic I was wearing my wrist knives and my rusty chain shirt which hung down far enough to cover my dingle and arse. I was already dripping with sweat from the heat of the sun, and so were all the men crowded around me, but I paid it no attention. I was very excited. There was a very light wind rustling the leaves of the trees along the river.

Our landing on the riverbank at the foot of the bridge did not go smoothly. It started with a mishap and went downhill from there. It was so crowded at the deck railing when John's galley bumped up against the riverbank that men were standing on the landing plank which had been resting on the deck. And that was not the only problem because in all the excitement John's sailors had somehow forgotten to bring forward the stool we would need to stand on in order to climb up and get on to the landing plank so we could walk ashore.

So there we were, all of us jammed along the deck railing with our weapons as a couple of sailors leapt on to the riverbank and endeavoured to hold the galley against it—with no way for me and my heavily burdened and sweating and swearing archers to get ashore.

It took us only a few moments to understand the problem. There was much shouting and pushing until the boarding plank was freed of the men standing on it, including me, and lifted into place with one end resting on the deck railing and the other on the nearby riverbank.

And then I could not climb up on to it because the stool was missing and I was much too overloaded to jump up on to the boarding plank. Similarly, because I was so overloaded, there was no way I could jump all the way across the two or three feet of water to the nearby riverbank as a couple of the galley's sailors had done so the mooring lines could be thrown to them.

The whole situation was damn embarrassing and, despite the fact that I was only wearing my chain and a lightweight tunic, I was rapidly getting very hot and sweaty being as I had heavily overloaded myself with weapons and supplies in an effort to impress my men.

My pride and the situation were saved when a three-legged stool was passed overhead on the crowded deck from one man's upraised hands to the next until it reached the deck railing where the boarding plank had been set in place. The plank stretched between the galley and the riverbank with one end resting on the galley's deck railing and the other on a couple of feet of French land on the riverbank.

At that point, I was finally, with John and the men around me helping to steady me, ready to step up on to the stool and then up on to the boarding plank. But when I started to do so, I found the plank tilting significantly downwards towards the galley. That was because the weight of all the men standing on one side of the galley's deck had pushed the top of the deck railing down far below the riverbank.

My foot slipped and I almost fell as I wobbled my way up on to the stool, and then from the stool up to the upward sloping plank. But I made it with a help of the archers standing on the deck around me who helped to steady me and boost me up. They continued steadying me until one of the sailors already on the riverbank grabbed my outstretched arm and pulled me up the plank and on to the riverbank.

"Good work; stay here and help the next men," I ordered the helpful sailor as I shrugged to shift the heavy load I was carrying on my shoulders to make it more comfortable. Then I started carrying my heavy load towards the nearby bridge, all the time expecting to feel the bite of a crossbow quarrel shot from the nearby city wall.

There were curious French men and women both standing around and walking nearby. They were watching as I began walking towards the bridge. I did not wait for either John or his lieutenant, or for my apprentice sergeant. I could not wait; the load I was carrying was so heavy it was all I could do not to drop it or fall to my knees and make even bigger fool of myself in the eyes of my men.

All I could think about as I staggered towards the bridge was that it was a good thing we landed unopposed as my hands were full and I surely would not have been able to defend myself. Even worse, if that was possible, the sweat on my forehead was running into my eyes such that I could barely see. And, of course, I had no way to wipe it away.

# Chapter Thirteen

*We take the bridge.*

People and horse-drawn wains were crossing the bridge in both directions as I trudged up to where the bridge began and put down my load with a great sigh of relief.

John and his lieutenant were right behind me and were putting down their loads by the time I was able to get my bow off my shoulder and start to pull an arrow out of one of the quivers I was carrying. Then I realized that I was confused about the need to pull an arrow out of my quiver, and tried to put it back. Pulling it out was just something I had done without thinking in the confusion of the moment. Three or four puffing and panting weapons-carrying archers and my apprentice sergeant joined us a few seconds later.

To my surprise, when I looked back at the river I could see men pouring off the galley I had just struggled to leave. Apparently, after I had climbed ashore with some difficulty, John's galley had somehow gotten close enough to the riverbank so the men could stand on the deck railing and, with a little help from those already on the riverbank, step ashore despite the rocking motion of the galley and the heavy loads they were carrying.

I could also see the sailors of my other two galleys jumping ashore to moor them next to John's and Henry's galleys landing men on the island. And then I thought I saw a splash on the island side of the river near the bridge as something went into the water, but I was not sure. I certainly hoped it was not one of my men; most of them did not know how to swim.

\*\*\*\*\*\*

The very first group of John's archers to reach us were only carrying shields and short swords in addition to their longbows and pikes. They were his best fighters, and John's lieutenant immediately began forming them up into their fighting lines. It gave me great satisfaction to see our ranks being formed; we were ashore in France with a rapidly growing fighting force. If the French did not sally soon we'd have the bridge and they would never get rid of us. So far so good, except that I suddenly realized that I was very thirsty and felt slightly dizzy.

To everyone's great surprise and pleasure, including mine, and just as it had been as we rowed up the river, the French people had not yet even recognized our hostile intent, let alone what was happening. There had been no effort to sound the alarm, let alone an attempt to repel us. To the contrary, the bridge's drawbridge had been lowered once the barge finished passing through the opening and people and wains were once again moving normally back and forth over the bridge and passing through the gate in the city wall that was near the entrance to the bridge.

The people who were crossing the bridge and those just standing around nearby were certainly curious and spent time looking at the galleys along the riverbank and the men pouring off of them. But they did not seem particularly concerned. And the ramparts on city wall near the open gate were still not manned. For a few moments I actually considered walking to the gate and taking control of it.

A young woman walking with a small child holding her hand, a girl from the looks of her neatly braided hair, noticed me watching as she and her child walked across the bridge towards me. She gave me a smile and a slight nod. I smiled back and nodded to them both.

"Bonjour, Madam and Mademoiselle," I said in English with an even bigger smile as she passed me whilst I was using the sleeve of my tunic to wipe the sweat off my brow. They were amongst the very few French words I knew.

"Bonjour, Monsieur," she replied as she continued on past me.

Our men instinctively recognized that there was no threat from the passing people and remained peaceful without any order being given. John's lieutenant, whose name I had forgotten, Charles I think, did a particularly smart thing. He sized up the situation and, without being told, formed up his galley's men on the bridge in a seven-men-deep fighting line that only closed off half of it. Then as the men from the other two galleys arrived with their weapons and bridge-destroying tools, he directed them to take positions that extended our fighting line into a column that stretched deeper into the bridge instead of across it.

As a result of where Charles positioned our men, the bridge was only partially blocked and the French civilians, riders, and horse-drawn wains and carts were able to continue moving unhindered in both directions across it. It was a good decision as it meant the local people were not immediately alarmed; yet all he had to do was march half of the men about ten feet to their right, and in only a few seconds the bridge would be tightly sealed. Alternately he could give them an "about face" order and double-time them out of crossbow range.

I caught Charles's eye and nodded my approval. He had done the right thing without being told to do it. Then I put a thought behind my eyes to remember his name, and started rapidly walking across the bridge to see how the men from my other three galleys were doing at the other end of the bridge. They were to similarly hold the other end of the bridge, the island end, whilst the men from all six of our galleys who had come ashore with their axes and tools destroyed it beyond repair. Freddie followed close behind as I went to see them.

Our initial moments of peace and tranquillity ended before I reached my men on the other side. I had slung my long bow and a quiver over my shoulder and was walking briskly across the middle of the bridge to see what was happening at the other end, when suddenly there were shouts coming from the other end of the bridge where we were headed. People began hurrying towards us along with a wain and several carts being pulled by horses and mules which were being whipped by their drivers to increase their speed.

"Well, Freddie, at least they know we are here," I said to my apprentice sergeant as I increased my pace and once again tried to wipe the sweat out of my eyes.

\*\*\*\*\*\*

When I reached the island end of the bridge, I found a large and rather motley group of French men, women, and children standing in front of three seven-man-deep battle lines of archers, one from each of the galleys that landed on the island-side of the bridge. There did not appear to any French fighting men, liveried servants, or nobles amongst them.

The archers of my other three galleys had closed off the entire bridge and were standing quietly in their ranks facing them. The people standing in front of them all looked like ordinary men and women who merely wanted to cross over to the Right Bank of the city.

My approach was noted and James, my second in command and one of the newly promoted captain majors, worked his way through the ranks of his archers and hurried towards me with a look of satisfaction on his heavily bearded face.

James was the son of a Ludlow Castle hostler who had run away from home and joined the company in one of our very first intakes of recruits. We had served together on several occasions and I knew him to be steady and dependable, even if he was not the sharpest arrow in the company's quiver. He had commanded the three galleys which landed their men on the island side of the bridge; and he seemed to have done a better job of getting his men ashore than I had.

"Hoy Commander," James said as we met and he knuckled his forehead to acknowledge my higher rank. In the background I could see many of his men had turned their heads around to watch us. The bridge was so narrow that James had the archers of each his three galleys in separate fighting lines, one behind the next, with each line being seven men deep as was the company's tradition.

Beyond James' lines I could see a gathering group of men and women who looked as though they wanted to cross the bridge and were unable to do so. James had been told to close off the bridge without killing anyone unless they tried to stop him, and it appeared that he had done exactly that.

"Hoy Captain Major. I see you have closed the bridge and caused some people and wains to hurry away from you and your men when you did. Did you have any problems getting ashore or closing the bridge?"

"Nothing important, Commander; nothing important. Just some fool noble in a carriage who tried to push his way through our lines and got cut down for his trouble. That is probably what set the common folk to hurrying, seeing him fall. Screamed like a pig when he got chopped, he did."

"Well done, James. Well then, strip him of everything of value and toss him in the river if you have not already done so, and get your lads started on tearing down the bridge.

"But first let everyone in that group of Frenchies in front of your lines cross over to the mainland unless they look like gentry. Then close off the bridge permanently to all men whilst letting the women and children continue to pass for as long as possible. Oh, and there will be more common folk we will be letting come across from the other side. Do not bother them; let them pass through your lines."

"Aye Commander; I will let them through. And you can count on me and my lads to hold the line for as long as necessary."

"I know I can count on you and your lads, James, I know I can." ... "Come on, Freddie. We can go back. The captain major has things under control over here." I said the last bit loud enough so his men could hear.

James was all puffed up with pride and pleased with himself as he knuckled his forehead and I turned to retrace my steps back to the other end of the bridge. Freddie followed close behind until we began passing over the now-lowered drawbridge. Uncle Thomas had not mentioned it, but I could see that it was important because it could be raised to stop traffic across the bridge even if we were attacked before we could finish destroying it.

"Freddie, draw your sword and stay here to command the drawbridge until I send someone to relieve you. I will send some archers to support you. Leave the drawbridge down so no French barges can pass in either direction, but be prepared to raise it on a moment's notice if any of our galleys or their dinghies want to pass."


\*\*\*\*\*\*

I felt quite unwell and more than a bit wobbly by the time I returned to the men of the galley companies I had led ashore. Both John and his lieutenant came out to greet me as I walked up to the men in our battle line that was continuing to block off half the bridge.

By the time I reached them and ordered the men to move deeper on to the bridge, to get them out of crossbow range from the city wall, I could hear pounding and shouting behind me. James' men were beginning to destroy the bridge, and it was time for my men to start helping them. People, mainly women and children and commoners from the look of them, were continuing to hurry across the bridge in both directions.

"You look a bit poxed, Commander. Are you alright?" I heard John ask. He sounded far away.

"I am fine. Just a little hot, that is all."

"Uh, Commander, should we start destroying the bridge?"

"Yes, it is time. Please start as soon as you have got all our men on the bridge and out of crossbow range."

I do not remember anything after that until I heard someone say "get him into the shade and pour more water on him." Later I learnt that I had ordered John to send some men to relieve Freddie at the drawbridge so he could re-join me. *I nodded my agreement when he mentioned it to me much later; but I never did remember that or anything else I might have said or done whilst I was asleep.*

# Chapter Fourteen

*Henry takes the island and Peter loses his reinforcements.*

After much discussion, William and I had decided to have all the archers assigned to take the island come ashore under my command at the same time and in the same place. We were supposed to do so in the middle of the island where the islanders lived in their hovels and had their market, and as close as we could be to the main gate in the wall around the king's castle whilst still being well out of crossbow range.

The possibility of landing my men simultaneously on both sides of the island had been given some consideration as had the notion I should leave some of the archers aboard their galleys as an additional reserve. In the end, however, it was decided to take the safest course of action and concentrate all of our men assigned to take the island into one strong fighting force under my command instead of dividing them in some way.

From bitter experience, very bitter, I was well aware that it is almost always better for a commander to concentrate his fighting men into one strong fighting force instead of locating them all over the place in smaller groups which might be attacked separately and overwhelmed one at a time. I had insisted on it because we did not know the strength and abilities of the king's forces inside the castle. It would be a disaster if we divided our archers into small groups and the French king had a sufficiently large force in his castle. Then the king's men would almost certainly sortie out and overwhelm us one group at a time.

As a result of my concerns, all eight of the galleys under my command followed George's six galleys into the north fork of the river that runs through the middle Paris and made for the riverbank in the middle of the island. George's six galleys had further to go up the river than we did, so my captains and I began landing our archers on the island at almost the same time as George and his men began landing at both ends of the bridge at the other end of the island.

Our landing went well despite the unexpectedly intense heat coming out of the cloudless sky from the sun passing over our heads. I led just over six hundred archers ashore, almost all the archers from eight galleys. My captains and I quickly formed them up into a battle formation far enough away from the walls of King Phillip's great castle to be safely outside of crossbow range.

As soon as all of our men were ashore, and our battle lines were firmly established in front of the castle, I ordered the captains of two pre-selected galley companies of archers to quick-march their men along the riverbank all the way around the island and destroy all the dinghies and small boats they came across. Every man carried a pike or battle axe for that purpose in addition to his longbow and one of our large land-fighting shields.

Some of the company's other galleys, eight of them under Harold's command, were also assigned to destroy the dinghies and other small boats everywhere along the river, and so were the galleys of the men who landed to destroy the bridges.

That was probably more than enough galleys to do the job, but I wanted to make sure the French small boats and barges were gone because their destruction was so important in terms of preventing King Phillip and his courtiers from escaping. Accordingly, I sent the archers of one of my companies upstream along the riverbank to walk all the way around the island and destroy any boats and barges they found.

At the same time, I sent all the archers of another company walking downstream to walk all the way around the island and do the same. The two companies would obviously meet and pass one another somewhere on the riverfront path on the side of the island opposite from where we landed.

Before they began marching I called the two captains to me and reminded them to keep their men close up against the castle wall as they walked around it in order to make it difficult for the defenders standing on the ramparts and at the arrow slits above them to see them and shoot arrows down on them.

Similarly and simultaneously with my men marching around the island, many of our galleys, including those of both George and Peter, were also searching for and destroying dinghies and small boats along the riverbank of both the mainland and the island. *Of course they were; we were determined to make sure no one was able to escape from the castle; we did not come all this way for nothing, did we?*

All the rest of my men, six full galley companies of them, stood in their ranks and watched as the archers of the two companies hurriedly departed to march all the way around the island in an effort to destroy all boats and barges they could find. The island was not all that large; even so, it would take the men of the two companies several hours to walk the waterfront path all the way around the island and arrive back to where my main force was waiting, and probably much longer since they were almost certain to find small boats and barges along the way that they would have to stop and destroy.

A few minutes after the two companies departed I ordered the captains of each of my galley companies to send some of their men to their galleys to fetch water skins, and to move the rest of their men to where there were some trees along the riverside further away from the castle gate. We would wait in the shade whilst the French king decided what to do.

*\*\*\*\*\*\* Peter Barrow.*

My six galleys were rowing their way up the Seine to take and destroy one of the two wooden bridges reported to be at the far end of the island, the one bridging the river channel between the island and that part of the city of Paris on left bank of the river. According to Thomas and the map, there was a wall around that part of city and it had a gate only a few feet away from the entrance to the bridge.

My main concern was that French soldiers would sortie out of the gate and attempt to drive us off the bridge before we could finish ruining it beyond repair. They were also likely to man the wall's ramparts and try to shoot crossbow quarrels at me and my men whilst we were working to destroy the bridge.

Since the French would sooner or later begin shooting crossbow quarrels at us from the city wall, I intended to have my men work at destroying the bridge far enough down it towards the island to avoid them. George and his similar mini-fleet would be doing the same thing to the other bridge, the one that ran from the island to the right bank.

We were still rowing in the middle of the river with the castle island in sight in front us when something important must have happened or been seen. I was on the roof of the forward deck castle of my galley and looking back at the string of five galleys assigned to me in addition to the one I was on. They were following close behind me just as they had been ordered to do.

Beyond my little mini-fleet, I could see Harold's galley coming up the river with Commander William on board and the galleys of his mini-fleet carrying the archers that would be my reinforcements if my men and I had to fight our way ashore at either bridge entrance, or were faced with a strong sortie coming out of the city gate.

As I watched, Harold's galley suddenly turned to the left, increased its speed dramatically, and headed straight for the other branch of the river, the one that came around the left side of the approaching island—instead of following me and my men to the bridge that was further down the branch of the river coming up on my right as had been the original plan.

The other galleys carrying my potential reinforcements followed Harold's. Something significant must have happened or been seen in the waters on the other side of the island. It was an unexpected change to our plan, and it seemed to mean that my men and I would have to take and destroy the bridge connecting the island to the left bank of the river all by ourselves, and we would have to do it without the reinforcements I expected to have available if I needed them.

# Chapter Fifteen

*Harold's men take the royal barge.*

William and I were on the roof of my forward castle as my galley led the galleys carrying our army's reserve force towards the entrance to the south stream of the Seine where it flowed down towards the sea from between the French king's river island and that part of Paris which was on the left bank of the Seine. We were following behind Peter's six galleys as they moved up the river to take and destroy the wooden bridge which connected the king's island to that part of walled city of Paris which was on the left bank of the river.

Our initial role was to standby and be ready to land our archers to reinforce Peter's men if they encountered serious resistance. If there was no serious resistance, on the other hand, several of my galleys, or the dinghies of all of them, would attempt to pass under the bridge and begin destroying all the small boats and barges they could find that were upriver from the island.

The rest of my galleys would turn around at the bridge and row all the way around to the other side of the island to see if George and Henry needed reinforcements. If George and Henry also did not need reinforcements, the galleys of my mini-fleet would then split up and begin moving back down both sides of the river destroying everything they could find that might be used to carry the French king and his courtiers to safety. At least, that had been the plan until it changed.

It was a shout from one of the lookouts up on the mast that changed the plan and gave William and me the first inkling that we might have caught the French king at home on his island in the middle of Paris. The lookout was up at the very top of the forward mast because he had uncommonly good eyes for seeing things far off in the distance that most men could not see.

"Hoy the deck. There be a fancy blue barge with little flags moored to the riverbank by the castle, and some men in coloured tunics are on it and standing about on the shore near it. Blue their tunics be. And there are great blue flags flying from the castle's towers. The castle's ramparts do not look to be manned."

William and I looked at where the man was pointing, and then at each other. My lookout was pointing to the branch of the river George and Henry's galleys were about to enter.

A second or so later William gave me a very specific direct order. He had a rather determined and satisfied smile on his face as he gave it; and at the same time he crossed himself, spit over his shoulder, and tapped the wooden railing around the roof of the forward deck castle where we were standing for good luck. He tapped three times as he gave the order.

"Signal Edward's galley to follow you and row hard for the barge your lookout sees tied up next to the castle, Commander. It may be King Phillip's royal barge. We must not let it get away."

"Aye Commander, Edward and I are to row hard for the barge moored by the castle and take it."

William had issued a formal order to me, and I, of course, had immediately replied in kind by repeating it back to him so he would know I understood what I was to do. It was a tradition and a requirement in the company for its men to become extremely formal and precise when giving and receiving important orders.

Our apprentices and the archers and sailors standing around us on the castle roof knew exactly what the sudden formality between two long-time friends meant—we were either going into action or something significant was about to happen.

My orders were quickly shouted to our rowers and rudder men by my sailing sergeant and then my loud talker repeated my "row hard for the barge moored by the castle and take it" order across the water to Edward from Heathrow's galley which was right behind us. For a moment I was uncertain what order I should give next. I had never gone after a barge moored on a riverbank with a galley before, or even drilled my crew to do so.

Finally, I gave the familiar and often practiced order for "boarding parties stand by to take a prize." It was the only order I could think to give under the circumstances. It would, at least, get my men into fighting positions that were more or less where I thought each man would have to be to take a moored barge. *I had never taken a moored barge on a river or even drilled my crew to do so, had I? For some strange reason, I began wondering behind my eyes if taking a moored barge was a drill I should begin requiring all of our galley captains to practice.*

The results of my order were instantaneous, and nothing less than what I fully expected.

Everyone in my crew rushed to their assigned positions: Some of the archers on the deck of my galley put down their weapons and ran to their oars, others of the archers swarmed up both our masts to the lookout nests with their longbows and quivers, some climbed on to the roofs of my galley's two castles, and my number one and number two prize crews assembled on the deck with their weapons. Similarly, the sailors stood by to work the sails, throw our grappling hooks, and raise the boarding ladders that our prize crews would climb.

My galley rapidly picked up its speed as our rowing drum began to beat faster and faster as more and more men reached their rowing benches on the lower tier of oars. The same orders were quickly repeated on Edward's galley, the one immediately behind us. Both galleys made directly for the castle with Edward's coming hard behind us.

We were not alone; the six other galleys in the line following mine saw the two galleys in front of them suddenly leap forward. They quickly began following us as they had been ordered to do. All the galleys in my mini-fleet were now rowing rapidly for the riverbank where the barge was tied up next to the castle instead of following Peter's galleys and rowing into river channel on our right.

William and I were soon able to see the barge for ourselves from the roof of my galley's forward castle where we were standing. It was moored against a little wooden wharf running along the river bank closest to the castle's entrance gate, and well within easy arrow range of the high castle wall that came out almost to the river.

As we got closer we could see several little blue flags flying on the barge and the dozen or more men standing and sitting in the barge and on the nearby riverbank. They were all wearing similar blue tunics and knitted caps. Our long-sighted lookout at the top of my forward mast had seen true.

No further orders needed to be given as we closed in on what was almost certainly King Phillip's royal barge. When we got close enough, arrows began to be pushed out towards the men in the blue tunics; first from the two archers in the nest on the forward mast; then at almost the same moment from the three archers standing on the castle roof with me and William; and finally from the archers standing on the deck.

Neither William nor I took part in the arrow pushing, although both of our young apprentice sergeants did. They were very excited; it was the first time either of them had pushed an arrow at someone.

There was immediately much scrambling about by the men on the barge and along the riverbank as our arrows began to fall on them, and some of the blue tunics began to go down. Within seconds every man on the barge or on the riverbank who was still on his feet was running for his very life.

In the rapidly shortening distance, we could hear a lot of screaming and shouting as they ran. Shortly thereafter we bumped rather hard up against the barge and the men of our boarding party swarmed aboard the barge. They promptly cut its mooring lines as I had loudly ordered them to do, and the barge and our prize crew began slowly, very slowly, drifting away along the riverbank. It was the smallest and most important prize we had ever taken.

We watched and listened to all the commotion as it occurred a few feet in front of us on the barge and on the nearby riverbank, and whilst Harold's galley backed away from the barge so it could float free with our prize crews still on board. As we watched, more and more heads began to appear on the castle parapets and peer down at all activity and noise below them. We could see the watchers clearly from where we were standing because the big castle's curtain wall looked to be no more than thirty or forty paces from the riverbank of the island.

"Well, Commander," William said to me with a smile as he rubbed his hands with glee at the sight of the barge moving out into the flow of the river. "Do you think they know we are here?"

Before I had a chance to answer, a crossbow bolt thudded into the deck below me and a few seconds later an archer on the barge screamed and went down with a bolt in his belly. At that moment, as I looked up at the faces appearing in the archers' slits above us, I was very thankful that William and I could not be singled out for special attention from the French crossbow men because all of us were all wearing the same light brown hooded tunics, the only difference being that William and I had more stripes on the fronts and backs of ours than did the everyone else.

William reacted immediately with another order, and our archers began responding; they pushed arrows out of their longbows whenever anyone showed himself at the arrow slits above us on the battlements of the nearby castle wall.

"Have your men throw a line to the prize crew on the barge, Commander," William ordered me, "and pull it farther away from the shoreline. We have no need to stay here any longer and let the French shoot their arrows at us."

Whilst all that was happening rather rapidly, and even though they were not in any way needed, the rest of my galleys began to arrive one after another at the riverbank under the castle wall—and unnecessarily put themselves in danger from the French archers on the ramparts above them. They had all dutifully followed my galley when we had sailed into the divided river to get the king's barge.

Using the booming voice of my loud talker and our own energetic arm waving and motions, William and I immediately ordered our galleys to move on up the river towards the bridge George was assigned to destroy. They obeyed immediately and moved off. The prize crew manning the sweeps of the royal barge followed them.

As my galleys began moving away from the castle and its crossbow men, I realized behind my eyes that it was time for them to return to their original assignment of being a floating reserve for our landing forces and patrolling the river in search of small boats and barges to destroy.

The French king's crossbow men were good and, by the time we all got out of range, we had paid an unexpectedly high price to get away with the king's barge despite our return arrows and the speed with which we took his barge and towed it away: Three of our men had been wounded during our brief encounter, including one whose wound was so severe and painful he would probably soon die of it or need a mercy.

Even worse, one of our very best archers was killed outright when a bolt shot from one of the arrow slits atop the wall took him in his forehead. He fell to the deck from the archers' nest on the forward mast and broke the arm of a sailor standing next to the mast when he landed on him.


\*\*\*\*\*\*

We towed the king's barge a short distance down the river and my sailors used our galley's axes to chop a hole in its hull and sink it in the middle of the river. And to send King Phillip and his courtiers a message, we did so in full sight of the large and rapidly growing number of watchers on the castle's walls.

William and I just looked at each other and gave a sigh of relief when the last of our men was out of range. We did not have to say a word—we both knew it was a good thing for us that the French were unprepared and it takes crossbowmen so long to reload their bolts; the same number of Frenchmen with longbows, or even regular bows at such a short range, might well have slaughtered our men and driven us off before we could attach lines to the royal barge and pull it away.

# Chapter Sixteen

*George's men begin destroying the bridge.*

My head hurt most severe and I was dizzy and unsteady as I got to my feet with Freddie and a young one-stripe archer I had never seen before pulling on my arms and elbows to help me stand up.  There was the distinctive and instantly recognizable sound of axes chopping wood in the distance. I was confused as I was helped somewhat unsteadily to my feet.

"What happened?" I demanded of Freddie.  My mouth felt dry.  "And why are not you at the drawbridge?"

"The captain major sent one of his captains to relieve me and told me to tend to you, Commander. It seems you went to sleep from the sun and fell down. Some of the other men did too.  That is why they dragged you over here and we were throwing water on you."

Suddenly I understood.

"Oh my God!  How long was I asleep?  Did the French attack?  What is happening?"

I looked around rather frantically as I asked my questions. What I saw were several men asleep on the bridge with their mates trying to wake them by slapping their faces and pouring water on them, and a number of other archers sitting and standing around us—and they all seemed to be staring at me as I struggled to my feet. *I did not feel humiliated at the time, but I did later—and that, as everyone knows, caused me to do something quite foolish in an effort to redeem myself.*

Some the men around me looked quite wane and their mates were helping them sit up and drink from water skins and bowls that must have been fetched from our galleys. We were on the bridge and the men who were near me were looking at me, and listening intently to our conversation. A few feet away I could see the backs of a seven-deep line of archers in battle formation. To my great relief, they were just as I had left them when I went off to visit the men at the other end of the bridge.

"How long was I asleep? What has happened?" I demanded again of Freddy. My mouth felt very dry and I seemed to be croaking as I spoke and unsteady on my feet. Freddy still had a firm hold on my elbow.

My apprentice sergeant brought me up to date on what had been happening whilst I was sleeping.

"The men are trying to destroy the bridge as you ordered, Commander, but it seems to be going much slower than we expected. The lads are having trouble. Some of the wood is so hard that our axes are bouncing off it, even when we sharpen them."

I was still trying to understand what I was being told when there were shouts of alarm and movement within our ranks. Men with weapons were starting to appear on the ramparts above the city gate. They seemed to be too far away to reach us with crossbow quarrels, but maybe not.

"Move the men to the other side of the bridge. And hurry," I shouted towards our battle lines. "Get them further away from the castle wall."

*I had made another mistake; I should have already ordered them to move to the other side of the bridge.*

****** *Captain Joshua Farmer.*

My galley was assigned to raid Harfleur along with Tony Priest's. Tony was the bastard son of a London cleric and still bitter about it although he had not seen his father and mother for many years. He, like me, did not know or care if any of his family were even still alive. At least that's what he always claimed although I was not at all sure he meant it.

In any event, Tony was senior to me so he was in command our little two-galley squadron. Working together, we took three large merchant transports from the Swede and Rus lands. They were anchored off the Harfleur quay and offloading their cargos into flat-bottomed lighters which were powered by great long oars called sweeps. Apparently the transports' hulls went too far down into the water to get up the river.

We also took a couple of single-masted French coasters. They were inbound and so heavily laden with firewood and black coales for Paris's cooking fires that they could not get all the way up the Seine.

Taking the five transports was quick and easy because there was no resistance. We just came alongside, climbed aboard them on our boarding ladders, and, a few minutes later, watched as our prize crews raised their sails and ruddered them for Cornwall.

What did take a good part of the rest of the day was going ashore to destroy the fishing boats we found. We usually do not destroy fishing boats. But this time we had to do it so they could not be used to help the French king and his courtiers escape from the king's island.

As you might imagine, the French fishermen were beside themselves with anger as they watched our men chop the hulls and main beams of their boats, but they mostly backed off when we waved our swords and pikes at them. Those few who did not back off, just three in all, were left to their mates to barber or bury.

After we sent our prizes off to Cornwall and broke the fishing boats' hulls, Tony and I followed the orders we had been given and our galleys began rowing along the French shoreline towards the entrance to the Seine whilst periodically stopping to destroy the small boats and barges we came across. The sun had finished moving overhead and it was getting dark by the time we reached the mouth of the river.

I was very satisfied as the day came to an end, and so were my men—we had taken a number of valuable prizes and destroyed everything that could float between Harfleur and the entrance to the Seine, and we had not lost a single man. Our only casualty was an archer who lost a couple of teeth when he was hit by an oar swung by an angry French fisherman.

In the morning we would go up the river at first light and continue destroying everything that we came upon that could float. The boats of the Harfleur fishermen who been out fishing would be destroyed when they returned with their catches—One of our three sister galleys assigned to remain at the river entrance and take prizes would do for them. To my surprise, there was no sign of our two sister galleys who had visited Honfleur on the other side of the estuary.

\*\*\*\*\*\*

Three of our company's galleys, the three assigned to remain at the river entrance, were the only sails in sight as we entered the river early the next morning and began rowing up the Seine towards Paris. After a couple of hours, during which time we twice put men ashore temporarily to destroy dinghies and small fishing boats, we met some of our galleys coming downstream. They were doing the same thing we were doing—destroying anything and everything the French might use to carry their king to safety from his island.

And coming downstream immediately behind our galleys were a number of prizes under tow with prize crews on board. They were the transports our galleys had taken in the river either before or after they delivered their cargos to Paris.

Our prizes were not actually being towed down the river, of course; they were floating freely down the Seine with their prize crews using lines attached to their prizes' dinghies to pull on their tow-lines when it was necessary to keep them in the river's deepest waters and guide them around sandbars and other boats. When they reached the estuary, our prize crews would recover their dinghies and set their sails and rudders for Cornwall.

To my surprise, one of the galleys we met was Harold's with William, our company's commander on board. After a brief conversation between the commander and Tony, we used our oars to turn around and we all rowed a little bit further down the river to where it widened out enough so we could stop and talk. We had to move downstream from where we met in order that there would be enough room for our somewhat unwieldy prizes to safely pass us.

It did not take long to find a wide spot in the river where we would be able to talk. Even then our galleys still could not get too close because we had to leave our oars in the slowly flowing water of the Seine so we could periodically row to maintain our positions. Tony, of course, did most of the talking since he was senior, but I was close enough to listen to the words being shouted back and forth as they came over the water to me.

Tony was rightly quite proud as he reported to the Commander on the prizes he and I had taken and sent off to Cornwall. But as I listened I suddenly realized something was not right. Why were Harold and his galleys sweeping the river of small boats this far downstream and asking questions if our two sister galleys came up from Honfleur yesterday afternoon? And why were they not with him?

I shouted out my question when there was a brief lull in the talking.

"Commander, what happened to the two galleys assigned to raid Honfleur? Were they successful? Are they behind your galleys and farther upstream?"

"I was about to ask you the same question, Captain. Have you not seen them?"

There was immediately a great deal of anxious shouting back and forth, and that was followed by orders being coming loudly across the water from the command galley. Less than a minute later, the first of three of the galleys which had been rowing periodically to hold their places just behind the Commander's galley came rushing past us with its rowing drum beating an increasingly rapid rowing pace and additional lookouts climbing its masts. Two more of the Commander's reserve galleys were right behind it.

My lieutenant and I just looked at each other and shrugged as our galley rocked back and forth from the waves and swells caused by the three galleys hurrying past us.

# Chapter Seventeen

*Henry and the French response.*

We did not have to wait long for the French to respond to our arrival and the battle lines I formed up just out of crossbow range in front of the main gate of Louvre Castle. William had not even returned from leading his men down the river to make sure all the small boats had been destroyed, when a Frenchman with a very loud voice showed himself and began shouting at us from the castle. He was standing on the ramparts above the castle's huge and beautifully carved wooden entrance gate.

The Frenchman shouted something at us in French which I pretended I could not understand. I did so by stepping forward from our lines and lifting both of my wide open hands above my shoulders and shrugging my head and shoulders to indicate I could not understand him.

A few moments later, a different man appeared on the ramparts next to him and a new voice began shouting something to me in church-talk. The new shouter looked to be a cleric of some kind.

I raised my arm to acknowledge the Latin words, and motioned for Samuel, my Latin-gobbling apprentice sergeant to come forward and stand beside me to interpret. Then we walked forward together a few more paces, all the time being careful to stay well out of the range of a crossbow bolt, and waited. We did not have to wait for long.

"My lord king demands to know who you are and what you want. Why have you come to Louvre Castle?"

Samuel repeated the Latin-gobbled question to me in English. *He is in there, by God. We have him.* I quickly gave Samuel my lies to shout back.

"We are axe men and mercenaries from the Rus and the Swede lands who have been contracted to fight for his excellency, Otto the Fourth, the Holy Roman Emperor, and King of Burgundy. Our commander is the emperor's son." *Otto does not have a son, he is very much like Richard and prefers boys. It was Thomas's idea; he said saying Otto's son was our commander would confuse everyone.*

What Samuel shouted back to the cleric on the castle wall was the very specific answer William told me I was to give if I was approached or questioned by the French before he came ashore. Besieging Louvre Castle and demanding a ransom in Otto's name would be believable, at least at first, Thomas had assured us, because King Phillip had actively supported another German prince to be the Holy Roman

Emperor instead of Otto who had an English mother and had grown up in England.

I brandished an axe at the French as I gave my answer for Samuel to shout back to the cleric in church-talk. Shaking the axe at the castle whilst I replied was a nice touch; my apprentice sergeant had suggested it earlier.

What we were trying to do, of course, was conceal and distort our connection to England and King John in case the French prince won and took the English throne.

There was what appeared to be an acknowledging wave from the Latin-gobbling cleric, and then a very long pause. It lasted several minutes at least. And then came the French response. It was in the form of a question.

"It is believed that Otto abdicated and is no longer either the emperor of the Germans or the King of Burgundy. Is that not so?"

"No, that is not correct. Our beloved emperor, Otto the Fourth, was chosen by God himself to be the emperor of the Holy Roman Empire and to be the King of Burgundy and the Germans. He did not abdicate despite being opposed by King Phillip and his fellow heretics."

I continued after a brief pause so Samuel could translate what I had said into Latin and shout it back to the castle.

"Because of the expenses and losses caused by King Phillip's foul opposition to our emperor's rightful place, what we want, indeed what we demand, in the name of God himself, is all of the many coins in King Phillip's chests so our emperor can use them to hire even more mercenaries and end the efforts of the usurpers who are attempting to claim his rightful throne."

I hoped I gotten it right; William had been very precise about what I was to say and not say, and particularly that I was to always deny we were English and always refer to Otto as "our" emperor because England was not part of the emperor's realm. I did not understand why, but both William and Thomas said it was important.

After another pause to allow Samuel to gobble my words in church-talk to the men above us on the castle's ramparts, I added more.

"It is "God's Will" that our emperor receive King Phillip's coins and use them to eliminate the evil men who are trying to replace him. Accordingly, the emperor has ordered us to hold the island, and to enjoy its food and women whilst we do, until the emperor receives a sufficiently large ransom from France to pay us and enable him to contract for even more mercenary companies. We will stay until our emperor gets his rightful coins and pays us no matter how long it takes."

There was another very long pause whilst the men on the ramparts conferred. Then the French threats began.

"In the name of God and King Phillip, I command you to leave immediately. God does not recognize Otto as emperor. He will curse you and send you to purgatory if you remain in France, and the armies of France will destroy you, if you do not leave the grounds of Louvre Castle immediately. Go quickly whilst you still have a chance to save your lives and your souls. God wills it."

I listened attentively whilst Samuel translated the French priest's words. When he finished, I made a very dismissive, some would say obscene, gesture towards the castle with my free hand, the one that was not holding the big axe, as I shook my head with disgust and turned away to walk back the few steps it took to reach the front line of our battle formation. I was feeling quite satisfied with myself as I did.

Even better, the sun was going down; there would be no more gobbling back and forth with the French today. William would be pleased; so far everything had been going as he said we should hope and expect. And the French would almost certainly launch a sortie out of the castle first thing in the morning. We were ready for them; there was no way there could be enough French knights and soldiers in the castle to defeat us.


****** *That evening.*

William and Harold arrived in Harold's galley and joined me just after the sun went down on a cloudless sky. The rest of the galleys carrying the reserve archers had followed them in such that there were now fifteen galleys tied up along the island's riverbank just past the castle. They had found us easily enough despite the growing darkness by rowing towards the cooking fires each galley's cook had lit with the firewood he had fetched from his galley.

The first thing William and Harold did was meet with the captains of the galley companies and then walk amongst their men as they stood at ease in the lines of our battle formation. I, of course, went with them and carried one of several candle lanterns so that William and his commanders and captains could see and be seen.

William's inspection was a success. Our men appeared to be ready for whatever might come, and much heartened by our successes that day and by the arrival of merchants bringing drink and women from the handful of taverns on the island. Afterwards we spent a warm and comfortable evening eating and drinking with our captains, and talking about what had occurred so far and the inevitable French sortie that would come out of the castle to test us. The enthusiasm and confidence of our men was very encouraging.

What was much less heartening were the reports that came in from George and Peter about the bridges that connected the island to the two parts of the walled city.

Their reports were almost identical—neither of them had been able to totally destroy his bridge despite his men being in total control of it and not being attacked. And they had each pulled their men back from the bridge entrances near the city walls because of quarrels that were coming from the French crossbow men who seemed to be infesting the walls' ramparts like a nest of biting lice. They had each suffered several wounded men until they did and one man was killed by a quarrel that went straight into his head.

So far all George and Peter had been able to accomplish was to take the bridges and cut off normal traffic over them by pulling their men back and destroying the drawbridges. The result for each bridge was a narrow and easily repairable watery gap between its two totally intact parts.

Also as a result, all of our men were now on the island side of the drawbridge gap in their bridges, and the French were on the other side sheltering behind the city walls. On the other hand, both George and Peter had totally succeeded in carrying out their most important assignments—taking the bridges and cutting off the island from Paris so the French king and his courtiers could not escape.

Our other problems at the bridges, and how the commanders on the scene saw them and were responding to them, were also very much the same. It seems the wood used to construct both bridges was uncommonly hard such that our axes were almost totally useless even when they were constantly sharpened.

Even worse than the hardness of the wood, according to both George and Peter, was the roundness of the long logs that were holding up the bridge planks. They were very thick and difficult to stand upon as was needed in order to swing an axe at them. Already one of the archers chopping on them, one of Peter's men, had fallen into the river and disappeared. Another had made a deep cut in his own foot.

Both of our bridge commanders also said the same thing about how they intended to proceed: They each reported that they had brought in candle lanterns from their galleys and would have their men work through the night chopping on the logs on the island side of his bridge. Neither Peter nor George had any idea when his men might be finished. All of their galleys were now moored on the island side of the river.

After we finished supping and drinking with the men, which involved much joshing, and the remembering of long-ago men and battles, William and Harold returned to their galley, which was moored nearby, to get a few hours of sleep. They would return before the sun arrived to stand with our men when the French sallied out at us in the morning, something which seemed inevitable. Both they and I pretended not to hear the sound of more than a few women talking and laughing in the darkness beyond the light of the campfires.

My captains and their men were fully prepared to receive the French expected French sally; they stayed in their ranks and slept on the ground so they would be ready in the morning as well as instantly prepared to jump up and fight in the event of a night attack. I thought a night attack highly unlikely, but stayed with the men and caught a few hours of sleep by digging a little hole for my hip immediately in front of our front line and sleeping on the ground as the men did.

Nothing happened in the darkness except I got a sore neck and my arm went numb from sleeping on it.

\*\*\*\*\*\*

We were at full strength and fully ready for anything when the sun arrived the next morning. I had all of the archers from my eight galley companies at the ready and William had gotten up in the middle of the night and brought in seven additional companies ashore from his reserve galleys.

In all, we had almost twelve hundred heavily armed men in front of the castle and ready to fight when the sun arrived in the morning on its daily trip around the world. It was a far stronger army than we could possibly need to defeat a sally no matter how many men the French king had in his castle. After the sally, the fifteen galley companies of archers and the men at the bridges would remain on the island as its garrison army, and our galleys would constantly patrol the river to prevent anyone from escaping until an acceptable ransom was paid.

Sure enough, as soon as there was enough light to see, a large number of watchers appeared on castle's ramparts, the castle's huge entrance gate swung open, and a force of French knights and soldiers sallied out of Louvre Castle in an effort to surprise us and drive us away.

There could not have been more three or four hundred of them, of whom less than a dozen were knights on horseback and forty or fifty men on foot who appeared to be household guards. Most of the rest of the disorganised mob appeared to castle servants who had been pressed into service for the sortie and did not even know how to carry a spear or use a sword.

We instantly recognized it for what it was—a force strong enough to hold the castle until it ran out of food, but one which was not anywhere near to being strong enough to defeat an army as large and powerful as ours. What we were seeing was a "forlorn hope," and the French knights and foot soldiers probably knew it even before the castle gate opened and they started towards us.

Why they decided to attack was uncertain. A few probably did it for the sake of their king's honour or, in the case of the French knights, their own honour because their king was watching. The poor sods on foot, of course, were like the village levies of the English and French barons; they did so because they had no choice. For them it was either fight with a chance of survival or refuse to fight and be immediately chopped or hung.

Afterwards, to give the French some credit despite our doubts, we decided the French sally was also to test us to see if we really would fight and, if we did, to see how we would fight—so they would know how to come at us in the future.

The fighting that resulted, such as it was, all happened in full view of the many watchers lining the castle's ramparts. And when it was over the watchers knew they were in very serious trouble, that we were like a tree standing in slow moving water and could not be moved.

A handful of mounted French knights carrying lances and swords led the way. They came galloping out of the castle gate as soon as it opened. The men on foot, mostly carrying spears, ran in a mob immediately behind them.

Our response would have surprised anyone who had fought with or against us in the past. For the first time in all the many years of the company we did not use our longbows when we were charged; we relied, instead, on our swords and bladed pikes. We deliberately did not use our bows in order to further confuse everyone, both now and in the future, as to who we were and for whom we were fighting.

It was a decision that confused our own men. They could hardly believe it and there was much muttering in the ranks when they were ordered not to use their longbows. For the most part, they obeyed and only a half dozen so arrows were pushed out. The small handful of archers who ignored the "no arrows" order were quickly prevented from continuing, and they and their sergeants immediately lost their stripes.

Our bladed pikes mounted on their long poles were more than enough. The French sortie neither succeeded nor lasted very long. About half of the mounted knights charged straight into our front lines with tremendous shouts. Our men were ready for them and the French knights immediately went down when they impaled themselves and their horses on the pikes which being pointed at them by the men in our first three battle lines, with the other end of each pike's long pole anchored firmly in a small hole dug by its holder.

Some of the pike poles splintered as the knight's horses ran themselves on to them, but in every case the horses were stopped in their tracks. Not a single rider on a horse broke into our lines. Our only casualties came from a couple of French knights whose horses were abruptly stopped when they were impaled by our pikes, which caused their riders to come out of their saddles and fly through the air until they crashed into our ranks.

Indeed, the possibility of such "flying knights," as everyone knows, was the reason why we always left a gap between the men in our third battle line and those in our fourth—because we knew from the company's many battles that knights coming off their pike-stopped horses usually stop flying about the time they reach the open area in front of our fourth line. That is where our men kill them if they are not already dead. A dagger pushed into an eyehole of an enemy knight's helmet or visor works wonders for keeping him down permanently.

The only surviving French knights were the handful who realized the futility of the sortie before they reached our lines. They turned their horses away from our battle lines and began galloping back towards the castle gate from whence they had come a few minutes earlier.

Most of the French foot also stopped and turned back when they saw the knights pull their horses around and begin galloping back to the castle. Indeed, the French foot suffered much more from being ridden down by their desperately escaping knights than from us. It happened when they were all desperately trying to get through the castle gate at the same time.

We made no attempt was to chase after the retreating French salliers or to finish off the French wounded. As our veterans knew, and our apprentice sergeants were taught, it was usually better under siege circumstances to let wounded enemy soldiers return to the castle to help eat up its food supplies.

The galley captains and veterans explained this to the younger archers. Besides, no one wanted to go forward into crossbow range unnecessarily. There was, however, much cheering in our ranks with many obscene gestures being made towards the French watching from the castle's ramparts. Spirits were high.

# Chapter Eighteen

*The siege.*

It had been several weeks since we landed on the island and simultaneously began destroying its bridges and the small boats that King Phillip and his courtiers might use to escape. George and Peter had taken much longer to destroy the bridges than we expected, but it was done and they had brought their men and galleys into our main camp in front of the castle.

The result was such a large camp that it stretched from one side of the island to the other and effectively cut off the castle from the rest of the island. Similarly, when our galleys were not out patrolling or bringing in food from the villages along the river, they were tied up along the island's riverbank in such a way as to be out of crossbow range from the other side of the river.

Nothing much had happened in the days that followed the French sally except for a few people trying to get across the river in makeshift boats and rafts. Most of the people trying to leave the island were commoners, residents of the island who were trying to escape from the island now that it was running out of food. A few were people who lived elsewhere and had been visiting the island when we took it; they just wanted to go home.

The company's noose around Louvre castle was as tight as my lieutenants and I could make it. And, so far as we knew, we still had King Phillip and his courtiers trapped in the castle, as the residents of the island had confirmed when we first arrived. His royal flag, at least, still flew from the castle's highest turret.

Our efforts to keep the French king trapped inside his castle residence were extensive: Harold had the company's galleys moored all around the island except where they would be within crossbow range of the castle or the opposite shore, and every night many of our galleys and their dinghies rowed around and around the island to prevent both escapes and the arrival of food supplies that might enable the castle to hold out longer.

We also moved men much closer to the castle gate as soon as it got dark each night and we had long lines of men constantly walking around the castle in an effort to catch anyone who might try to climb down, or be lowered down, from its walls.

It was all intended to prevent anyone from leaving the castle or helping to resupply it, and it seemed to be working. It also helped to keep our men busy and out of trouble.

As a result of our efforts to keep the king and his courtiers isolated, however, the food situation for the commoners on the island became increasingly desperate.

More and more people were begging in the streets and particularly at the outskirts of our camp, and women were increasingly trying to come into our camp to sell themselves for food for their families.

We, on the other hand, had more than enough food because we had brought so much with us and were bringing in more. We were taking no chances because we had no idea how long our siege would last. Already several of our galleys had been sent off to fetch corn and cheese from Cornwall even though we were still able to buy all the food we needed in the market towns both up river and down river from Paris.

It was our good fortune that not every French merchant or farmer with food to sell was as loyal to Phillip as he was to getting his hands on the silver coins we had in our pouches. On the other hand, and despite our siege-related efforts that kept them busy, the periodic idleness of our men when they were not rowing or walking about to maintain our siege was starting to cause a discipline problem. The main source of trouble was the women seeking coins for their protectors or food for their families. They were coming into camp despite our efforts to keep them out.

What we did not do to keep the men busy in their off hours was require daily archery practice and hold periodic tournaments. To the contrary, we forbade the men from using and carrying their bows for the same reason we repeatedly told them they were on the island as part of an army of Swedish and Rus mercenaries employed by King Otto who was also the Holy Roman emperor, not as English archers—because we wanted to do everything possible to avoid being in conflict with Prince Louis in the event he succeeded in his quest to replace King John as England's king.


\*\*\*\*\*\*

It was seeing a desperate woman begging for food with her children in her arms that caused me to order a change. *She reminded me of my mother.*

"Let every commoner who is not from the castle leave the island if they want to leave," I ordered Harold after my lieutenants and I got together and discussed the situation. "Ferry them across the river on our galleys and tell them that they have Emperor Otto himself to thank for their freedom.

"At the same time," I told Henry who was in command of our camp and also of all of our men when they were ashore on the island, "I want you to tighten up our lines around the castle even more. We need to make sure no one gets out to mix in with those who are being allowed to leave."

I really did not think it was necessary to tighten our siege lines, but I did not want the company to think that my letting the commoners leave the island, and helping them to do so, meant I was going soft behind my eyes.

"And we need to be damn sure every person who asks to leave is carefully inspected and questioned to make sure they are not gentry from the castle. That is now your main task, George. Make sure your men check every man carefully before he leaves. And especially check any woman that looks like she might be a man wearing a woman's clothes. The French men are well-known to be good at that sort of thing."

My decision to let the common folk leave the king's island occurred at about the same time that more and more French soldiers began to appear on both sides of the river, and particularly on the west bank. That is where the French set up a tent camp just south of the city walls. The river separated them from us, of course.

As a result of the river being our moat, at least so we dearly hoped, we would be able to conduct our siege in peace because the French army would not be able to do anything more than look across at our camp in front of the castle, and at our galleys as they moved up and down the river.

There was a minor exception to our ability to conduct our siege without being bothered by the French army. It occurred when our galleys strayed within the range of the French soldiers who were carrying crossbows. When they did stray and get to close, the French soldiers shot crossbow quarrels at our galleys and then, of course, the archers on the galleys had replied by pushing their "longs" back at the French crossbow men.

The minor skirmishes were all rather meaningless. Even so, the arrival of the French soldiers along the riverbank forced our galleys to take the common people leaving the island further down the river before we unloaded them. It also resulted in the company suffering several wounded men; one of whom quickly died despite his captain's best efforts to get him to a barber.

Soldiers from the rest of France were not the only ones who had come to Paris in response to our raid. Word had arrived from London last week, via Cornwall, that Prince Louis had suddenly galloped to Dover and immediately sailed.

Prince Louis was obviously in a hurry because the Channel had been a bit rough and it was well-known that Louis suffered from the sea pox and refused to sail unless the sea was calm and the winds favourable. My lieutenants and I were not at all surprised when there was a report of a royal flag flying over a large tent on the far side of the main French camp.

Immediately upon hearing of Louis's arrival, I sent a parchment to Sir William Marshal, the commander of King John's army, informing him that in response to the agreement he had signed on behalf of King John, the company of archers had immediately sailed for France and joined with axe-carrying Swedish and Rus mercenaries in a major attack on France.

I also confirmed what I was sure Sir William already knew—that our attack had succeeded in causing Louis and a number of his knights to leave England in order to reinforce the French army now in Paris. It therefore might be, I gently suggested, a good time for the king's army to launch and offensive and begin driving what was left of the French invaders out of England.

What I did not tell Sir William was the real truth—that we had only taken the island in the middle of Paris and were besieging Louvre Castle because King Phillip was in it and we hoped to fetch a great ransom for his freedom. Nor did I mention that we had no intention of fighting the French army if it could be avoided, or that we were pretending to be Swedish and Rus mercenaries fighting under a commander from Sweden, or that we intended to leave France as soon as we received a sufficient ransom.

\*\*\*\*\*\*

The first indication that our fortunes might be about to improve was a loud blast of a horn from the ramparts above the castle's gate. It was repeated several times. A few moments later a small door in the castle gate opened wide enough to let a man duck his head and slip out.

What emerged was an elderly priest carrying a cross in one hand for protection against the unknown and wearing a hooded black robe with its hood thrown back. The priest was a tall and skinny fellow with a long and wispy white beard that hung down all the way to his belly. The black robe indicated he was priest of the Benedictine order. The door in the castle gate was immediately shut behind him.

Our priestly visitor walked a few steps forward from the gate whilst the horn blew again several times from the castle's parapets to once again announce him to us. Announcing him thusly was intended to assure us that he was coming to us with the castle's approval, and was not intended to be a surprise. It was a request for a peaceful talk.

After a few more steps towards our lines, the old priest stopped and waited for someone from our side to respond.

I was in the camp scribing a parchment to send to Cyprus with a list of the prizes we had taken when I heard the distant horn sounding from the castle's ramparts. Moments later the news reached me that "a priest is coming out of a door in the castle gate."

The message came to me informally by word of mouth as our men shouted the news to each other. It rippled from man to man across our camp like an ocean wave moving faster than a man could run. It similarly and simultaneously reached everyone in the camp including my principal lieutenants: Henry, Peter, George, and Thomas. Harold was not there; he was out with his galleys patrolling the river in search of boats to destroy.

My lieutenants and I met as we were walking briskly through our camp towards the priest who was apparently waiting near the castle gate. And we were not the only ones heading in that direction. A surprising number of our men were walking that way as well, and some of them seemed quite excited by the news. My lieutenants and I were pleased at the priest's arrival, but we were neither excited nor surprised by his appearance; it had been expected.

Our only surprise was that it had taken the French so many days to contact us. They must have had either more food and firewood reserves in the castle than the island's residents told us, or fewer people. In any event, we had expected to hear from the castle sooner or later and had long ago determined how we would respond.

Henry would pretend to be the Swedish captain of Emperor Otto's "mercenary army" and do all the talking on our behalf. Henry was chosen for several reasons. For one, he spoke French fluently which was much better than any of the rest of us. Accordingly, he could pretend not to understand either English or French and use his Latin-speaking apprentice to translate for him—whilst he listened to what the French said to each other in French thinking that Henry would not be able to understand what they were saying. It was a good gull and had worked for us a number of times in the past.

Secondly, and it would be very important if Prince Louis succeeded in getting the English throne, Henry intended to return to Cyprus and stay there permanently after this campaign. That meant he was the only one amongst my lieutenants who could pose as a Swedish mercenary captain without the risk of anyone in Louis's English court, if there ever was such a court, discovering that he was, in fact, one of the company's archers.

*Of course we were using Henry. We wanted Phillip's ransom coins and intended to take them no matter who it made unhappy. But it would be better for the company and Cornwall, in the event Louis ever did become the King of England, if Louis was angry with a Swedish mercenary claiming to be in the pay of the German Emperor instead of the archers of Cornwall.*

# Chapter Nineteen

*Negotiations and a big surprise.*

Henry and his Latin-gobbling apprentice sergeant, Samuel, walked only a few feet out in front of our lines. They stopped walking in order to remain out of crossbow range, and motioned for the French priest to come forward and join them. Samuel, just as he had been told, put on his priest's robe and walked out behind Henry. He then stood somewhat behind him such that Henry would have to turn his head away the French priest in order to speak to him.

The meeting caused quite a stir. All the archers in our battle lines climbed to their feet, and it was obvious that every one of them would be trying to listen to what was said. The castle ramparts were suddenly lined with watchers. This was an important meeting and everyone knew it.

****** *Henry*

"I am here to translate in case you cannot speak Swedish or Rus," Samuel immediately explained in Latin as the old priest walked up to us and gave a stiff little nod of his head to acknowledge us.

The old priest immediately looked at me and asked me in French if I spoke French or English. I just looked at him blankly, as if I could not understand what he was saying, and shrugged my shoulders. Then I turned back at Samuel with a questioning look on my face, and indicated through a "give me" gesture with my hand, and a very quiet, almost mouthed, "tell me," to indicate that Samuel should translate what the priest had just said. He promptly did. *Of course I turned my head away and spoke quietly; I did not want the priest to know I was speaking English, did I?*

"Tell him I do not speak French or English, and that you are a priest from Austria and will translate. Also tell him I am Eric, son of Eric, from the Swede lands and that I command the emperor's mercenaries here in France."

The old priest, nodded his head towards me after he heard Samuel's explanation, and proceeded to identify himself as Father Pierre from someplace called saint something or other. It was the name of a city or village I neither recognized nor cared to know. Then Father Pierre stood up as straight as he could, took in a great breath, and became quite direct; he said that he had been sent to ask me what would be required "for your galleys to sail away and leave France in peace." It was the question we had all been waiting to hear.

"England paid one hundred and fifty thousand silver marks to ransom King Richard a few years ago," I replied. "That is about eighty thousand pounds of silver coins. Phillip is certainly a much more important and richer king.

And the emperor does not wish to insult King Phillip by suggesting he is not worth more than Richard; so we will leave in peace as soon as we receive one hundred and twenty thousand pounds of silver coins.

"But that is impossible," the old man gasped. "That is more than the revenues of the kingdom for an entire year." The priest's gasp and sincerity were impressive. *He was a good negotiator; he would have gasped and said it was impossible if I had said it would take ten silver coins and two chickens.*

"Certainly it is possible and we both know it. King Phillip already has those coins in his household chests. And if he does not have enough, he can certainly borrow whatever he needs from the Templars who have that much and more right here in Paris." *Do we actually know that about king's household chests and the Templars? Of course not. But it was a good story and it could be true.*

"Would you let food and servants into the castle if the king agrees?" the old man finally asked as he pondered my response.

"Only if the castle surrenders," I answered with the sincerest possible look on my face I could muster.

"But if the castle does surrender peacefully, the king and his family and courtiers will be treated with the greatest respect and allowed to remain in their rooms and keep their servants, and no one in the castle will be harmed in any way. Emperor Otto swears it."

"I will tell the king what you have said," the priest finally replied after staring at me for some time as he if was trying to get behind my eyes to learn the truth. After a few moments, he turned away and trudged slowly back to the castle.

****** *Henry*

The French priest had no more than gone back inside the castle when the men around me began shouting and pointing towards the river. One of the three galleys we left at the entrance to the river was coming up the river towards us as fast as its men could row. There was an urgency to its booming drum and hard-rowing, and we could all sense its urgency as it came closer and its rowing drum got louder and louder.

I shouted an order for my men to remain in their ranks as William and I and many others, including George, Peter, and Thomas, hurried to the riverbank to meet the rapidly approaching newcomer. Harold's galley was just tying up further along the riverbank and I could see him climb on to the roof of his stern castle to get a better look.

A few minutes later the new arrival's overly excited captain jumped ashore, knuckled his head in response to all the many stripes on our tunics, and reported that a large French fleet accompanied by at least a dozen English-built war galleys "and maybe more" had been seen entering the Seine estuary and might already be coming up the river. He had followed his orders and come immediately to sound the alert; he had not waited to count them. *English-built?*

All of William's lieutenants, including Harold who had just come ashore, were gathered around him on the riverbank as he began giving his orders.

"All captains report to the commander's galley; all men report to their galleys *except* those in Commander Henry's fleet." The order was repeated loudly by every sergeant as he began running to his assigned position.

The captains were given their orders by William as soon as they reached him. As a result, he had to repeat them several times for late-arriving captains. They all heard the same thing.

"French galleys and a fleet of transports are in the estuary and may be coming up the river as a relief force. All of our galleys, except the eight in Commander Henry's fleet, are to go down the river and into the estuary looking for prizes. If you find one, take it. Turn around where the estuary meets the sea and immediately come straight back if you do not see any potential prizes.

"Commander Henry," he said as he turned to me, "you are to keep all of the archers from your galleys on the island to make sure King Phillip does not get away whilst we are away. Be very alert. The French may be trying to cause confusion in our ranks so Phillip can escape.

"You are to be prepared for a French sortie out of the castle, and be ready at all times to rapidly send quarter-companies from the galleys in your fleet to fight off multiple landings coming in from either bank of the river. Deploy your quarter-companies and use them just as we planned. Everyone else is to man their galleys and row down the river for French prizes."

I responded by repeating back my orders to William so he would know I understood them.

"Aye, Commander. I am to keep my men on the island and be prepared to fight off a sortie from the castle and multiple landings on the island's riverbank, all coming at the same time."

Then I double-timed back to my battle lines with my captains who had, quite properly, answered the "all-captains" call. I began giving them my own orders as we ran. As we did, everything around us suddenly became hectic.

Captains were still arriving to get their orders, and all around me men were shouting and running to their galleys or, in the case of the men in my galley companies, shouting and running to their assigned places in our major battle formation in front of the castle and the quarter-companies of my fast reaction forces.

*My quarter-companies were each composed of three files of men under a steady sergeant and stationed at various places around the island. They were charged with running to wherever enemy soldiers might be attempting to come ashore and preventing them from landing.*

****** *William*

I jumped from the riverbank to the deck of Harold's nearby galley as soon as I finished giving orders to Henry and the captains who had rushed to my side. After I vaulted over the deck railing, I headed straight to the roof of the galley's forward castle to join Harold. Thomas came with me and so did our apprentice sergeants.

Harold was already on board and shouting out the orders needed to get his galley underway. He had come aboard a few moments earlier whilst I was still giving orders to Henry and the late-arriving captains. All around me sergeants were shouting and men were running, and I could see men on shore hurrying towards their galleys in an effort to get aboard them before they pushed off and began going downstream in search of the French. It was very exciting.

The scene on Harold's galley was similar to that which was simultaneously occurring on many of the galleys moored along the island's riverbank: Arrow bales were being brought up from the galley's cargo holds by its sailors and opened, pikes and other weapons were being laid out in their appointed places, men were settling themselves onto the rowing benches and picking up their oars, and some archers carrying their longbows and extra quivers of arrows were climbing masts to get to their fighting positions whilst others were hurrying to their fighting positions on the galley's deck and on the roofs of its two deck castles.

It everywhere looked chaotic because so much was happening at the same time, but it really was not; rapidly getting ready to fight his galley was something every captain had his men practice constantly.

Only Henry's galleys were quiet, with their sailors crowding their decks and watching, as everywhere our galleys began pushing off from the riverbank and their rowing drums began beating. Whilst Henry's sailors quietly watched the activity on the galleys around them, his archers were gathering in their battle ranks in front of Louvre Castle and in smaller groups scattered about the island.

****** 

"Cast off all lines and push off; cast off all lines and push off," Harold loudly ordered as I joined him. As I did, Harold's sergeants all loudly repeated his order and my apprentice sergeant handed me my bow already strung all nice and proper. He had alertly nipped into the forward deck castle I shared with Harold to get it and a couple of our bigger land-fighting shields.

"Wave the 'attack' and 'follow me' flags if you would, Commander Lewes. And keep waving them," I ordered.

As he repeated his orders back to me and we pushed off from shore, a late-arriving archer from Harold's crew literally dived headfirst into the galley in order to avoid being left behind.  There were cheers from the crew as he did and Harold smiled broadly.

The sound of rowing drums was all around us as we started down the Seine, and faces were beginning to appear all along the battlements of the king's Louvre Castle to watch us go.  I would imagine the French also watched from the city walls across from the island.


******

A goodly number of our galleys, as many as half a dozen of them, and perhaps more, had pushed off before we did.  They were ahead of us as we started down the river.  Harold wanted to lead the way so he had his men rowing hard with a man motioning those we caught to get behind us, including one poor sod whose galley had almost immediately run aground on one of the Seine's infamous and ever changing sandbars.

When we reached the point where the river straightened out just past the island, the lookouts reported they could see some of our galleys strung out ahead of us including several who appeared to be moving particularly fast and pulling away.

Harold was not happy when he heard the lookouts' reports that we had thrusters trying to be the first to the battle, not happy at all. The mouth of the river was hours away and he wanted the men somewhat rested for the battle that might be coming.

On his galley, Harold had already ordered the men of his entire upper rowing tier to stop rowing in order to save their arms. He had also ordered the hard chargers amongst the galleys which came up behind us to slow down and fall in behind us.

*I knew Harold. He was not unhappy with the fact that our galleys were dashing towards the mouth of the river where I had ordered them to go; he was unhappy with himself for forgetting to remind me to order their captains to save their men's arms—which, of course, was something I should have remembered on my own and ordered myself.*

Thomas thoroughly understood Harold. He immediately rolled his eyes at me and began trying to soften Harold up and distract him by pointing to the people moving along the riverbank. Many of them were stopping to watch as our long line of galleys rowed past them with their drums pounding. It did not work; Harold remained angry with himself. It did not last long.

"Perhaps it is best that some of our galleys hurried on ahead of us," I finally added in an effort to cheer up Harold. "We have got two more galleys still at the mouth of the river or around out there somewhere. If the report of a large number of enemy galleys is accurate, they are badly outnumbered and will need help as soon as they can get it. Help from tired arms is better that no help at all, eh?

"Aye, that is true, William.  But it is past being too late if there are as many French galleys as Tommy reported.  Our lads will have already been overwhelmed no matter how much better they are or how hard they fought."

"But English built galleys; how can that be?  He must be wrong," I said.

"Oh aye, it is possible alright, damnit.  There are yards in Bristol and on a couple of the Channel Islands that could be building them, and then there is the big French yard at Toulon.  They can build anything there.  But I am thinking they are galleys from the Channel Islands.  Some of the islands changed sides and went from supporting John to supporting Phillip, at least that is the rumour I heard.  And there is a yard on Sark where I heard rumours that a couple of galleys were being built for that God damned Eustace, the Benedictine monk who turned pirate."

"Eustace the pirate monk?  Is he still around?"

"Oh aye, he is.  His base is on Sark, at least it was the last I heard.  He used to support King John by taking French coasters and fishing boats.  And then he turned for some reason and began supporting Phillip.  At least that is what I heard.  His men are supposed to be mainly sailor men who cannot find berths and need to eat.

"Good sailors they are, but not much bottom as fighters, or so it is said. But they do not need to be much in the way of fighters to wave swords and scare people into surrendering, do they? At least, not for taking small boats off honest sailors and fishermen.

"The word is that Eustace is now earning his coins carrying French men and supplies back and forth from France, and taking everybody's coasters and fishing boats and such as prizes as he has done for years. He used to sell the prizes he did not keep and their cargos in Scotland and England, but now he sells them in France and to the merchants in the Low Countries, especially Amsterdam. At least that is what everyone says."

# Chapter Twenty

*Our galleys fight.*

We were in the Seine estuary with two sister galleys for the purpose of blocking the entrance to the Seine and taking prizes from unsuspecting arrivals. My captain, Ralph Shoemaker, was resting in his deck castle when the lookout gave us a loud "hoy the deck," and reported seeing a couple of masts coming up over the horizon.

Ralph was the fourth son of a shoemaking family from Plymouth. He woke up and rushed out of his castle as soon as he heard the first report. He did not, however, immediately order the sailing sergeant to rudder us in the direction of the masts that were reported. That was because only two masts were reported. We had taken the squadron's last prize such that it was turn of our two sister ships to take the next two.

A minute or so later everything changed. There was another "hoy the deck" from our lookout. This time our lookout reported seeing numerous masts coming up over the horizon. This was fine news and the men who heard it cheered loudly; it meant there were more than two prizes available to be taken.

The captain responded by ordering me to "remain here Lieutenant Sudbury" and going up the rope ladder of our forward mast to see for himself. Everyone was quite hopeful as the captain climbed the mast because we had just watched as first one and then the other of our two sister galleys dropped its sails and began to row rapidly into the wind towards the oncoming sails and masts. They were doing the right thing by going to check out the approaching vessels instead of waiting for them at the mouth of the river.

After a few minutes, the captain climbed down from where he was perched in the lookouts' nest and ordered our sails to be dropped and our rowing benches manned. We began following behind our two sister galleys at a good speed.

Our galley and our two sister galleys had already taken a number of prizes from unsuspecting transports arriving with Paris-bound cargos, and everyone in the crew was hopeful these would be more of the same, perhaps an entire merchant fleet. It was quite surprising to us, then, when one of our sister galleys, the one farthest out in front, suddenly spun around and made straight for the mouth of the river at its best speed. Its sails were quickly raised to get the wind and the distant sound of its rapidly beating rowing drum carried across the water to us.

Even more surprising, its "follow me" flag was being waved at us from the galley's forward mast. Our second sister galley in our little squadron of three immediately spun around and joined it.

That was when Ralph made the first of several mistakes that cost us dearly—instead of trusting his fellow captains and making for the mouth of the river with them, he climbed the mast once again to see for himself.

Both of our two sister galleys were almost at the river's mouth by the time our white-faced captain came down off the mast with an uncertain and questioning look on his face. The first thing he did was to come back to where we were standing to tell us what he had seen.

"It is a big fleet and some of the sails in the van are galleys of a type I have never seen before. They might be enemies," the captain said as he came up the steps to the roof of the forward castle. He then himself loudly gave the order to the rudder men to turn us around and head for the river at our highest possible speed. And then he went down to the rowing decks to make sure his order was obeyed.

*The captain was a very fearful man and unsure. He never believed anything was done right unless he saw to it himself; and he was constantly worried about doing something wrong and losing his command. Plymouth men are like that as everyone knows.*

Alex, the sailing sergeant, and I just looked at each other and shrugged—not a word was spoken, but we both knew the captain should have called down from the mast and ordered us to get the galley turned around instead of waiting and doing it himself. Both of our sister galleys had already turned and raised their sails.  They were hurrying towards the river.

"Raise the sails and keep ruddering us straight towards the river," I finally said as I headed for the forward mast. "That is an order, Alex.  I am going up on the mast to look for myself."  Our galley was finally beginning to turn and the captain had not remembered to raise our sails.

A great number of enemy sails and many of the hulls under them were already fully visible from where we were standing on the roof of the stern castle.  Their thrusters, galleys similar to ours, were leading the way.  It was clear that the French fleet was heading for the mouth of the Seine just as we would soon be doing. Captain Shoemaker was still down amongst the rowers.


****** *Lieutenant Sudbury, the son of a Sudbury slave.*

What I saw when I climbed the mast was the captain still down to the lower rowing deck and our galley just beginning to turn. I also saw an entire armada of galleys and other sail coming towards us. They were led by eight or nine big war galleys somewhat similar in design and rigging to ours.

The big galleys were in front of the armada, but behind them were the sails of numerous transports of various types and sizes, including at least a dozen of what looked to be small galleys with ten or twelve oars to a side compared to our forty.

Eight or nine of the biggest enemy galleys were close to us by the time we finally finished turning and our sails were raised. After a while, and to my immense relief, I got the impression that the French fleet was moving slowly and we might be widening the gap between us and our pursuers. It made me feel much better behind my eyes. *Thank you Jesus; that was close.*

From where I was on the mast, I could see our two sister galleys. They were some distance ahead of us and entering the mouth of the Seine, just as we would be in a few more minutes. That was worrisome to me because, unlike the galleys in our fleet which had gone up to Paris, we had never sailed in the river before and did not know its dangers. All we knew about the Seine was what we had heard—that it was filled with many dangerous sandbars and there were false channels in various places between its mouth and Paris.

For some reason, as I moved my eyes back and forth between our pursuers and the approaching mouth of the river, I began to worry that the captain would remove me as his lieutenant because I ordered our sails to be raised without waiting for him to give the order himself. After considering my prospects, I decided to stay up on the mast a while longer to give him a chance to cool off. It was from there that I watched as the captain moved to the bow and summoned a number of sailors to join him in looking for threatening sandbars.

*Ah well, better to be a live sergeant than a dead lieutenant. Maybe he will let me transfer to another galley or let me leave as the master of a prize that the company is likely to buy for its own use.*

****** *William.*

It was an interesting voyage down a river that was different in every way from the crowded waterway we had seen and travelled when we first arrived—it was different because the Seine was now totally empty of traffic. No big transports were moving down the river, probably because they had all been taken earlier. And none were coming up the Seine because they were all being taken as prizes at the river's mouth; and no small boats and barges were to be seen because we had destroyed all we could find.

What had not changed were the fishermen standing and sitting along the riverbanks, and all the carts and people on foot moving along the cart paths on either side of the river. It would have been quite a pleasant and relaxing scene if we were not on our way to a sea battle, and traveling too fast for our own good as a result. As it was, Harold and I just stood on the roof of the forward castle with our apprentices and Harold's sailing sergeant, and watched the people going about their lives on either side of the river.

Twice we passed a scene of frantic activity on the deck of one of our galleys that had hurriedly pushed off from the island ahead of us only to run aground on one of the Seine's many sandbars. We all knew we were going too fast, but it could not be helped.

What did help save us from a general disaster was following in the exact path of the galleys rowing immediately ahead of us on the simple premise that if they could make it through the instant waters, so could we. Even so, there were a number of sailors in the bow of every one of our galleys, each of whom was looking out for sandbars. And many of them were carrying long poles and pikes to push their galley off if worst came to worst and it ran aground.

Several hours later there was a hail from our lookout on the mast.

"Hoy the deck. Hoy the deck. There be a gaggle of galleys ahead of us in the river. Three or four of them, maybe more. .. Dead in the water and in a galley raft they be. … No, there be six or seven of them, maybe even eight."

Harold and I looked at each other for a brief moment. Then we both jumped down on to the deck from the castle roof, took the few steps needed to reach the forward mast, and began climbing the mast's rope ladder to see for ourselves. I went first as was traditional and expected of the man with the most stripes. As we jumped down to the deck and ran for the mast, Harold shouted out to his sailing sergeant to "take over the ruddering and set a fine course."

What Harold meant, and his sailing sergeant fully understood, was that Harold wanted his galley to continue closely following the twists and turns taken by the galleys rowing immediately ahead of us.

"Wait down here," I told our apprentice sergeants as I grabbed the rope ladder and began climbing with Harold right behind me. They had dutifully followed us to the mast and the rope ladder lashed to it. But we did not need them *or want them* climbing with us; all they would accomplish by following us up the rope ladder would be to cause it to shake and jiggle even worse than it otherwise would.

Everyone had heard the lookout's "hoy" to the deck and his report. As a result, the heads of all of the archers and sailors on our galley's deck were moving back and forth as they turned from looking ahead to see what might be coming into sight in front of us, to looking up to watch Harold and me as we climbed. I went all the way up the swaying and jerking rope ladder as far as I could go which was just under the lookout's nest which was now manned by two of Harold's best archers.

Harold was right below me and making the rope ladder move back and forth as he kept leaning around this way and that to get a better look. I was doing what I always do whenever I climb a mast's rope ladder to get a better look—

clinging to it for dear life and only moving a hand or foot when everything else was firmly in place.

I truly hated climbing a mast; it had scared me ever since I almost fell. That was years ago off Constantinople when Harold was still using his old galley with forty-four oars to a side, the one we took off the Algerians.

For a few moments after I reached a spot just below the lookouts' nest, I was not sure what I was seeing in the river ahead of us. Harold, however, knew galleys and understood immediately. The rope ladder jerked and swayed as he leaned away from the mast so he could look at me as he explained what he saw.

"It is one of the galleys we had stationed at the entrance to the river. Around it there appears to be a couple of strange galleys, and around them there appears to be some of the thrusters who pushed away from the king's island before we did."

A few seconds later a surprised Harold exclaimed with an incredulous sound to his voice, and a move so sudden to lean away from the mast for a better look that it gave the ladder a such a jerk that it put a quivering chill on my ballocks and cause them to shrivel.

"Look there. By God, there is another gaggle of galleys all together in another raft further on down. Something is amiss for sure."

I waited until Harold had finished climbing all the way down to the deck before I started slowly climbing down. For some reason I had suddenly become so very fearful that my legs began trembling and I was afraid to even slide my hands down the ladder's rope so I could take a downward step.

It was not long after I finally, and very slowly, finished making my way down to the deck that we reached the first group of galleys. Harold and the lookout were right. They were all grappled one to another and locked together into one great galley raft next to a sandbar in the middle of the river.

At first it was not at all clear what had happened. After much shouting back and forth whilst the galleys behind us backed their oars and dutifully waited, Harold and I understood, or thought we did—all three of our galleys from the mouth of the river had been chased up the river by an unknown number of enemy galleys.

One of the three galleys we had left in the estuary, the first to enter the river, had somehow made it all the way up the Seine to Paris and sounded the alarm. Its captain and crew were not aware of the fate of their two sister galleys. They did not even know if they had followed them into the river. Obviously at least one of them had done so.

In fact, both of the other two galleys had followed the first into the river, and neither had made it all the way up to Paris; they had both ended up going aground because they were unfamiliar with the river and moving too fast in an effort to escape their pursuers. The first of our galleys we reached with the enemy galleys around it had gotten the further up the river.

According to Henry, the stranded galley we had come upon first was captained by Jack Shoemaker. He and his crew had obviously been involved in a desperate battle and had only been saved by the timely arrival of our thrusters — the galleys which had pushed off before us and we had tried to catch in order to slow them down and save their men's arms.

The last of our three galleys from the river mouth was almost certainly among the gaggle of galleys Harold and I had seen further down the river when we were on the mast. If so, its crew was almost certainly engaged in a similar desperate battle against an overwhelming enemy force. That was almost certain to be the case because Captain Shoemaker's battle-scarred galley, the one we had just relieved, was the last of our three galleys to enter the river and had rowed past its stranded sister galley and gotten further up the river before it too had gone aground.

We had come upon Jack's galley first, even though it was the last of the three to enter the river, because it had gotten further up the river before stranding itself. I started to say something harsh to Harold about Jack's galley not stopping to assist its sister galley, but I caught myself just in time when I remembered that I myself had told the captains of the three galleys assigned to the mouth of the river that hurrying up the river to warn us of an approaching danger was their primary task, and much more important than going after prizes or fighting the French in some way.

In any event, according to what we were quickly told, Jack's galley had been taken after it had gone aground and been attacked by four enemy galleys which had followed it up the river. The enemy galleys, in turn, had been attacked, and two of them taken, when the thrusters from amongst the galleys I had ordered down river reached the river battle and fell upon the enemy galleys from behind.

By the time Harold and I reached the scene, the fighting to relieve Jack and his crew was all over. The thrusters leading our galleys down the river had joined the fighting and taken two of the enemy galleys as prizes. But they arrived too late for many of our men.

Jack's galley had suffered severe casualties including the deaths of almost half its crew and the wounding of many of the others, several of whom were wounded so terrible that they needed mercies. From the looks of where many of the enemy bodies were located, and the number of arrows sticking in them, it appeared that Jack and his crew had given a good account of themselves, but had been overwhelmed.

According to the somewhat confusing initial reports being shouted out to us, two other enemy galleys had initially been in the fight. But they had managed to cast off their grapples and escape back down the river when their crews saw our thrusters coming. In any event, we still had no idea as to the size of the enemy force we would soon be confronting, or who they were.

All we knew after stopping for a few brief moments at the scene of the battle was that there were enough of enemies coming to cause all three of our galleys to try to get up the river to warn us. We could not stay to learn more; we now knew another of our galleys was fighting for its life further down the river. It too might need reinforcements.

"Go. Go. Hurry," Harold shouted, and his loud talker repeated. Harold and I emphatically motioned for the galleys coming down the river behind us to hurry on past us and head towards the second gaggle of galleys further down the river and join the fight. We both pumped a fisted arm up and down as they came towards us, the age-old signal to hurry. Harold's flag waver did his part too, by pointing to each of them as they came past us and shaking his "attack" flag at them.

The result was exactly what we expected—the rowing drums of the galleys that had followed us down the river stepped up their beat dramatically as their captains got our clear and emphatic message. There was immediately a lot of shouting and activity on their decks, and the boarding parties already formed up on their decks cheered and waved their weapons as they hurried past us.

# Chapter Twenty-one

*William and the second galley.*

We left our stricken galley and our prizes behind and hurried down the river to see what we could see at what was almost certainly the site of another river battle between one of our galleys and a French relief force. At first all we could see from where we were standing was a great raft of galleys and men running all about on them.

Some of the galleys we saw were clearly not ours. One in particular had some kind of catapult on its deck. And the sounds of a battle could be clearly heard in the distance. As a result, Harold gave orders for a large boarding party to be formed that included every archer, even those less experienced men now rowing on the lower rowing deck. They were to put down their oars and join the fight as soon as we grappled the galley raft; they would be our second wave of boarders.

Harold's boarding party was not needed even though its highly excited members swarmed aboard and across the empty deck of one of our own galleys as soon as we bumped up against it. My lieutenants and I led the way. I had my longbow slung over my shoulder and was carrying a sword and a ship's shield.  Harold and Thomas were right behind me and similarly armed.

I was very excited and the first man to step over our deck railing and begin to run towards where a great group of men were gathered on a couple of distant galleys on the far side of the galley raft.  All of my lieutenants and all the archers from Harold's galley were right behind me.  My run took me across two of our sister galley's empty decks, and then across the empty decks of two strange galleys whose decks were covered with dead and wounded men.

The casualties I saw as we ran across the galley decks included several of our archers who appeared to be dead and half a dozen others who had been wounded and were being barbered and offered water by their mates.  We ignored them and continued climbing over deck railings and running across decks whilst holding our swords and pikes as we ran.  And, of course, every man had a longbow and quiver of arrows slung over his shoulder.

I did not get very far in my running before I was overtaken.  I may have been the first over the railing to leave Harold's galley, but many of Harold's boarding party were younger and faster.  They soon passed me, including one lad with a sword in his hand who literally jumped over two deck railings that were lashed together without breaking his stride.  I was already puffing and had a pain in my side as I carefully swung my bad leg over the railing and chased after him and all the others who had passed me.

Running across galley decks is not easy. I was breathing hard when I finally ended my mad dash. I slowed down, and then stopped and put my hands on my knees to rest when I realized the decks of the galleys I was approaching were crowded with men wearing archers' tunics. There was the noise of a lot of shouting, but none of the usual sounds of fighting. The battle was obviously over and we had won.

After taking a couple of deep breaths to regain myself, I cast off and got underway again, and an instant later reached the great mass of our men, all of whom were standing about with weapons in their hands and looks of great anger on their faces. What my lieutenant commanders and I saw and heard when we pushed our way through the crowd of angry archers was appalling.

"It is Harry Farmer's, by God. I recognize the carved figure on its bowsprit," I heard Harold say behind me.

What had occurred soon became clear despite all the confusion and anger around me: Harry's galley had run aground, and then been attacked and outnumbered by men from a large number of enemy galleys.

Harry and all of his men had all fallen, but they had given a good account of themselves before they did if the many dozens of dead and wounded enemy men on the galley decks near them were any indication. The victorious enemy galleys and their crews were still there trying to get Harry's galley off the sandbar as a prize when the first of our galleys arrived, the ones Harold and I had waved past us and ordered to hurry.

After a short and intense battle which had ended just as we reached the scene, our men had re-taken Harry's galley and also taken four of the enemy galleys as prizes—two large ones the same size as ours, and two very small ones. Four or five enemy galleys, including two as large as ours, were reported to have cut their grapple lines and escaped down the river when our relief force arrived.

The report of the captain of our first galley to reach the scene said it all as he reported to me with his tunic covered with blood. *Fortunately not his from the look of him and his jaunty gestures.*

"Had we known that Harry and all of his men were dead we would have stood off and showered the enemy galleys with arrows until their crews surrendered. But we did not know, did we? So we closed with them and fought our way across their decks to Harry's galley—and took many unnecessary casualties because every one of Harry's men was already dead."

"All his men are dead?" I asked incredulously. "How can that be? There are always wounded men lying about after a battle."

I was appalled by the numbers and names of the men we had lost, and so were my lieutenants. And I was so angry when I learned that our wounded and our men who had surrendered had been immediately murdered, that I staggered as if someone and hit me and almost fell down for a sleep.

Of course I was shocked. It was almost certainly the company's greatest loss of men in a single battle, over a hundred here plus as many as fifty more from the battle for Jack's galley further up the river. So far as I was concerned, there was no ransom large enough to justify such losses.

My face was turned towards Peter and George and I was looking at them most intensely when I leaned forward and snarled out the thoughts behind my eyes. *Thomas told me later that he had never heard me speak with such a vicious sound in my voice.*

"No one murders an archer and escapes. No one. Our revenge will be most fearful on them and whoever sent them, eh?"

The company's next commander and his number two solemnly nodded their agreement, and so did everyone else who heard me including some nearby one-stripe archers who would surely spread the word. I hope they spread it for I truly meant it. Revenge is required by both our contract and the holy book, and the men know it.


****** *Harold.*

William was clearly shaken by what he had seen and heard as he and I and the rest of his lieutenant commanders walked across the decks of the galleys where the fighting had occurred. He was as angry and distressed as I had ever seen him in all our years together. We were returning from what had been our second look at the galleys where the fighting had occurred.

The first time we looked had not taken long because we were moving fast and trying to understand what had happened; this time we were everywhere asking questions and looking carefully to make sure all of our wounded men were being properly barbered by their mates and given flower paste for their pains.

More and more French people were gathered along the nearby riverbank and silently watching. The cries of the wounded were terrible to hear, especially those of the men from the enemy galleys. They were not being given any of the flower paste to eat. They would not need it where they were going.

"Bill Long and Thomas can gobble French," William said to us as he gingerly lifted his bad leg to climb over a deck railing to get on to yet another galley.

"So we are going to leave them here with the men of Bill's galley to barber our wounded and question the prisoners. We need to find out who they are and who sent them. Thomas and his apprentice are to put on their priest's robes and make sure that our dead are all buried on the shore with the proper Church words gobbled over them to get them to heaven sooner or later."

We had just finished once again visiting Harry's galley so we could see for ourselves what had happened, and we were all quite shaken by what we had seen. After a moment of deep thought behind his eyes, William told us more about what he wanted the company done next.

"We will assign prize captains and crews to our prizes when we return after we deal with the French fleet. Then we will take them up the river to Paris so King Phillip can see them. They might help him understand why the number of coins required for his ransom just increased.

"Now it is time to find Bill long," he said with a vicious snarl in a voice loud enough for the men on the deck to her. "I am going to tell him to throw all the prisoners in the river for the fish to eat after he and Thomas finish questioning them. Every goddamn one of them, dead or alive, except for any young boys, of course. Otherwise, they are all to go into the river for the murder they did to our wounded."


****** 

We left our murdered men and our burial party behind and spent the rest of the day rowing down the river in search of the French galleys which had escaped. We did not find them even though we rowed all the way down to the mouth of the river and reached it just as the sun finished passing overhead on its endless voyage around the world.

There were fewer and fewer people to be seen along the shoreline of the river as we neared the mouth of the Seine. The river itself had been empty except for an enemy galley which had stranded itself on a sandbar next to the riverbank. It was one of their small ones with ten oars to a side. We viewed it with distain—it was only good for carrying messages and taking fishing boats and small coasters.

The men on the stranded galley had waded ashore and run away as we approached. We had seen them go. But we only slowed down to look at the enemy galley for a few moments before we resumed rowing and continued on down the river.

Before we resumed rowing, however, Harold shouted out an order to Richard Kent, the captain of one of our galleys, to stay behind to try to retrieve it. If Richard was able to get it off the sandbar, he was to send the little galley up the river as another prize for the French king and his army to see, and then continue down the river to re-join the main fleet. *I was thinking behind my eyes that it was much too small for us to use in the east; we would either sell it or destroy it.*

The sun had almost finished passing overhead by the time we saw the mouth of the river in the distance. After briefly talking things over with Peter, whose galley was immediately behind ours, William and I decided our galleys should tie up along the northern bank of the Seine, and sally out into the estuary in the morning as soon as the early light of dawn appeared.

And tie up along the riverbank is exactly what we did. Within minutes there were galleys moored one after another all along the riverbank. The men were allowed to go ashore to stretch their legs, but cooking fires were forbidden in the hope that any enemies in the estuary would not know the size of the force coming for them, or how near to them we might be.

It was a deserted stretch of the river. There was nary a Frenchman or hovel in sight, not even a fisherman or a traveller on the roads or someone working in the nearby fields. There were a lot of bugs though and we were constantly waving our hands to keep them out of our eyes; France is full of them.

******

William called an "all captains" meeting for the deck of my galley almost immediately after we finished mooring for the night. He wanted to explain what the fleet would do in the morning and give his captains their orders.

The captains who assembled on my deck in the moonlight to listen to William were uniformly grim; they had all heard about the murders of Harry Farmer and his men, and many of them and their crews had seen their bodies. Their men, the captains reported, were beside themselves with anger and, to a man, they were spoiling for a fight. None of us would have expected anything less; the archers considered themselves to be what we truly were—a band of brothers.

William's basic plan was simple, and appeared to be agreeable to everyone: The fleet would follow my galley, with William on board as the fleet's commander, into the estuary at sunrise with almost eighteen hundred archers on twenty-three ocean-going war galleys. More specifically, our entire fleet would follow my galley into the Seine estuary, and when we got there we would search it and take or destroy everything we could find that was afloat, including fishing boats.

If there was no enemy fleet in sight when we entered the estuary, we would split up into three mini-fleets and go off in different directions and spend the entire day searching for the enemy. Afterwards, when the sun was going down at the end of the day, all of our galleys would reassemble at the mouth of the river except those who were in hot pursuit of prizes.

All prizes were to be sent to the mouth of the river. Those with shallow enough drafts would be taken up to Paris so King Phillip and the French army could see them; those too large to get all the way up the river would be sent to Cornwall with prize crews.


****** *Harold Lewes.*

All of William's lieutenant commanders and their seconds remained aboard my galley after the "all captains" meeting to talk whilst we ate cold bread and drank bowls of ale. The atmosphere as we ate and talked was very much like the "all captains" meeting that had just ended—one of great anger and quiet determination; our casualties had been far too high for there to be any elation about the prizes we had taken.

The fact that we had successfully driven the French galleys from the river was never mentioned at the meeting. To the contrary, there was an intense feeling of bitterness and vengeance-seeking as we went over our plans for the morning—and a growing feeling of unease about what might be happening in Paris whilst we were gone.

*Me? I did not say a word to anyone about it, not even to William, but I was particularly concerned about the trebuchet I had seen on the deck of the one of the small French galleys we had taken. It was obviously a catapult the French galley was carrying up the river to use against the army we had in front of the king's castle. As it turned out, I was wrong and should have said something: we were unprepared for what happened next and it cost us dearly.*

# Chapter Twenty-two

*We are surprised.*

The first light of day had barely appeared when William nodded to me. It was an order to proceed. I nodded back and immediately ordered our mooring lines cast off and the "follow me" flag waved from both masts. My mini-fleet with eleven galleys was to be first into the estuary, Peter's mini-fleet was next with six, and George's six galleys brought up the rear. Once we got into estuary we would split once again into three mini-fleets and sail abreast with each mini-fleet following its commander.

We were as ready as we could be: Our arrow bales and weapons were laid out in readiness for an instant sea battle, our best archers manned the decks, castle roofs, and the archers' nests and positions on our masts. Our men were well-fed and their arms were fresh; we were ready for anything, or so we thought.

Our galleys did not exactly charge out of the river and into the estuary. To the contrary, we had no idea where we would find the French fleet, or if we would find it at all. As a result, we were going rather slowly in order to save the arms of the men who were rowing, and most of the men were not.

The wind was somewhat unfavourable, but very light as it often is in the early morning. Our sails were ready to be instantly raised, but we did not raise them in order to reduce the chances that we would be seen by our enemies. We did not want them to see us in time to escape.

Every galley's lower tier of rowing benches was empty and its oar holes plugged. The archers who usually rowed on the lower tier, mostly our newer men and their experienced sergeants, were all rowing on the upper tier where they could more quickly get into the fight if one developed. The upper tier men were in their deck, castle roof, and mast positions, and ready to immediately begin pushing out arrows.

Only the three sailors who were each galley's rudder men and drummer, and its inevitable handful of dullards and "punishment men" who constantly bailed out the in-coming water, remained below in the stench and dim light of the lower rowing deck. The rest of the sailors on my galley, as on each of the other galleys in our fleet, were standing ready to raise our sails and throw their grapples. As I said earlier; we were ready for anything, or so we thought.


****** *William*

Harold and I stood on the crowded roof of his galley's forward deck castle as we led the fleet out of the Seine and into the estuary. It was the first hour of what promised to be a fine morning with a clear blue sky. A long line of our galleys followed close behind us. They would form into their mini-fleets as soon as they cleared the river. There was not a sail or mast in sight in the estuary. Even so, our troubles began almost immediately.

Long rolling Atlantic waves were coming in from the ocean beyond the estuary and making our galleys shudder and move up and down as they reached us. Our men had been up the river at the castle island for several weeks—long enough for many of them to lose their sea legs. Within a few minutes the sea pox struck and the decks railings of our galleys were thronged with men losing their breakfasts and being poxed with weak legs.

My apprentice and I were among them. And so were several of the archers in the nest on our forward mast—much to the outrage of the men on the deck below them. Fists were shaken and threats were made and muttered.

We were only a few minutes out of the river and the deck was still being sloshed with seawater from our wooden bailing buckets when there was a cry from our lookouts.

"Hoy the deck. Hoy. There be masts and sails off to the east towards Harfleur."

Harold shouted "stay here; I will be right back" at me as he jumped down from where he was standing next to me on the roof of deck castle roof. Within a couple of heart beats he began climbing the rope ladder next to the forward mast to see for himself. I stayed behind along with both of our very sea-poxed apprentices.

*Of course he told me to stay. Harold was an experienced sailor man; he knew that pox-weakened men should not be climbing rope ladders if it could be avoided. I nodded my understanding and appreciation when he told us to stay where we were.*

Harold had barely reached the mast and grabbed the rope ladder to begin climbing when there was another shout from the lookout on the forward mast.

"Hoy the deck. Many masts and sails to the west towards Harfleur. They look to be coming towards us."

Harold went up the rope ladder next to the mast very fast, as only an experienced sailor could manage. He had climbed no more than half way before he suddenly began climbing down just as fast whilst shouting out a string of orders.

"Turn towards west by northwest, sailing sergeant, west by northwest."

And then he added, after a very brief pause, "Wave the 'follow me' and 'attack flags,' sailing sergeant, wave them."

The first of the enemy masts and sails began to come into sight even as Harold's orders were being repeated by his loud talker. We could see there were a large number of them. And we still did not know for sure who they were or how well they would fight. No order was given to increase our speed.

"The sun is behind us so they may not have seen us yet. But they soon will if they have not already," Harold said as climbed the three wooden steps to once again stand by my side on the castle roof. "And by God, there are a lot of them, including some big galleys like ours out front. They must have spent the night off Harfleur.

"But here is the thing, William, there are many sails in the French armada, but most of them do not look to be very large and some of them appear to have cargos on their decks. That is strange, is it not? I wonder what it means?"

****** *William*

No order had been given to increase our speed. There was no need. The enemy armada would have seen us and it was still coming towards the mouth of the river. In a few more minutes we could see it clearly. It was huge. There were war galleys out front that were similar in size to ours, and a large number of smaller galleys of the type we had seen and taken in the river.

What was interesting was that most of the French fleet consisted of single-masted transports, and even some of what appeared to be large fishing boats. Their decks appeared to be crowded with men and cargo.

It was hard to get an accurate count, but there were easily over a hundred smaller single-masted transports and big fishing boats, and perhaps twice that many or even more.  There were also at least twenty small galleys and nine or ten large war galleys comparable to ours.  A number of the transports and small galleys seemed to have some kind of cargo on their decks.

The French had the wind somewhat at their backs and their sails were up.  It could only be an armada carrying a relief force to Paris, with the small galleys intended to be used to pull the transports up the Seine and the large ones intended to fight off enemy attackers such as ourselves.  Their intention to go all the way up the Seine to Paris would explain why there were only smaller transports and galleys.

"They mean to fight us to get through to the Seine instead of turning back," Harold said quietly as he stood by my side and we watched the French fleet come slowly towards us.  "And I do not understand why.  They are either world-class fools or they know something we do not."

"Maybe those are troop transports taking soldiers and supplies up the river to fight us in Paris, and the galleys are for pulling them up the river and carrying soldiers the way we use our larger galleys in the Holy Land to carry passengers," I suggested. *That had to be it.*

"You may be right.  But I am not sure, am I?  It's what is on their decks that does not look right to me.  It could be we are seeing more of those trebuchet catapults like the one on the small galley we took as a prize," Harold suggested.

"That is the only thing they could be," I agreed. "They are probably carrying them up the river so they can use them to throw stones and such over the river and into our camp on the island."

Harold's thoughts and concerns were similar to mine. I could not understand the behaviour of the approaching armada either. They should have turned away and started running by now. Perhaps they did not understand what they were facing.

"It could be that they do not know how strong we are and their commander is determined to push through us and get into the river. He has the wind," I suggested.

Harold agreed.

"It is more likely their commander did not know how strong we are when he gave his sailing orders, and now he has no way to tell his captains to do something different. But why has he not turned and run for it? The others would follow him or scatter if he did."

"Perhaps he fears for his life and lands if he does not at least try to get through and relieve our siege on his king?" I said it with more than a little uncertainty in my voice.

*We were both totally right and totally wrong.*


\*\*\*\*\*\*

What followed was a surprise for all of us. The huge and slowly moving French fleet continued sailing for the mouth of the Seine and we split into our three mini-fleets and continued slowly rowing straight for them. As we got closer we could see that the transports and galleys of the French fleet were sailing close together, very close together.

I led the galleys in my mini-fleet straight at the middle of the French armada. And, as we had planned, George split off and led the galleys under his command to the left, and then he increased his speed and led them in to hit the French in the side of their formation; Peter did virtually the same thing on the other flank of the French formation.

I was standing on castle roof with Harold and close enough that I could clearly see what happened next as we closed on the French.

There was a burst of movement on the decks of some of the French boats and, moments later, what appeared to be great large rocks began flying through the air and landing with big splashes all around the galleys leading our attacks. At least one of Peter's galleys was hit. I saw its forward mast go down and great splashes all around it.

We were closing with the French ourselves when we were distracted and could not continue watching. We were still not with arrow range of the French galleys when it happened—a great hail of big black rocks began to rise out the French fleet and seemed to coming straight at us.

"Oh my God," I heard Harold say as the big rocks began flying through the air towards us from the French fleet and, a few seconds later, began splashing into the water all around us. One of them went right over the top of my head and almost hit our mast. They were rocks for sure, and big ones from the size of the splashes they were making as they landed all around us.

"Emergency turn around," Harold shouted to his sailing sergeant with urgency in his voice. "We have got to break off and get out of range. A hit from one of those damn things will sink us for sure."

\*\*\*\*\*\*

We spun around and retreated back towards the entrance to the Seine with the closely packed French armada continuing to slowly follow behind us. As we did, our sailors began frantically waving the "follow me" flag. The other galleys in our mini-fleet turned around and followed us as we fled. We raised our sails and everyone rushed to the oars; our galleys soon pulled ahead of the French fleet in the race for the mouth of the Seine.

I did not say anything to anyone, but I thought I heard the triumphant cheers and shouts coming from the French as we turned away and started our run for the mouth of the river. I became greatly vexed and out of sorts. It must have showed for everyone stayed far away from me, and no one said a word.

George's galleys followed ours; Peter's did not, however, and his absence was ignored in the first anxious and confusing moments after we turned back. Only one thing was certain: Our effort to destroy the French fleet had been a disaster; we had not even gotten close enough for even our very strongest archers to push out their longs.

Something suddenly dawned on me as remembered what I had once heard Thomas say about catapults when the crusaders were trying to take Constantinople. I ran back to the stern castle and climbed on to its roof to join the archers standing there. Rowland, my young apprentice sergeant, dutifully followed me. Harold stayed where he was and watched me.

A few moments later I saw, I least I thought I did, what I had hoped I would see. What had happened and caused me to run back to the stern castle for another look was remembering what Thomas had said. In addition, of all things, I remembered something I had seen many years ago at Acre when we were fighting there with Richard. It suddenly came out of nowhere and popped into my head behind my eyes.

"Rowland, run back to Commander Lewes and tell him I want him to slow down and let the French catch up with us. Tell him to stay ahead of them by just enough to keep out of range of their catapults."

My apprentice sergeant did as I ordered, and shortly thereafter I could hear Harold's shouts as he gave the orders and listened as his loud talker and sergeants repeated them. The beat of the rowing drum immediately slowed and we began to slow down. A worried Harold was by my side a few moments later. He had immediately obeyed my order, but he had a questioning look on his face.

"Look at the men around their catapults," I said as I pointed towards the tightly grouped French fleet. "Most of them are still trying to reload—and look where they are aimed."

Harold looked and initially did not understand. Then he did.

"By God, you are right. What shall we do?"

"Wave the 'follow me' flag and turn away. Head towards Harfleur. The French have catapults so it's a new type of war for our captains. We will need to have an 'all captains' meeting to tell our lads what to do and how to do it." *Now if I can only figure out what that might be before the captains come aboard.*

\*\*\*\*\*\*

The French fleet did not turn change either its course or its slow speed when Harold and I led our galleys towards Harfleur. To my great relief, the French fleet continued to plod slowly on its way towards the mouth of the Seine. A few minutes later Harold had the 'all captains' flag waved from his masts.  It did not take long at all for most of our captains to reach Harold's deck since almost all of our galleys had caught up to us and were rowing nearby, all except those in Peter's mini-fleet.

Harold and I talked briefly and firmed up our plans as we waited for our galleys to finish forming into a big galley raft surrounding Harold's galley.  Within just a minute or two the galley captains were climbing over deck railings and running across the decks of their fellow captains' galleys as they hurried towards us.

There was not a minute to waste and we encouraged them to hurry by standing on the forward castle roof and pumping our clenched right fists up and down in the age-old signal to hurry.  Harold and I continued talking and planning as we pumped.

"It just might work," Harold said to me as the captains began hurriedly arriving on his deck and we watched the close-packed French fleet continue to slowly move towards the Seine.  From where we were standing it looked like a virtual forest of sails and masts was slowly moving toward the entrance to the distant river.

"There is nary a hull in that lot with a deep draft such that it could not get all the way up the river to Paris," I said to my hurriedly assembled captains.  "So now we know the French fleet is almost certainly carrying a relief force of soldiers and weapons up the Seine to confront us and try to break our siege.  I suspect it means that chasing our galleys and fighting them in the river was never the main goal of the French."

"Aye commander," Harold added. "They just wanted to clear them out of the way so their armada could pass."

"Aye, you are right about that, Harold, yes you are. And the French fleet is obviously going no faster than their slowest transport so they can stay tight together and fight us off. How long do you think it will be before they get into the river?"

# Chapter Twenty-three

*We have another go at the French.*

Harold thought the French relief force was only a couple of hours away from reaching the relative safety of the Seine. Accordingly, time was of the essence if we were going to have another go at the French before they entered the river. As a result, our 'all captains' meeting only lasted a few minutes, and mainly consisted of me pointing at each of the captains and telling him where he was to place his galley and what he was to do after he got my signal.

Not all of the fleet's captains attended. Peter and his captains were still missing. He and his men had been on the other side of the French fleet and probably did not see our signal flags. But we had not yet begun to wonder why none of them had attended; we did not have time.

My plan was for our galleys to fall upon the French relief fleet as soon as the meeting with our captains was finished, and then chase them all the way up the river to Paris. The captains listened intently and were as ready as Harold and I could get them with less than five minutes of orders and explanations.

By the time the meeting broke up and the captains had rushed back to their galleys, every one of them had been told where he was to be in the circle of galleys we would be using to surround the French fleet, and what he was to do once the signal was given for the attack to begin. The question, of course, was whether or not each of the captains was up to carrying out his orders, and how the French would respond if and when he did.

Harold and I were increasingly optimistic about my plan and made much of our optimism during the brief minutes in which we had available to convey it to our captains. And there was good reason for our optimism; every one of our captains was a veteran who had spent years fighting and practicing to fight, and so were all of their sergeants, lieutenants, and chosen men;

All in all, Harold and I had good reason to be quite hopeful about what we were going to do, and it showed in everything we said to the captains during our short meeting. *And I was so worried when it ended that I had to fight the urge to run the deck railing and lose my breakfast after the captains gave a cheer and began running back to their galleys.*

\*\*\*\*\*\*

Our galley raft came apart even faster than it had been formed. As soon as each galley pushed off, and its oars were safely clear of the others, orders were shouted and its rowing drum began beating as it headed at its best speed for the position it been assigned in the loose circle of galleys we were putting around the closely packed French fleet.

Until the signal flag was waved to commence our attack, each of our galleys would fight only if one or more of the French galleys came out to challenge it, and then only if a fight could not be avoided by sailing away from them or driving them off with our arrows. Breaking up and destroying the French relief force was every captain's goal, not the taking of a single prize, no matter how impressive.

The only exception, I had told the captains, would be if a number of French galleys came after one or two of ours, and ours could use a 'wounded bird' to draw a large number of them away from the French fleet.

And it actually happened. The large galleys leading the armada did leave the French fleet to chase a couple of our galleys, but not for long. Eustace the Monk followed and then turned away to escape back to the Island of Sark with what was left of his galleys. In a sense, Eustace and his men abandoning the French fleet evened up the odds by offsetting our lack of Peter and his galleys.

*Harold and Thomas think Eustace understood what we were about to do and used chasing after one of our galleys as an excuse to abandon the French. It had not hurt at all that Eustace's men were pirates who had no interest at all in fighting anyone who might fight back; their survivors from the fighting on the river had already spread the word about our fighting abilities and the modern weapons we were using.*


\*\*\*\*\*\*

My initial plan was for each of our galleys to remain in sight of one or two of their fellow galleys whilst forming an entire circle around the French fleet. Then, when I waved the 'attack' flag, it would be seen by the galleys spread out on either side of Harold's. Each would, in turn, wave his attack flag such that my order would sweep from one of our galleys to the next until it reached all our galleys.

The plan was for all our galleys to hit the French armada at almost the same moment from many different directions. Hopefully, this would not give the French enough time to aim their catapults, and, once we closed tight up against the French armada, they would not be able to use them at all. We had to do something and this is all I could think to do at the time.

I stood by anxiously as Harold's galley rowed towards the French armada. After we reached it, we took up a position that was just out of range, we hoped, of the French catapults. Then we commenced rowing along with the French towards the mouth of the river. Others of our galleys were spreading out and similarly moving into their assigned places.

Some of our galleys had quite a bit further to row than others to get to get into place. Accordingly, I knew I had to wait to give the attack order until my captains all had time to get their galleys into position.

Waiting to give the order was difficult for me because the French fleet was getting closer and closer to the mouth of Seine. But wait I did with our galley rowing only hard enough to keep pace with the slowly moving French and remain out of catapult range.

Finally, the anxieties behind my eyes got the best of me as the French were less than an hour from the river. I could wait no longer. *Where the hell is Peter?*


\*\*\*\*\*\*


As you might imagine one of the most important orders I gave to my captains in our brief meeting was to always remain in sight of the galley charged with waving its attack flag at him, and not to leave his position and commence his attack until he saw the next galley in the circle acknowledge his signal by waving its own attack flag at the next galley in our encircling chain.

Relaying an attack signal from one galley to the next in such a way was something we had never practiced. In any event, as a result of the need for each galley to keep in sight of those on either side of it, our twenty-one galleys were only able to stretch about half way around the French armada. I, of course, did not know this when I gave the order for the attack flag to be waved.

"Wave the attack flag, Commander Lewes," I finally said. "Wave the flag." I felt a great relief when I did.

My order to wave the attack flag was immediately and loudly repeated by Harold and by the sergeants throughout his galley. The heads of everyone on deck then began moving back and forth as we watched the masts of the galleys on either side of us in the distance. Almost immediately they too commenced waving their attack flags. A few seconds later, at almost the same moment, they both stopped waving them and began changing their positions.

I breathed a great sigh of relief. My signal had been successfully reached the galleys nearest to us and been repeated by them. Now their flags had apparently been seen and repeated by the galley next beyond them in our encirclement; it meant that it was now time for them to begin their attacks.

We could only hope that the rest of our galleys further on down the line had also gotten the message. Now, for better or worse, we and each of our other galleys which had both received and passed along the order were on our own; it was time for us to launch our attacks on the French, and continue them even after the French fleet entered the Seine.

Harold's galley immediately did what we both devoutly hoped every one of our galleys was also doing at that moment—it spun around and began traveling as fast as our men could row along the outside edge of the French fleet in the opposite direction. Now we were heading as fast as possible away from the mouth of the river. We continued on that course whilst Harold slowly counted to three hundred.

Harold and I and everyone else on deck had begun nervously scanning the French fleet as soon as our galley spun around and the beat of our rowing drum rapidly increased. Both tiers of oars had been temporarily manned and all of our rowers pulled hard as if their lives depended on it, which they probably did. Our galley's oars instantly dug in and we began a fast run in the opposite direction along the outside edge of the French fleet. The rowing would continue until Harold reached a count of three hundred. We were staying just out of crossbow range.

What we watchers on the deck castle roof were anxiously looking for, of course, were signs that the French were trying to re-aim their catapults—not that we could do anything about it if they did; but we wanted to know just the same.

Catapults were something we had never before encountered at sea. But we were fairly sure that they were hard to aim and slow to load. Accordingly we had kept up with the French armada for a few minutes of slow and steady rowing in order to given the French time to aim their catapults towards us in the expectation that we would suddenly dash towards them. Now we were trying to quickly change our position in preparation to dashing in for an attack before they could adjust their aim.

There was activity everywhere as soon as Harold finally said "three hundred." For one, our galley heeled dramatically as our rudder men, rowers, and sail tenders turned us hard to the right and we commenced running straight towards the French fleet. For another, the entire lower tier of rowing benches emptied as soon as the turn was completed. It had been temporarily taken over by our deck archers for our sudden dash back along the edge of the French fleet; now they poured back on deck and picked up their weapons as we headed straight for the French fleet and closed on it.

The lower-tier men now rowing on the upper tier cheered as the deck archers ran past them and redoubled their efforts at the oars. Their weapons were close at hand in case they were needed.

# Chapter Twenty-four

*Death and destruction.*

We closed rapidly on a French fleet that was suddenly in an ever-increasing state of total confusion and disarray. It began when the transports and galleys with the catapults tried to turn in order to re-aim them at our new positions. The result was collisions and chaos as every French captain began trying to turn and twist in order to avoid colliding with everyone else.

Overall, however, the French still kept going towards the entrance to the Seine. It was as if their orders had been to stay together and head for the Seine no matter what. Or perhaps it was that the French did not yet fully comprehend what was happening; or perhaps they thought they could rely on their catapults to drive us off again.

Some of the French catapults were used as we all changed our positions at almost the same moment. A great cloud of rocks churned into the sea well off to the right of Harold's galley. Another somewhat smaller cloud of what appeared to be even bigger rocks went right over the top of our mast as we got closer to the French fleet and began to push out our arrows. The catapult hurling them at us had been re-aimed but its rocks went over us because we were too close by the time its deadly rocks were flung.

Our sudden change of direction had been a success; we were not hit by any of the rocks and neither, so far as anyone could tell, were any of our sister galleys, at least not those we had in sight in front of us and behind us after we all changed our positions at the same time and began running directly towards the French convoy.

The confusion, collisions, and disorder in the French armada intensified as soon as we reached the armada's outermost transports and could see the sea-poxed French troops packed on their decks. They were all small transports and galleys with shallow drafts that would allow them get all the way up the river.

*It was when we saw the shallow drafts of the French transports that we finally knew for sure that the French were attempting to bring an army up the Seine to Paris to relieve our siege. That realization and the murdering of the crew of our stranded galley made me more determined than ever to destroy the French armada and increase the ransom the French would have to pay to free their king.*

\*\*\*\*\*\*

When we got close to the transports of the closely packed French armada, we turned again, this time hard to the right, and began rowing once again towards the entrance to the Seine. Now we were moving so close along the very edge of the French fleet, that we constantly had near collisions and Harold frequently had to shout "in oars" to avoid having them sheared off.

Harold kept us so close to the French transports and galleys as we moved along the edge of the French fleet that those of us using our longbows on Harold's deck were periodically staggered as our hull scraped along the hull of a French boat we were passing. Our archers could hardly miss at such a close range and rarely did. The shouting, screams, and other noises on our deck and the nearby French decks were constant and deafening.

We began moving as if to go in a circle around the massive French fleet, always keeping them on our left and rowing close alongside of them at a much faster speed than the French were moving. Despite our constant attacks and their collisions and disarray, the French doggedly continued sailing towards the mouth of the Seine. As a result, we were constantly coming up on new French transports and wreaking death and havoc on the soldiers and sailors standing on their decks.

It was as if our galley was a sheep dog and the transports and galleys of the French armada were the sheep we were herding into an ever tighter flock by biting at their heels. The difference was that we were biting them with arrows and our bites were often fatal.

*Referring to the boats of French armada as a flock of sheep and each of our galleys as a sheep dog was what William told our captains during his brief meeting with them.*

*That was the first and only time he told them what they were to do when they closed with the French armada. Most of them understood and complied; I subsequently relieved those few who did not. /Harold Lewes/*

As you might imagine, our archers were under the strictest of orders to conserve their arrows. Every galley had many bales of them, but once they were gone they were gone. Accordingly, the archers were under the strictest of orders to only to push an arrow at someone on a French deck when the archer was absolutely sure of a hit.

Taking down a Frenchman with every arrow was so important that by the time we had raked the decks of the first four or five of the French transports we overtook Harold had his sergeants chanting "only push when you are certain; only push when you are certain."

Several times I watched as a sergeant ferociously rounded on an archer who taken a bad shot or missed an easy one. They were right in doing so; there was no excuse for one of our archers to miss at such a short range, particularly since every captain was supposed to be using his company's very best archers.

The reactions of the French crews and the sea-poxed soldiers who were the passengers on their decks were a sight to see as we overtook and passed them. Almost every French captain, if he lived long enough, reacted in the same way as we came alongside and began sweeping his deck with our arrows—he inevitably made an effort to escape the storm that was descending on him by making a hard left turn to get away from us.

What the French captains were doing was a desperate and all too human effort to get to safety—and it inevitably took them straight into the closely packed mass of the French armada. The result was more collisions and even greater confusion.

And the fighting was not all one-sided. Some of the French soldiers we overtook had bows and crossbows, and they began using them as our galley came alongside and began passing their transport.

The French archers rarely lasted long enough to take more than one shot since our archers especially targeted the French bowman in an effort to protect themselves and their mates. That the French archers inevitably took an arrow from one or more of our archers was small consolation for the archers and sailors on our deck whom they killed or wounded.

I distinctly remember seeing the blur of an arrow that narrowly missed me and the sound it made as it hit my apprentice in the thick part of his leg near his dingle. What I remember most was the look of despair and shocked surprise on Rowland's face as he stared at it and his blood began to run down the shaft and drip on the deck. There was no time to console or barber our wounded. All we could do was hurriedly drag them into the relative safety of one of the deck castles and keep fighting.

******

We had passed and killed men on the decks of ten or eleven of the French transports and a couple of small galleys when there was a chilling call from one of the archers in the nest on our forward mast.

"Galleys. Big'uns they be. Coming fast from the south. Four of them."

I had just finished pushing an arrow into the neck of a heavily bearded Frenchman on the crowded deck of a single-masted cog our galley was bouncing up against when I heard the lookout. I stepped back and turned to look.

Harold was already heading for the mast to see for himself as I turned. He had barely climbed ten feet up the rope ladder before he literally slid back down. By the time he returned, we had already gone past the transport carrying my most recent victim and I was picking out a target on the crowded deck of the next French transport. We were so close that I was instinctively bracing myself for the shock when we scraped up against it.

"They are ours; coming to help. Four of Peter's," I heard him shout to someone; me I think.

A moment later I grunted and pushed an arrow towards another Frenchman just as his single-masted transport turned a hard left and its bow collided with the side of a small French galley that seemed to be trying to work its way free of the armada.

My arrow came close, but it missed; the collision saved my target—by causing him to stagger to one side just as I grunted and pushed my arrow at him. I swore under my breath and suddenly, once again, became aware of all the shouting and screaming around me.

There was an open stretch of water before we would reach the next French transport. Its crew had seen us coming and it was already beginning to present its stern to us as it tried to turn away, only to be rammed amidships by another transport.

I took the opportunity to turn around to look for Peter's galleys, and saw them immediately. They were close and closing fast. From the looks of where they were positioned, and the direction they were headed, they had hit the French convoy somewhere behind us.

Ahead of us, from where I was standing on the castle roof, I could see the French transports at the front of the armada starting to enter the Seine; behind the French armada I could see several transports that appeared to be sinking, quite a few that appeared to be drifting aimlessly, and a dozen or more that had turned back and were heading every which way as they tried to run away to safety.

For a brief moment I wondered aloud why we had not yet encountered the larger French galleys which we had chased out of the river. They had last been seen leading the French fleet. Where had they gone? It worried me.

\*\*\*\*\*\*

The entrance to the Seine was a scene of chaos, desperation, and French heroism when we finally reached it. Many of the French captains had obviously had enough. They were everywhere running their boats aground with their sails still up, and their crews and the soldiers they were carrying were jumping off into the shallow water in an effort to wade ashore and escape.

Others of the French were trying to continue up the river as they had been ordered to do; they had lowered their sails and were attempting to attach towlines so the remaining French galleys, the small ones, could pull them. Some had already succeeded in setting their tows and were being pulled up the Seine; the river was filled with them.

Two of our galleys were in sight in the river and I could see them attacking the French transports. They were following my orders to continue harassing the French all the way up the river. I watched as the archers on one of them poured out arrows as their galley moved along a tow of three transports being pulled upstream by a small French galley. *Damn, I should have told them to concentrate on the galleys once they got in the river.*

"Stop here, Harold," I ordered. We were in the middle of the entrance to the river and still taking periodic French arrows, and pushing out our own arrows, as more and more French transports and galleys arrived. Some of the French transports and some of our galleys, I had no idea how many of each, had already made it into the Seine and were continuing to try to get to Paris.

Using Harold's loud talker, I shouted an order over the water to the captain of the galley that had been rowing immediately behind us, but was now almost up to us because we had stopped.

"Hoy Tommy. Turn around and go back out to accept surrenders, kill those who do not surrender, and take whatever prizes you can find, even small ones. Tow them back here if it would be safer than putting a small prize crew in amongst a lot of French soldiers. And pass the word to any of our lads you come across that they are to do the same."


\*\*\*\*\*\*

We waited at the mouth of the Seine for about an hour whilst I received quick reports and gave orders and new assignments to those of our galleys which were still arriving. Some were sent back into estuary and beyond to round up French prizes; others were sent to one side of the river or the other to take possession of the growing number of abandoned French transports; and others were told to proceed up the Seine and attack any French vessels and troops they encountered.

Our time at the mouth of the Seine became a particularly difficult time for me because one of the first of our galleys to arrive was one of Peter's. It brought terrible news. Peter and his galley and most its crew were gone. Their galley had been holed by a deluge of large rocks during the initial catapult attack. It had gone down quickly and only a few survivors had been able to cling to its floating fragments long enough to be rescued. The next commander of the company was not amongst the survivors despite an intensive search of the area.

It was with a very heavy heart that we began rowing up the Seine to Paris.

Everywhere there were signs of the death and destruction that had occurred as our galleys overtook the Frenchmen who had attempted to carry out the orders they had been given. We passed several bodies that were drifting down the river and saw others sprawled out on sandbars and along the shoreline. We similarly passed a number of abandoned single-masted French transports and several small galleys, including a transport that was drifting down the river sideways with no one on board.

Also along the river were wounded French soldiers and sailors as well as a number of live ones who could not swim and were stranded with deep water between themselves and the sandbars where their transports and galleys had gone aground. Many of them regarded us with fear in their eyes, but none of them looked to be dangerous; we would return later to deal with them.

Overall, we did not see as many dead and wounded French soldiers as I would have expected. It appeared that seeing our galleys coming up the river after them had caused many of the French transports to head for the riverbank and be hurriedly abandoned.

Twice in the initial stretches of the river we came upon one of our galleys rowing hard to slowly tow a string of prizes up the river. We waved and cheered as we passed them. What we did not see were many travellers on the road or the local serfs and slaves who would normally be working in the adjacent fields.

We were about half way to Paris when we began to encounter some of our galleys coming back down the river to gather up more prizes. Seeing the cheerful enthusiasm of their crews, and hearing their shouted reports, distracted me from the particularly black mood I had been in as a result of thinking about Peter and the implications of losing him after all these years.

# Chapter Twenty-five
*The new surrender terms.*

It was growing dark and prizes were continuing to arrive and be moored along the riverbank in the middle of the island next to our siege camp. The galleys which had towed in the early arrivals, including George's and Harold's, had turned around and gone back for more. The more recent arrivals did not; it was much too dangerous to travel on the river after dark, so they were stopping to rest. They would go back down the river and start again in the morning.

I had stayed behind to get things organized at this end when Harold took his galley back down the river to fetch more prizes. As the last of the day's light disappeared, I was ashore on the island, wolfing down bread and cheese, and sinking my teeth into an onion that made my eyes water.

Henry and Thomas joined me whilst I ate, and they had just finished telling me what had happened in Paris while I was gone. It could be summed up in two words—not much; we were still buying food from the merchants in the villages along the river and nothing had been heard from the castle.

My two lieutenants and their apprentices were leaning forward and listening attentively as I told them some of the details as to what I had seen and what I thought had happened to the French fleet and why. Everyone was still in a state of dismay at the extent of our casualties. The significance of our losing the man who was about to take over the command of the entire company had not yet hit them.

"Not all of the French soldiers were killed or drowned. A large number of them escaped when they abandoned their transports and waded ashore, that is for sure. And many of them probably took their weapons with them. But not a one of their catapults reached Prince Louis's army here at Paris, at least I do not think so."

Then I told Thomas and Henry of my intention to increase our ransom demands. They listened to what I proposed and agreed enthusiastically. And from the expressions on their faces, although they never said a word, so did the archers and sailors standing near enough to us to overhear what I had in mind.

Harold and George had apparently returned in the darkness. They walked up just as I finished telling Thomas and Henry what I thought we should do about the ransom. So I began again and repeated my thoughts a second time. The light from the flames of a nearby cooking fire flickered across everyone's faces as I did.


****** *Henry and what happened the next day*

Our galleys had been coming in all day towing additional prizes. They were mostly from the French transports and galleys that their crews had abandoned along the shoreline and on the sandbars of the estuary and the river. Many of them still had dead and wounded Frenchmen aboard.

As we had done yesterday, we brought the French wounded ashore for barbering and tossed the dead Frenchmen into the Seine. We did it within sight of the large number of watchers on castle's ramparts. We would decide later what to with the prizes. They were almost all too small for our own use; they would have to either be sold or destroyed. But where could they be sold?

In the middle of the afternoon William had a horn blower, Joe Horn from Harold's crew, walk out in front of our first fighting line and blow some toots on his galley horn to get the castle's attention. It was the first time either side had attempted to make contact with the other since I had given the castle our ransom demands. Faces soon began to appear on the castle's battlements.

A few minutes later, I called Joe back and walked out of our lines to take Joe's place and once again stand in front of the castle gate. William walked out a few steps behind me to be my translator. If asked, William would identify himself as a Swedish priest who had long ago left the Church "due to an unfortunate misunderstanding" and was now a member of a mercenary company of axe men. I, of course, was still Eric Eric's son, an axe carrier from Sweden and the commander of the emperor's army in France.

Both William and I were wearing tunics my apprentice had bought in the island's little market, and we were each carrying a great battle axe of the type often carried by fighting men from the north. I had carried one each time I had met with someone from the castle. It was part of our on-going effort identify ourselves as Swedish and Rus mercenaries employed by one of King Phillip's enemies, a German king who was a claimant to the throne of the Holy Roman Empire.

More time passed than it should have taken for the French to respond to our call for a meeting. I was just about to suggest to William that we give up and return to our lines for something to eat, when the small door in the castle gate opened. Father Pierre stepped out a moment later and began walking towards us.

"He is the same one as who came out to talk the last time," I said to William out of the corner of my mouth as the white-bearded elderly priest began walking towards us. The door in the castle gate was immediately closed behind him.

"Greetings, Father Pierre," I said rather sourly as he walked up to us. "And God's blessings on you, even though God is clearly no longer blessing your king and your cause."

I said the words in English with a deliberate mumble to my voice. Then William, who was standing somewhat behind me as an interpreter should, repeated them in Latin.

As he translated my greeting to the priest, I gestured towards the recently captured French transports. They were moored two and three deep all along the nearby riverbank in addition to our own galleys and the prize galleys we had taken. *We were continuing to try to hide the fact that we were English.*

"Many things have happened since we last spoke, as you can see," I said as I again gestured towards our long line of prizes. As I did, there was a shout and a splash nearby as another body was tossed into the Seine from the deck of one of our prizes.

As you might imagine, the timing of the dead Frenchman going for one last swim was not a coincidence. What was not planned, but was very real, were the periodic screams and moans of the French wounded. They were being loaded into dinghies and rowed across the river so their own people could barber them and, in so-doing, learn for themselves the folly of fighting with the emperor's men.

I did as William ordered and was very direct, and more than a little sarcastic, when I spoke to the French priest.

"It appears your King Phillip made a big wager and lost it. He bet he could ignore the emperor's generous surrender terms because his son's army would be able to drive us away. As you can see, King Phillip has lost his wager—the emperor's galleys have totally destroyed King Phillip's armada and the army it was bringing to help relieve his castle."

As I spoke I again gestured towards the prizes moored two and three deep along the nearby riverbank, and then I waited for William to gobble my words in Latin. I continued in the same manner when William finished.

"Unfortunately, the emperor's men suffered some dead and wounded in the process. As I am sure you can appreciate and understand, the emperor's men are entitled to be paid for their losses. Accordingly, instead of the ransom for the king and Louvre Castle being one hundred and twenty thousand pounds of silver coins, it is now one hundred and fifty thousand so the emperor can properly pay his men.

"Oh yes, I almost forgot," I snarled. "Because of the unnecessary delays and the need to continue to pay his men, the emperor now also requires, starting today, an additional one thousand pounds of silver coins for every additional day that passes without the castle surrendering, and an additional one thousand pounds for every day the emperor has to wait for the ransom to be delivered to him.

"Those who make wagers and lose them must pay, even kings whom God has blessed; I am sure he will understand that. Do you?"

The mouth of the old priest opened and he seemed to stagger as he pretended to be surprised at the new and higher amount.

"But that is impossible," the old man finally croaked as he appeared to struggle to regain control of himself after hearing such unexpected bad news.  It was a fine pretend and both William and I appreciated his efforts and skill as a negotiator.

"Ah, but it *is* possible," I responded with a heavy emphasis on the word *is*.  "The Templars have that much and more right here in Paris.  And being Templars, they will gladly part with it on generous terms, especially for King Phillip and his son." *Thomas said the Templars have the coins so they probably do; I did not realize they were so rich until he told me.*

We talked for a few more minutes.  Among other things, I repeated the "emperor's promise" that the king and courtiers would be treated well when the castle surrendered, and I offered to have a parchment from King Phillip carried across the river to Prince Louis with whatever orders the king might wish to give his son about obtaining the ransom coins.

When I finished, I nodded towards Father Pierre as if to reaffirm my own words.  Then I turned and began walking back to our lines whilst William was still gobbling at the priest in Latin to tell him what I had said.  When William finished, the priest gave a great sigh of resignation and trudged back to the castle.  There was the smell of rain in the air.

A few hours later our siege became partially successful. Louvre Castle surrendered.

Louvre Castle surrendered peacefully in exactly the way I had specified to Father Pierre. The huge entrance gate swung open and men began to emerge with armloads of the weapons that had been in the castle. We watched silently as they placed them in a great pile just outside the gate.

The gate remained open after the weapon carriers returned to the castle. At that point, a heavily armed force of about fifty of our men, all carrying battle axes and recently captured swords and shields, marched into the bailey to the beat of a marching drum. They entered cautiously and ready to fight in case there was French treachery involved. There was not.

Our initial entry men were standing "at your ease" in their ranks in the castle's bailey, and Father Pierre was waiting for me at the gate, when I arrived with William, George, and Thomas. All of us were wearing tunics from the local market and carrying axes. There was not a bow or quiver of arrows anywhere to be seen.

Father Pierre was surprisingly affable. He welcomed us in the name of the king, and handed me a "parchment from the king" with a request that it be carried across the river and delivered to his son, Prince Louis. It directed his son to contact the Templars and borrow the ransom coins. *I know it did because William unrolled the parchment and read it before it was delivered. Of course he did.*

George, Harold, and Thomas waited on the ground stones covering the castle's bailey with some of our men whilst William and I, accompanied by Father Pierre and about twenty heavily armed archers, thoroughly inspected the entire castle from top to bottom. We started under the castle in the dungeons where the prisoners and the castle's food supplies were stored. There were a handful of very hungry prisoners, all apparently French and being held for petty reasons, and absolutely no food.

After I briefly questioned the prisoners using William and Father Pierre as translators, William quietly told me to free them. A couple of our guards were ordered to take them to the bailey and tell Harold to transport them across the river to freedom. "And tell Harold to give them each a couple of coppers so they can buy themselves some food."

We saved the king's great room for last. King Phillip was there with his wife, some of his courtiers, and a few servants wearing blue tunics. When he saw us in the doorway, the king drew himself up and looked away from us in an effort to be quite dignified and every inch a king whom God had favoured; his courtiers gasped as we appeared and looked at us with eyes that were both worried and curious.

William and I merely looked in through the doorway at the king and his attendants, bowed respectfully, and withdrew. The king and the fops of his court obviously had no weapons and clearly would not be a threat to anyone even if they did. The expressions on the faces of the servants never changed in the least.

When we finished, I realized that several things about Louvre Castle had surprised me.

What surprised me most about the castle were the wooden plugs in the windows of King Phillip's personal room that keep out the dangerous night airs—they were not made of wood. A man could see through them as if there was nothing there!

I touched one of them and it was real. It was a good idea because it would keep out the rain and the night smells that cause the pox, and yet a man could look out and see whatever there was to see.

"My wife would love them," I told William. And I immediately reminded myself to ask Thomas who made them and where he thought I might be able to get some for my new villa on Cyprus.

The other thing that surprised me about the castle, both because it was not there and because I had not thought of it before, was that the castle had no moat to protect it and provide some of the delicious fish with flaky white meat that one finds in most moats. And, of course, no moat meant there was no drawbridge that would have to come down if someone wanted to get in or out.

*Later I wondered why the French had not dug a moat; they certainly had enough water nearby. They must have thought the river would be enough of a moat. Bad mistake, eh?*

\*\*\*\*\*\*

We delivered the king's rolled up parchment to his son by blowing a horn and then putting a courier's leather parchment carrier containing it on the riverbank in front of one of the city gates. It was the gate which opened on to the bridge George and his men had taken and finally destroyed.

Four days later a little door opened in the same city gate. Two men ducked their heads and emerged. One of the men was carrying a horn and began a great tooting to get our attention on the island. There was also much waving of arms and distant shouts. They obviously wanted to talk.

A French-speaking volunteer, a two-striper from one of our galleys, promptly rowed a dinghy over close enough to be able to hear them. George offered to go with him in case a Latin gobbler was needed, but William would not allow it.

Our man listened to what the two Frenchmen had to say, shouted back and forth a few times with them, and then promptly rowed himself back to give his report. He was very excited and proud of himself for being the bearer of good news. And it was good news. The French had the ransom coins in hand and wanted to arrange for their payment. The Templars and Paris's other moneylenders had come through for King Phillip.

Having the French agree to pay the ransom was something we had expected after reading the king's message to his son, and we were ready to receive it. Three dinghies set out for the French side of the river almost immediately. Each was towing another relatively large dinghy that was empty except for two pairs of oars.

As the empty boats were being moored in the shade of the city wall, a courier pouch with a parchment Thomas had scribed in Latin was held up by the sergeant in charge of the rowers so it could be seen by the many faces watching from the city wall. After he had waved it several times to call the watchers attention to it, and was sure it had been seen, he placed it in one of the empty boats and the three men immediately rowed their dinghies back across the Seine to re-join us on the island.

The message was scribed on the parchment in Latin. It told the French to use the empty boats to bring the ransom coins to the island. It also offered all the prizes we had taken, except for five of Eustace's large galleys from the Channel Islands, for another five hundred pounds of coins. We had already decided to keep Eustace's five galleys to replace the two we lost and expand our fleet; we also decided to keep the catapults and, of course, all the swords and other weapons.

Our men were not bothered in any way as they moored the empty dinghies and then rowed back to the king's island.

# Chapter Twenty-six

*I make a costly mistake due to good weather.*

Chests full of coins almost immediately began being rowed across the river to the island. Thomas set up a tent with a rough wooden table near where the chests were being unloaded, and my lieutenant commanders and I began counting the coins with the help of our apprentices.

Harold's lieutenant and the men of Harold's crew took care of everything else. His sailors handled the unloading of the chests and carried them to the nearby tent, and his galley's archers set up and manned a "do not pass" line of guards in a great semi-circle around the counting tent and the unloading area.

At first hundreds of excited archers and sailors stood watching from just behind the line of guards. They faded away as the hours passed, particularly when marching and sword practice assignments began being made and were conducted under the determined eyes of our captains major.

Examining and counting the ransom coins was a tedious business and something we had forgotten to consider. George solved the problem. He rushed to the island's little market and returned with a crude scale that had been used to weigh sacks of corn at the rate of twenty pounds at a time. There was nothing we could do except use it.

Counting the ransom coins was a simple but laborious process: Big handfuls of coins were taken out of a chest and piled on to an empty plate hanging from one end of a wooden pole until it lifted the plate carrying a twenty pound weight at the other end of the rod off the wooden table on which the crude scale sat.

There were twenty pounds of coins on the plate each time there were enough coins on the plate to lift the weight at other end off the table. When that happened, either George or I lifted the coin plate off the end of the pole and dumped the coins into an empty chest. Some of the coins we emptied came from chests that appeared not to have opened for many years. Twice we found a small amount of jewels and gold coins hidden under the silver.

Each time we dumped a plate with twenty pounds of coins into a chest, we put one of the coins into a "counting chest." The ransom would be paid in full when the counting chest had seventy-five hundred coins in it for the ransom, plus two hundred and fifty for the daily delays. It was a tedious process and ended up requiring more than one counting chest, but my lieutenants and I set about doing it with the greatest of smiles on our faces and much happy talk and banter.

We talked about many things as we counted, including the clear window plugs we had seen in the king's rooms. Thomas said they were called glass and very similar to the coloured window plugs that had begun appearing in certain wealthy churches and cathedrals.

Everyone agreed that glass window plugs were a fine idea because it would please our women in addition to keeping out the rain and the night vapours that caused the pox. We also agreed that we should look into it as soon as possible, both for our own use and as a cargo we could carry and sell to merchants just as we do with the flower paste that stops pain and the weapons we capture.

"We will have Father Pierre ask King Phillip's chamberlain where the plugs came from," William announced.

\*\*\*\*\*\*

The coin deliveries and counting continued all that day and through the night that followed. There were so many chests that we had to erect an additional tent. It was a cheerful time. My lieutenants and I talked about many things as we counted, and we made a number of decisions about other matters related to the company and our personal lives.

We were all tired, but content, by the time the counting and weighing was finished late the next afternoon.

A side effect of handling so many coins was that we quickly learned to spot pretend coins made from lead, and set them aside to send back to French for replacements. There were some, but not too many, and they were quickly replaced by the French.

In the end, we were about a hundred pounds short of having received the required number of coins. It was a number that could easily be explained by the crudeness of our weighing device or the sticky fingers of the men on the other side of the river who did the counting for the French.

It did not take me long to decide that the loss of a questionable hundred pounds of silver was a small price to pay to keep our word to free the king and return Louvre Castle to him. Accordingly, as I poured the last plate of coins into a chest, I told Henry to nod his acceptance of the ransom to Father Pierre. The Franciscan had been waiting anxiously since early morning to see if we would keep our word. He nodded back from just outside the circle of Harold's archers who were keeping everyone away from the counting tent and its coins.

Father Pierre was standing by himself and very much alone when he nodded his understanding that we had accepted the ransom.

That the French priest was standing alone was no surprise; an order had long ago gone out, and had been constantly repeated, that anyone who was seen talking to someone from the castle, or told any islander, even the public women, that he was English or an archer, would instantly lose all his stripes, promotion prospects, and prize coins. To the contrary, our company was, our men were repeatedly told by their captains and lieutenants, part of a much larger mercenary force of Swedes and Rus contracted to the emperor of the Holy Roman Empire for one campaign.

*Accepting the ransom coins without demanding another hundred pounds was an easy decision and one with which my lieutenants agreed. We knew that there would almost certainly be more ransom opportunities for the company in the years ahead, and sooner or later word was almost certain to get out that we had ended up with some or all of King Phillip's ransom. If so, it would be helpful in terms of negotiating future ransoms and contracts if it was known that the company always honoured its agreements and did not come back for more.*

\*\*\*\*\*\*

We distributed the coin chests amongst our galleys and sailed for Cornwall on a warm day in September. As you might imagine, the chests were divided somewhat evenly amongst all of our galleys to insure that as many as possible would get through to Cornwall if we ran into trouble.

Louvre Castle and the king's island were soon behind us as our huge fleet of galleys and prizes moved one right after another down the Seine, and then spent the night waiting together in the estuary. In the morning we sailed across the Channel to English coast in one great fleet. We stayed together in case the French or anyone else had heard about our newly acquired wealth and was inclined to try to take some of it from us.

The small galleys we had taken and a few of the larger transports from amongst our prizes sailed on their own with prize crews from our galleys; the rest were towed behind our bigger galleys with a couple of rudder men on board to help steer them.

No one tried to interfere with our passage from the French coast to the relative safety of the English coast. That was their good fortune and salvation, although perhaps those who thought about having a go at us did not know it.

Taking a galley crewed by the company's archers was difficult in the best of times; trying to take one whilst its crew was carrying their own prize coins was so close to suicide that anyone who tried would spend eternity in purgatory, at least that is what a smiling Thomas had suggested whilst we waited out the night in the estuary. We, of course, agreed with him because we were certain it was true.


\*\*\*\*\*\*

Our initial plan was for each of our galleys to tow a string of small prizes across the Channel to England and then up the coast to Cornwall.  Others of our prizes would sail and row with our grand fleet with prize crews on board.  We would all be together in one great fleet guarded by more than thirty war galleys.

Everything changed the next morning.  It was a fine and balmy September day.  The weather was particularly good, the sky was clear, and the wind in the calm Channel waters was favourable for London—so I made a great mistake:  I ordered all but Harold's and two other galleys to sail for Cornwall without the prizes they had been towing.

After consulting with Harold about the weather, I ordered most of the prizes to sail for London.  Why?  Because that was where they would almost certainly fetch much higher prices than if we sold them in Cornwall.  The only prizes that went with our galleys to Cornwall were those with catapults on their decks.  It seemed like a good idea at the time.

Hurriedly assigned small prize crews went aboard the prizes which had been under tow, and set their sails and rudders for London.  Harold's galley, with me on board, and three others of our galleys accompanied them.

Also sailing for London were the nine small galleys we had taken off the French with an archer at every oar.  They would help guard our prizes along the way and then, as would almost certainly be necessary for many of them, help pull them up the Thames to where it widened below London.  The merchants located on the riverbank along the

Pool where the Thames widened were the best potential buyers.

Both Harold and I went with the prize fleet to London. Normally George or Peter would have led the prizes to London. But poor Peter was gone, George needed to return to Cornwall to see if his poxed wife and her new infant were still alive, and Thomas was anxious to get back to his school. As a result, George and Thomas were on their way to Cornwall, and the fleet of prizes heading for London was under my command with Harold as my lieutenant. Harold's galley would lead the way with me on board.


****** 

We made a fine voyage. No one tried to interfere with our fleet and we easily made our way into the Thames estuary below London. Our only excitement came when one of our prizes, a small single-masted cog, began taking on water somewhere off of Dover and sank so rapidly that it had to be quickly abandoned. Its skeleton crew of two sailors and three archers would have almost certainly been lost if their desperate cries for help had not been heard.

Our arrival in the estuary and our towing of our prizes up the Thames to the Pool was quite normal. The merchants and ship buyers descended on us in great force— and, to my surprise, everyone in London seemed to know that the company had taken a big ransom off of King Phillip in addition to our many prizes.

All I could do when they did was nod my thanks for their good wishes, and lie through my teeth by saying that Emperor Otto's Swedes and Rus got the ransom coins and we got the prizes. And then I would sigh deeply and complain that our men would get most of whatever the prizes fetched for their prize money and back pay.

The evening of our arrival was most enjoyable. I spent it drinking and eating in the White Horse, my favourite London tavern, with Harold and the other two galley captains. And I had made another mistake. In response to the entreaties of so many of my men for coins to spend whilst they were in London, I began passing out the prize money my lieutenants and I had agreed to pay for the ransom—twenty silver coins for every stripe on a man's tunic with the possibility of more to come if the prizes were sold for good prices.

More than a dozen of our men took their prize money and ran. It was a huge amount of money for a common man—twenty silver coins for every archer and sailor, forty for a chosen man, and sixty for a sergeant. It was enough to buy a farm or a village tavern, and the news that we were paying large amounts of prize coins to every man quickly went out from the prostitutes and taverns to become the talk of London.

Passing out the prize money to our men had an evil effect—King John learnt the French king had paid a ransom and a large number of French prizes had been taken. He assumed, rightly although I forthrightly denied it with a sincere expression on my face, that I would be keeping a large number of the ransom and prize coins for myself and my family.


****** 

I was just barely stepped ashore the next morning and was listening to a proposal from the son of the merchant, David Levi. He was in the process of offering to buy all of our prizes for seven hundred and twenty pounds of silver coins, when a party of a dozen or more of the king's guards trotted up on their horses. They pulled them to a halt between where I was standing and our nearest galley—and presented me with a parchment ordering my arrest and directing whomever caught me to take me directly to Windsor.

"We have been looking for you, their captain said with a smile as he dismounted. We were told to arrest you and fetch you to Windsor without delay, and that we must do." Then he reached for my short sword and plucked it out of its scabbard as he named himself as Sir Percival Fiske, a lieutenant in the king's personal guard.

I looked around for possible help in a fight, but there were no archers close enough to assist me. I had foolishly walked too far from the quay to be able to suddenly make a break for it and run to our closest galley. Even worse, there were too many of the king's guards between me and my men, and the only weapons I was carrying were the wrist knives hidden under my tunic, and the short sword which Sir Percival had already pulled from my belt.

My capture was my own fault. In my enthusiasm to sell our prizes I had gone ashore without a party of guards, and compounded my stupidity be walking too far from where our galleys were tied to the quay. My only protection was the rusty shirt of mail I always wore under my tunic and the knives I wore on each wrist that were hidden by my tunic.

"Tell Harold I have been taken to Windsor and to sell the prizes to Master Levi,"

I shouted my orders over my shoulder to Rowland, my apprentice sergeant, as a couple of Sir Percival's guardsmen grabbed me by my elbows and moved me towards a nearby horse with an empty saddle. They were big and strong as might be expected of a king's guardsmen, and moved me so fast that my feet dragged along the quay. David Levi's son and the onlookers around us just

stood there and watched with their mouths open in surprise.

# Chapter Twenty-seven

*Lies, betrayals, and my death.*

We dismounted and entered Windsor Castle on foot through a small door in the castle's south wall. After a short walk across the castle bailey I was taken up some narrow stone stairs directly to a cell in one of the towers. It was a small room with a great wooden bar sealing the door. My cell had three openings in its stone walls from which I could look out the castle bailey and part of the nearby town, a wooden stool with three legs, and a raised wooden plank for sleeping. There was a bowl for pissing and shitting.

The door closed behind me and I heard the distinctive sound as the heavy wooden bar was dropped into place so I could not escape. To my surprise, I had not yet been properly searched and was still wearing my chain shirt and the wrist knives hidden under my hooded archer's tunic.

The king's guards obviously knew about my chain shirt from when they grabbed me, and probably had not been surprised by it because they themselves were wearing chain. Chain, after all, was becoming quite common. The possibility that I might also be wearing hidden wrist knives or carrying other weapons had not occurred to the king's men. My gaolers, whoever they turned out to be, probably assumed I had already been searched.

It was not a surprise that the king's guards had not searched my wrists or anywhere else under my tunic where I might be carrying a hidden weapon. People who carried weapons typically displayed them in order to discourage attacks. And wrist knives were not commonly carried by nobles and merchants, or anyone else for that matter. As a result, the guards' failure to search under my tunic was understandable. It probably also helped that they were in a hurry to get me away from the quay before someone came to my aid.

The king's guards and my gaolers were not the first to make the mistake of failing to thoroughly search me. It had happened before and explained why Thomas was so keen on George and I always wearing our knives and practicing with them every day. I had done so for so many years that I could bring them out in the blink of an eye. The guards probably never thought to look at my wrists because no one in England and France carried knives there.

On the various times in the past when my brother and I had actually been searched under our tunics for weapons, our knives had not been found because we had dutifully raised our arms high over our heads whilst a searcher patted and grabbed at our ankles and felt around our dingles and bellies. Not finding them was a common mistake and my brother and I had taken advantage of the searchers' failures more than once, usually with very fatal results for those who searched had us and the people around them.

Having my knives still available to stick in someone's throat or eye was a comfort under the circumstances, but a very small one. I might kill a man or two before I was cut down, but there was no way I was going to fight my way all the way out of Windsor with two very small knives. Meanwhile I was thirsty and getting hungry.

A worldly monk had told Thomas about the need to have such knives hidden under his robe and how to use them. That was when Thomas was but a boy and had first been carried off to the monastery by the old abbot who fancied him.

Thomas had later rescued me and taken me crusading, and the monk had become the new abbot. It had all happened at the same time—when the first abbot had given his life to stop some robbers who were making off with the monastery's silver. The robbers had escaped after stabbing the abbot in his eye and throat, but the church's silver had been saved by the abbot's willingness to sacrifice his life for the Church.

*That, of course, was years ago. Rumour had it that after a few more miracles the Church would be elevate the old abbot to the sainthood. He had already been dug up so his bones could be relics.*

\*\*\*\*\*\*

My first visitor came as a total surprise. It was Sir William Marshal, the commander of the king's army. He walked in with a big smile on his face. For a brief moment, I thought about pricking his liver with the point of one my knives and trying to walk out of the castle with him arm in arm as if we were the best of friends. But then I decided it was not much an idea since so many people came with him and were standing in the corridor outside my cell.

"Sir William," I demanded with as much irate dignity as I could muster under the circumstances, which was a considerable amount as I was truly shocked and displeased, "what is the meaning of me being treated like this? I thought we were allies. And I am thirsty and hungry and without proper bedding."

"It is not my doing, please believe me. I went to the king as soon as I heard." He said it as if talking to the king absolved him of any responsibility even though he himself had personally guaranteed our agreement.

"Well, it may not be *your* doing that I am here, but it certainly is *your* responsibility to get me out, is it not? It was *you* who made *your* mark and seal on the contract. And it *you* who guaranteed the king would honour our agreement. And it is *you* who will be dishonoured and my men will hold responsible if this injustice continues." *I heavily emphasized the words 'you' and 'your' as I spoke; I was very unhappy.*

"I know. I know. Believe me, I know. And that is what I told the king. But he just laughed."

"But why? We did all of what we agreed to do. It was a great victory."

"Yes, I know. And the king was very pleased. But it is the ransom that is the problem. He wants it, the king does; him and the nuncio, that is."

"The nuncio? What has he got to do with this?"

"He told the king that God would forgive him for taking you for a ransom because his need for money to pay his army and hire mercenaries was so great. And that he could buy an indulgence to make sure. He said I could also buy one, for that matter."

I could not believe what I was hearing. Finally, I asked him.

"Did the nuncio tell you that God would keep you and the king alive if you did this, or just that you would avoid purgatory after the archers killed you?"

It was the first of a number of conversations between Sir William and me. He seemed to enjoy them, and we learnt a lot from each other. Sir William was a surprisingly simple man with an astonishing knack for knocking other riders off their horses at tournaments. Indeed, you were not much of a man at several courts unless Sir William had put you on the ground.

Until I mentioned it, however, the idea that the archers were certain to take a terrible revenge as a retribution for my being taken for ransom had not dawned on him. I, of course, regaled him with stories of the ferocity of our many revenges and retributions, some of which were true.


\*\*\*\*\*\*

I spent entire next month alone in my cell in one the defensive towers in Windsor's inner wall. Strangely enough, it was not all bad. I was properly fed twice a day, had warm bedding, and the pot provided for my piss and shite was emptied regularly. It helped that the weather was not cold.

What made my days surprisingly acceptable was that Sir William brought me empty parchments, scribing supplies including a plentiful number of goose feathers that he ordered my guards to keep sharp, and a piece of slate on which I could scribe my initial thoughts before I scribed them on a parchment.

With nothing else to do, I began scribing my orders for the behaviour of the family in the years ahead, the orders I had told George I intended to scribe after I turned over the command of the company to Peter. I also began scribing a history of the company so he and the rest of my family would know from whence we had come.

I never did see the king in all the weeks I spent at Windsor, although an increasingly worried Sir William came to see me a number of times. His latest visit was this morning when he and one of his sergeants came to visit. The sergeant, whose name was Richard, had come with Sir William previously.

Richard listened without saying a word as Sir William literally wrung his hands in despair whilst telling me there was nothing more he could do—I was to be taken to the wooden block in the castle bailey tomorrow morning and chopped for not paying enough ransom. At least, that was the excuse the king had given Sir William.

My response was one of anger and resignation. I asked that Father Albert, one of the priests in the nuncio's household come to help me with my prayers *and carry my orders for revenge to my son.* I also shocked Sir William by suggesting that he himself might want to take the last rites with me because he too was unlikely to be alive much longer.

"Why should I do that?" Sir William wanted to know even though I had explained the company's commitment to revenge and retribution to him a number of times previously.

What followed was a long talk during which I once again explained, with even more details and examples than the previous times, why the continuation of Sir William's life was tied to the continuation of mine. This time Sir William listened more carefully. There was little wonder in that—an army of archers was reported to have reached Okehampton whilst on its way towards Windsor and London. Richard, his sergeant, who seemed to be some kind of confidant, listened even more intently.

*Sir William was a fine tournament jouster, but more than a little dense about the world beyond his tournaments and the king's court. He had not understood at first that the king had learnt about the archers war-fighting abilities from his spies and realized he'd gone too far. Now, if I understood Sir William correctly, the king thought that if I was chopped the company would be leaderless and there would be no retribution.*

\*\*\*\*\*\*

It was somewhat my fault that the king had decided to chop me. Throughout my time in the tower at Windsor I had held to the lies I told when I first arrived—that most of the ransom coins had gone to the Swedes and Rus, and that almost all of the company's share of the ransom and the sale of the French prizes had gone to our men as prize money, and to pay their arrears in pay from the previous two years.

"All that is left of our share of Phillip's ransom is in the chests on the three company galleys in the Pool. They were carrying the coins to Cyprus to pay the arrears in the pay of the men who are on Cyprus and stationed in the ports throughout the Holy Land and elsewhere."

I had repeated my lies with all the sincerity I could muster. And, at first, my lies had succeeded. The king agreed to free me in exchange for all the coins in the chests of the three galleys. An agreement was quickly reached and a message from me to Harold resulted in him quickly getting the coins. But after he was paid, the king refused to release me; he had heard about the additional coins from the sale of our French prizes. He wanted those coins as well.

By then I was spending my time thinking of ways to get all the coins back, and then some, just as we had done to King Phillip for holding Thomas. But I had to be free to do it. And I wanted to be free, both so I could start taking a profitable revenge, and because winter was coming and I found myself increasingly unhappy about being away from my family. Accordingly, and only because I could see no alternative, I ordered Harold to also turn over to King John the coins from the sale of our prizes.

Harold and our galleys had stayed in London. And he obeyed my order and turned the coins from the sale of our prizes over to a party of priests and knights representing the king. But once again the king would not release me; now he wanted the rights to Cornwall's stannaries returned to him. I had no choice; I made my mark on the parchment the nuncio drafted. That was two weeks ago.

\*\*\*\*\*\*

It was a difficult night and I could not sleep at all, not for a single moment; there is nothing to better sharpen the thoughts behind your eyes than knowing you will soon be dead.

I spent the entire night pacing around my cell in the darkness whilst terrible thoughts raged in my head. I wondered what it would like to be dead and if it would hurt. And I worried about my women and children and what would become of them. Finally I resolved to go down fighting. I began practicing, as I had every night in the darkness, by bringing out my knives over and over again from under my now-filthy tunic. It helped to distract me, but it never stopped me from thinking or being angry.

My arms were tired from my constant practice as the dawn's early light began to arrive. Almost immediately I heard many steps coming down the stone floor of the corridor.

I stood up, flexed my hands to ready myself, and waited. With luck, I grimly decided, I would get a few of the bastards before they cut me down. It was the twentieth day of October in the year 1216, my last.

The door rattled as the great wooden bar that sealed it was lifted off so it could be opened; and then the door was pulled open with its usual loud creaking sound. Richard, Sir William's sergeant, entered first and the bastard was smiling. Right then I resolved to take him first. Behind the sergeant came Father Albert carrying a cross and a number of guards.  I flexed my hands, even though they were shaking, and stepped forward.  I barely heard Richard speak as I stepped towards him.

"You are free to go home, Commander.  King John and the nuncio were suddenly poxed and both shite so much that they died last night.  And please do not believe the rumours that it was caused by their bellies being cut by some of Sir William Marshal's men; he is lamenting their deaths most fiercely.  It was bad eels from what I heard."

End of the Book

There are more books in the *Company of Archers* saga.

All of the other books in this great saga of medieval England are available as eBooks, and some of them are available in print.  You can find them by going to Amazon or Google and searching for *Martin Archer fiction*.

Additional eBook collections of the novels in the saga are available on Kindle as *The Archers' Story: Part I, Part II, Part III, Part VI, and Part V.*  And there are more stories after those.  A chronological list can be found below.

And a word from Martin:

"Thank you for reading my stories.  I sincerely hope you enjoy reading about Cornwall's *Company of Archers* as much as I enjoy writing about them.  If so, would you please consider writing a very brief review on Amazon and Goodreads with as many stars as possible in order to encourage other readers.

"And, if you could please spare a moment, I would also very much appreciate your thoughts about this saga of medieval England and whether you would like it to continue.  I can be reached at martinarcherV@gmail.com."

Cheers and thank you once again. /S/ Martin Archer

**Amazon eBooks in Martin Archer's exciting and action-packed *Soldier and Marines* saga:**

*Soldier and Marines*

*Peace and Conflict*

*War Breaks Out*

*Our Next War*

*Israel's Next War*

**Amazon eBooks in Martin Archer's exciting and action-packed *The Company of Archers* saga:**

*The Archer*

*The Archers' Castle*

*The Archers' Return*

*The Archers' War*

*Rescuing the Hostages*

*Kings and Crusaders*

*The Archers' Gold*

*The Missing Treasure*

*Castling the King*

*The Sea Warriors*

*The Captain's Men*

*Gulling the Kings*

*The Magna Carta Decision*

*The War of the Kings*

*The Company's Revenge*

*The Ransom*

*The New Commander*

*The Gold Coins*

*The Emperor has no Gold*

*Fatal Mistakes*

*The Alchemist's Revenge*

*The Venetian Gambit*

*Today's Friends*

*The English Gambit*

## Collections

*Soldiers and Marines Trilogy – books I, II, III*

*The Archer's Stories - books I, II, III, IV, V, VI*

*The Archer's Stories II - books VII, VIII, IX, X,*

*The Archer's Stories III – books XI, XII, XIII*

*The Archer's Stories IV – books XIV, XV, XVI, XVII*

*The Archer' Stories V – books XVIII, XIX, XX*

*The Archer's Stories VI – books XXI, XXII, and XXIII*

## Other eBooks you might enjoy:

*Cage's Crew* by Martin Archer writing as Raymond Casey

*America's Next War* by Michael Cameron Adams — an adaption of *War Breaks Out* to set it in our immediate future when a war breaks out over the refugee crisis in Europe.

## An Extract from the next book in the series "The New Commander."

.... The first of the fleeing people to reach us were still loaded down with the personal possessions they were trying to carry to safety. The people behind them, however, were mostly empty-handed; they must have dropped everything except their children in order to run faster.

A mob of rioting looters and robbers was coming down the land towards us right behind the fleeing people. I saw them immediately as I turned a corner to get on the narrow lane that led to St. Mary's Church.

As I turned the corner, I saw a couple of thrusters from the mob catch up to a fleeing man, a merchant from the look of his clothes, and throw him to the ground along with the howling child and the rough linen sack he was carrying over his shoulder. They were scarcely twenty paces in front of me.

A woman wearing a black hooded gown and holding tightly to the hands of two young children was even nearer to me, less than ten paces away. She was up against a door in the wall of a nearby hovel watching with a look of absolute horror on her face at the man and infant who had been thrown to the ground.

The aghast woman was not the only one watching man and child being attacked. Some of the shutters were open above us and there was much shouting back and forth amongst the people looking out from the tightly packed hovels lining the lane. The air was full of smoke and noise.

Everyone in the lane was running towards us for one reason or another, including a couple of wide-eyed families who ran past the downed man and the robbers without even looking at them. A mob of shouting men was right behind them. Some of them looked to be carrying clubs and I caught the glint of at least one blade.

The two robbers were bent over their victim. They had clubbed him to the ground and were roughly searching under his robe for his coin pouch when I reached them. It did not take long as they were only a few steps away. I could clearly see what they were doing.

It was instantly apparent that the would-be robbers were looking for whatever coins the man might have been carrying. They were both carrying clubs and I was carrying my galley shield in my left hand and a short sword in my right.

I dropped the sack I had over my shoulder, and it only took three or four strong steps before I was on them. And so were the archers I had been leading who were immediately behind me. I screamed a great oath as I brought my sword down on the head one of the robbers just as he lifted his victim's coin pouch and turned towards his companion with a look of triumph on his face. That was when he first saw me.

The look on the robber's face turned to surprise, but only for a very brief moment as I chopped down with my sword as hard as I could. The merchant's pouch and some of its coins went flying as my blade missed the robber's turning head and bit deeply into his body between his neck and his shoulder.

I had used both hands and swung it so hard that afterwards I had to put my foot on the man's still-wiggling body to pull it out. He had not even had time to throw up his arm in a futile effort to block my downward chopping sword.

Almost at the same moment, one of my newly assigned archers from the galley's crew, also loudly screaming, ran his sword so deeply into the back of the other robber that its bloody point came at least a foot out of his chest. The second man was on his knees grabbing at the bloody blade as some of my men ran past me and I saw the archer begin trying to get his blade out so he could use it again.

All the rest of my shouting and charging men came boiling around the corner and into the lane as I began waving them forward with one hand whilst at the same time I was trying to retrieve my sword with the other.

The damn thing was stuck so deeply into the would-be robber's shoulder bone that I actually dragged him for a few feet along the lane as I tried to continue running towards the on-coming mob. My men were excited and shouting as they rushed past me to get at the mob of men who had been pursuing the refugees. They fell on them like a pack of wolves charging into a herd of sheep.

It was not much of a fight. By the time my men reached the thrusters at the head of the mob, most of the rest had stopped and were trying to turn around so they could run away and escape. Some of them made it; but many did not. We took no prisoners and our only casualty was a young one-stripe archer from the galley who slipped on some shite in the alley and broke his arm.

Made in the USA
Middletown, DE
05 February 2021

33143521R00191